# Celebration

An anthology of original short stories commemorating the $50^{th}$ anniversary of the British Science Fiction Association

Edited by Ian Whates

NewCon Press
England

First edition, published in the UK March 2008
by NewCon Press

NCP 006 (hardback)
NCP 007 (softback)

10 9 8 7 6 5 4 3 2 1



ISBN: 978-0-9555791-3-4 (hardback)
978-0-9555791-4-1 (softback)

Cover Painting by Vincent Chong
Cover layout and design by Andy Bigwood

Invaluable editorial assistance from Ian Watson

Printed in the UK by Biddles of Kings Lynn

# Contents

# The BSFA
## An Appreciation

Watch now as I do something I have always wanted to do: become British.

The British Science Fiction Association is 50 this year. Three cheers somehow seem insufficient. Perhaps a 21-gun salute, or even a fly-past, including historic British aircraft of the period. I would hope, at the least, to see the TSR2. After all, any appreciation of the BSFA is also an appreciation of 50 years of the fantastic.

The BSFA was born in a Britain that is very different from the one we live in today. The Cold War had been going on for over a decade, there was full employment, the post-War consensus was still in force, and Harold Macmillan was the Prime Minister: a man who affected an Edwardian benign paternalism. All very different from Britain today, in the front line of the 'War on Terror', with every politician in the country having a team of spin doctors; with globalisation and the rise of the new powers in the East, China and India; a consumer society in full flow. And yet: how different really? For the Cold War read 'War on Terror'; for the promise that nuclear power would bring us all unlimited energy at virtually no cost, the promise that nuclear power will bring us energy at competitive cost and save us from global warming; and leadership around the world still at the mercy of 'events, dear boy, events'.

Science fiction has never had a very good track record when it comes to actually predicting the future – as opposed to speculating about different possibilities, and warning about some of them – and yet we find ourselves living in a science fiction world, as strange as anything that could have been imagined by the founders of the BSFA and the writers they so much admired. London looks more like the set of *Blade Runner* every day; the psychology of our society was imagined by J G Ballard in the sixties, barely a decade into the BSFA's life; and – pardon my immodesty – I might mention the existence of the 'news porn' and 'food porn,' which figured heavily in my second novel, *Synners*, published in 1991. Science fiction, as a cultural form, is no longer in the ghetto; it has colonized everything else. And a significant part in that colonization of the 'mainstream' (that is, everything) has been the work of lovers of the stuff of imagination, like those early BSFA founders, and the legions that came after them.

Every one of those who spent time in the service of the BSFA was an amateur in the true sense of that word: they all did it (and do it today) for the love of science fiction, and because of a desire to communicate that love as widely as possible. In the worlds of film and television, there are probably few people left to convince. After all, our most popular TV drama recently is *Heroes*; and science fiction or fantasy films like *ET*, *Star Wars* and Harry Potter are among the highest earners of all time. Not to mention that the Terminator is now governor of California.

However, there is still much to be done to encourage people to read the literature of the fantastic. It seems to me that it is here that the next 50 years of the BSFA lies – exactly as it was the place for the BSFA in its first half century. The BSFA has always served an invaluable function by acting as a link between inquisitive readers, keen to make contact with other lovers of SF, and the more organized SF community of professionals and amateurs. It has brought people in from isolation, and many have gone on to be important members of the field. One has only to think of Michael Moorcock (briefly editor of the BSFA's critical journal *Vector*) or Malcolm Edwards (former *Vector* editor, now exalted high in the ranks of British publishing).

Science fiction, as a literature of the fantastic, exists in its purest form in literature, for here it actually takes place in the mind of each individual reader – an unlimited terrain, knowing virtually no boundaries. Where better to play out the ideas, the speculation, the imaginings of SF? In a society where reading faces unparalleled competition from other demands on people's time – including of course the virtual worlds of computer games, Second Life and online communities, all of them among the scattershot prediction of SF writers – literature has to struggle ever harder for those precious hours. Long may the BSFA continue to be in the vanguard of that struggle, attracting more and more people to read the books and stories, and linking up lovers of SF with each other.

I wish that I could say I participated. Instead, as a recovering American, I can participate in celebrating what has gone before and what is to come. And I'm sure there's plenty more to come.

Nothing can stop the dedicated amateurs of the BSFA; not even 'events, dear boy, events'.

*Pat Cadigan* – January 2008

# The Jubilee Plot

## Stephen Baxter

Murmurs ran through the crowd. "She is coming! The Queen is coming!" "Listen – you can hear the whistle of her Trevi!" Under the high sun of this June morning, top hats were raised and lacy parasols twirled.

Giles Romillie was as thrilled as the rest at the sound of the steam whistle. Above all he dreamed of the race across the Channel bridge at six that evening, after which he himself was to be presented to Her Majesty – if he won! And somewhere in the crowd around him was Edith Wilcox, and he imagined her warm gaze on him when he returned from the French side and raised the trophy in victory.

It was 20th June 1887, the day of Victoria's Golden Jubilee. Later Giles would remember these heady morning moments and marvel at how little he had anticipated of the hours to come, when, as the Jubilee Plot unfolded, at peril would not be racing glory or the love of a serving girl, but his very life – and the life of a Queen-Empress.

His immediate problem was that he couldn't see what was going on. Lost in a forest of tall men wearing shiny black morning suits and women in elaborate gowns and bonnets, he could see nothing but Kentish sky. Giles, twenty years old, already dressed in his bright scarlet racing leathers, was stocky and strong, but tall he was not. He must witness the Queen's arrival. He cast about, looking for inspiration.

He was a hundred paces away from a raised bandstand that stood on the bridge slip road. That might do. With muttered apologies he pushed his way through the crowd. He knew most of these people, by sight if not by name; his father's class, the land-owning aristocracy, was powerful and supremely wealthy but not numerous, and everybody knew everybody else. He was rewarded with irritated glances from the loftily pompous – and, in his tight-fitting leathers, frankly lustful looks from some of the ladies, and one or two men.

He reached the bandstand. Its delicate wrought-iron roof was supported by slim pillars. In its shade, players of a Grenadier Guards band were sorting out their music and brass instruments. They ignored Giles. He stepped onto the stage, but he was only eighteen inches off the ground, and could see little more than he had before.

A trombone player, a big man wearing campaign ribbons from the Ottoman War of a decade ago, took pity on him. "Looking for a view, sonny? Why don't you follow the other lad's example and go up top?" He indicated the iron roof.

"What other lad?" But the man had already turned away. So Giles, relishing a bit of adventure, set his peaked cap back on his head and scaled a pillar's ornate ironwork. His thin-soled boots slipped on glossy white paint.

A hand in a black leather glove reached down. "Let me help you."

Giles looked up at a handsome, grinning face, a shock of blond hair silhouetted against the sky. "Ulrich," he growled. "It would be you."

Ulrich Zuba laughed. "You may as well get used to me finishing first today!"

Giles grudgingly took the offered glove, and let Ulrich haul him up to the roof. So they sat side by side, Giles in his red racing leathers, Ulrich Zuba, Giles's deadliest rival, in his black.

At least the view, over a sea of top hats and parasols, was as magnificent as Giles had hoped.

He was only a hundred yards from the mighty abutment of the Jubilee Bridge, whose iron roots had been planted firmly into this chalky coastal ground a few miles from Folkestone. The bridge was a cantilever design, with iron trunks striding away towards France, supporting dual-level trackways inside shaped boxes of girders. It was hard to grasp the scale of the structure until you remembered that the lower track bore a four-track rail line, a route for the continental railway companies to reach the British Isles, and the upper, a route for autocars, was as wide and true a road as anything the Romans ever built. The vision of Sir Benjamin Baker, architect of the Forth Bridge, the whole was painted post-box red, bright against the blue of the sea. Tall ships passed under its mighty spans.

And it was across that upper roadway that, later that day, Ulrich and Giles would be racing for the honour of being the first to cross the freshly opened bridge.

Away from the bridge, a broad new Telford road ran straight as an arrow off to the north to join the main south coast route. The rail link rather petered out, ending only in the rusty old military line to London. One short troop train stood idle on the tracks, its carriages black with soot. Around the bandstand milled the select crowd, looking from this vantage like a flock of exotic birds. A pavilion sheltered the most notable, including several foreign heads of state, and there were distractions, including a fair and a display of country dancing.

But most eyes were turned north, where a short road train was approaching. As its mighty ten-feet-diameter wheels turned steadily, the Trevi's whistle blasted again, a puff of steam rising like a flag, and the onlookers cheered. Giles strained to glimpse the little woman who must be riding within one of those ornate carriages, in her black widow's weeds, on the throne of Britain since the death of her father fifty years ago today. Beside her should be her son, Edward Prince of Wales, the heir to the throne to whom would fall the honour of starting the race, as well as driving home the bridge's last rivet, of solid gold.

"It was good news for you, Giles," Ulrich said in his slightly laboured English. "The Queen herself drives your autocar to the starting line."

"Oh, very witty. I'll have you know that famous old omnibus drew her carriage to her coronation. One of Gurney's designs, I believe, deriving from Trevithick's prototypes. The Queen cleaves to tradition. That is her role."

"She chose not to risk her royal neck in a put-put coal-gas autocar like your Boulton. Very wise! Perhaps she has merely been waiting to purchase a sound petrol-driven design like my Daimler."

"If so she might change her mind after she sees you lost in my dust this evening."

"We will see." Ulrich glanced around. "Chancellor Bismarck is intending to be here in time to witness my triumph. He will be travelling, in fact, on the very first railway train to arrive from the continent over the bridge."

"Trains. Pah! The rail carriageway spoils the line of the bridge, if you ask me. They should have left it as a dual-level roadway."

Ulrich raised plucked eyebrows. "But without the money from the continental iron-road companies, who are impatient to get at your ore and coal, the bridge would never have been built in the first place. Surely you know that. Do you read the newspapers, Herr Romillie?"

Actually Giles rarely did, save for the reports on motors and racing – and in particular on himself.

Ulrich laughed again. "I will not tease you. Look." He pointed. "A young lady is waving to you."

Giles"s heart beat faster.

She was a slight girl, her complexion olive, her jet black hair set off well against the cream-coloured gown she wore. She grinned up at Giles, and mouthed, "I've been looking for you!"

"You have found me!" he called down.

"You lucky dog," Ulrich said.

"She is called Edith."

Edith Wilcox worked in the royal household. Giles had met her when his father took him to Hampden Court to discuss protocol surrounding the race events. Today Edith's duties would start when the patient Trevi brought the Queen to the royal pavilion.

"Such a pretty girl," Ulrich said. "But such poor taste in men! And forward too, if I may say so. She has an exotic look about her – Mediterranean, is she?"

"Actually she's from London – Euston. Her father is Irish, her mother black, a freed slave."

Again Ulrich raised his eyebrows. "A half-caste, then! Well, she's a beauty for all that. But she's hardly a marriage prospect, is she? Not for a scion of such a family as yours."

The very question surprised Giles. "Well, of course not. She's just a bit of fun."

"That's the attitude," came a growling voice from the ground. Sir Joshua Romillie spoke around a fat cigar, his face as red as Giles's racing jacket.

"Good morning, Father."

Ulrich tipped his peaked cap. "Sir Joshua."

Sir Joshua grunted. "Should have known I'd find you up there, Giles. Can't resist making a spectacle of yourself, can you? Like a ruddy peacock in those leathers."

Ulrich defended him. "I rather think more eyes are drawn to Her Majesty this morning, Sir Joshua. Or else to the loveliness of Edith Wilcox."

"Who? Oh, Giles's latest flibbertigibbet. Well, I was young once. Any engine must be run in. Just so long as you don't wear out your piston, eh, boy?"

Giles, blushing, glanced at Edith's sweet face. She was whispering to her friend, another palace servant, a flame-haired Irish beauty called Gemma whom he had met once or twice. Perhaps they were talking about him. Edith winked at him boldly. He felt his heart soften, just a little.

But he said, "Of course not, sir."

"Oh, for heaven's sake get down from there, you pair."

They made their way to pillars and began their descent from the roof.

Ulrich asked, "And what do you think of the bridge, Sir Joshua?"

He frowned, an intimidating expression exaggerated by his dense grey sideburns. "I heard you taunting the boy over the rail deck. I'd have nothing to do with that if it was my choice. Shunting the poor around the country might be good enough for you continentals, but it's not the English way, and never has been. The English yeoman lives on the ground his ancestors have tilled since before the Conquest, and he's best left there. My own father opposed George Stephenson himself..."

Ulrich responded with words about the efficiency and economic growth delivered by rail transportation.

And as they politely argued, Edith came pushing past Sir Joshua, towards the grandstand. Her face was drawn. "Oh, Giles – Giles, it's awful!"

"Edith?" He was shocked. He had lost sight of her while he climbed down. From the smiling coquette of just a minute ago she was transformed, on the verge of tears. "Whatever is the matter?"

"Gemma's been telling me things – oh, Giles! *You must not race*," she said, her voice earnest, a half-whisper. "You mustn't go on that bridge. Promise me!"

He was bewildered. "Edith – the race, it's everything to me – how can I possibly promise such a thing?"

"But you must." She glanced around, evidently scared. "I'll get myself in the most frightful fix if I say more. Please, don't race – I must go –"

With that she was gone into the crowd. Ulrich had witnessed the little scene, and watched Giles curiously.

And there was a bang like a clap of thunder, so loud it was like a physical force, a blow in the chest.

Everybody flinched. There were screams. Sir Joshua took his cigar out of his mouth and turned around. "What in blazes was that?"

Giles shinned quickly a couple of feet back up the bandstand pillar. And he saw, over the heads of the crowd, that the Queen's Trevi steam omnibus had exploded. Its big boiler was broken open like a burst paper bag, and it had careened off the roadway. The passenger carriages had become detached, but seemed unharmed.

Soldiers were already running towards the shattered road train. People seemed stunned, but now the screaming started again, shouts of fear and anger. Sir Joshua strode into the crowd, trying to exert control.

And Giles, clinging to the pillar, sensed that his life had changed forever.

Sir Joshua insisted Giles stayed close to him in the chaos that followed, for the sake of his safety.

Police and even senior military officers knew who Sir Joshua was, and deferred to him; he spoke to members of parliament, ministers, members of the royal household and other senior figures as an equal, giving advice and commands. Indeed Sir Joshua held a parliamentary seat of his own, representing a 'rotten borough' on the outskirts of Luton whose few hundred electors were mostly his relatives or employees.

And through his father's conversations Giles, shocked, learned that although the royal party was unharmed by the explosion, an elaborate plot was unfolding this day of the Queen's Jubilee.

The detonation of the Queen's Trevi had been no accident. A bomb had broken the seam of its high-pressure steam boiler. The saboteurs had got their timing wrong, as the road train had been running too slowly to do any harm. But that wasn't all. There had also been an attempt to blow up Westminster Abbey, intended, presumably, to detonate at the time of the Queen's attendance at a thanksgiving service tomorrow. That had been uncovered thanks to a stray remark in a London pub by an Irish labourer. The Metropolitan Police had quickly broken the man, using techniques honed against strikers and other agitators over the decades, and had exposed a conspiracy by Irish Home Rule campaigners.

So two attacks had been thwarted, but the police and senior soldiers wondered aloud if there were more plots to be uncovered. Giles fretted over what Edith had said to him, which seemed to imply that there must indeed be such a threat – something to do with the race perhaps. He needed to talk to her.

But Edith and the other girls had been sent home, whisked away in a fast road-train to London. He knew her address, though he had never in his life been to such a place as Euston. But how was he to get there, on this day of confusion?

He mused on this with Ulrich, who had witnessed his fraught conversation with the girl. Ulrich disappeared for a while.

Then he returned, and tapped Giles on the shoulder. "I have found a way. Come with me."

"Found a way to do what?"

"To get you to Euston in a hurry. Isn't that what you want?"

Giles hesitated. "And leave me stranded in north London and out of the race – is that the game?"

Ulrich sighed. "Oh, do not be a fool. I know you say you care little for this girl, Edith. But I saw her agitation for myself. Might this not be more important than a mere race? Anyway you will be back by six. I will accompany you, so you can be sure there is no deceit involved! Will that satisfy you?"

Giles felt mollified, and faintly ashamed; the man did seem to be trying to help him. "All right. But how are we to get there and back in a few hours? In your smelly Daimler?"

Ulrich grinned. "I have been speaking to a few of your soldiers. I know soldiers. I have relatives in the military."

"*All* Germans have relatives in the military."

"Well, with a little sweet talk, and a promise of a grandstand seat to see the race's finish, I have secured us places on the next troop train back to London."

Giles wrinkled his nose in disgust. "A train? The railway? I've never ridden the railway in my life!"

"Then it is a day of novelties. Come *on*." He led the way.

Giles followed with a backward glance at his father, who had apparently not yet noticed his son was slipping away. Sir Joshua never paid him much attention at the best of times.

The troop train was a row of grimy wooden carriages behind a hissing locomotive of a French design. Ulrich talked them past the corporal guarding the train with a smile and a promissory note. There was no station here, no platform; they climbed into the carriage up a short wooden ladder directly from the rusty tracks.

The carriage was like a barn on wheels, with a wooden floor and slats for walls, and rows of simple, backless benches. There were only a few troops aboard, tired-looking men cradling packs and rifles with red coats unbuttoned. They glanced at Ulrich and Giles, uninterested, then turned back to their cigarettes and card games. Giles settled reluctantly on a bench, trying to keep his leathers clean.

Just minutes after they boarded, a whistle shrieked and the train jolted into motion. Giles had to grab the bench to avoid being thrown to the floor. As the train picked up speed the breeze whistled through the slatted walls, and Giles was glad it was such a hot day, but was dismayed when smoke and soot and even sparks came blowing into the carriage.

Ulrich laughed at his discomfort. "You are an iron road virgin."

"I told you, I never rode a rail train before in my life. And this is why."

"But you should visit Germany some time." He had to speak up over the chuffing of the locomotive, the rattle of the wheels on the track. "There you travel in heated coaches, with dinner served to you by a pretty waitress. Why, German cattle are transported in better conditions than this!"

"But even so, who wants to ride a train? To be shunted from fixed point to fixed point – you have none of the freedom you have in an autocar. *And* you can't choose what sort you travel with. No offence."

"But look at the economics. As I explained to your father, the rail can transport high volumes at low cost and high speeds. For industry's needs –"

"Canals will do for England, and turnpike roads, as they have always done. My father owns shares in the Silver Cross, the country's greatest canal system, connecting the Thames, Trent, Severn and Mersey. Once we had a cruising holiday, a summer in a houseboat. The canals were fair crowded with commercial vehicles and cargo."

Ulrich grunted. "Lumbering along at the pace of a broken-down horse! The British *invented* modern industrial society. You have an empire that spans the world. Yet you are the poor man of Europe! Continental entrepreneurs will come over the Jubilee Bridge to take away your coal and iron ore and other raw materials as if you are a colony to be exploited. You should come to Germany, my friend," he said again.

Giles was relieved when the train picked up more speed, and the noise drowned out Ulrich's voice.

The train cut briskly across the country, heading north-west. It stopped at Ashford, Maidstone and Sevenoaks, where troops and equipment were disembarked, and others loaded aboard. Then it turned north towards the capital, and joined the London Loop south of Greenwich. This grand circle of rail track, designed to ferry troops rapidly to trouble spots around the city, was the only major rail development to have taken place in Britain for forty years.

On the Loop, the train headed west and rattled through Deptford, Peckham and Camberwell. Ulrich peered out curiously at the capital's sprawling, grimy acres, houses and factories jammed in together under a pall of smoke, cut through here and there by the tracks of the motor roads – shining paths kept empty of pedestrians by law, to make way for the coal-gas-powered autocars of the rich, and the occasional steam omnibus.

Giles felt proud of this vision of London's roads, for his own family had had a great deal to do with its creation. In the 1830s a man called Sir Goldsworthy Gurney had run a trial steam-driven road train service between Gloucester and Cheltenham. After the railways failed, the Romillies and other interested parties had argued for Gurney's system, and poured money into resolving the attendant technical problems: high pressure boilers to make engines powerful enough, road surfaces toughened by Thomas Telford's expensive processes, pneumatic tyres to make the journey itself bearable for passengers. Sir Joshua always said that it was a much more civilised solution to Britain's transport needs than the rail, a solution that did *not* involve laying waste to whole swathes of ancient English countryside with bridges and cuttings and embankments, and shrieking locomotives putting the cows off their milk.

But Ulrich did not seem impressed. "London is not like Berlin."

"Well, I should hope not."

"The roads are so poor, save for the motor routes. And without rail how do people travel to work?"

Giles was puzzled by the question. "In their autocars."

"Not the rich," Ulrich said. "The workers, the ordinary people."

"They don't. Well, they walk. If everybody travelled about it would ruin the character of the place, wouldn't it?"

"Why, look there – a cow!" Behind every grimy house or terraced row was a scrap of green, populated by cows, sheep, chickens. "Cows, in your capital!"

"How else are you supposed to get fresh milk in the city?"

"You transport it in from the countryside. By rail!"

"Maybe you like your milk sour in Berlin," Giles said defensively. "Here we take it warm and udder-fresh."

"How medieval!"

Giles cast about for a way to shut him up. "Look – you're starting to sound like an agitator."

"Oh, I would not dream of causing trouble." But, glancing at the soldiers with whom they shared the carriage, he fell silent. The line swept over the river at Vauxhall, and Ulrich peered out at the crowded, grimy Thames.

The train stopped at Marylebone, and here Giles and Ulrich alighted. It was a walk of only a mile or so east to Euston. But this was a slum area. The old Marylebone road was lined by shabby houses and tenements and jammed with traffic, most of it horse-drawn. In one doorway they saw a man fallen down drunk though it was barely past lunchtime; in the next a sad-looking prostitute bared bony ankles. And over it all hung the foetid stink of the city.

Ulrich muttered, "In Berlin such areas have been cleared. The penetration of the railways into the city saw to that alone. In Berlin we have a *hauptbahnhof*, a big central station from which tracks push out in all directions. This is the north of London, is it not? Perhaps a great rail terminus might have grown up in Euston, if the iron roads had come this way, connecting the city to the provinces. Instead –" he waved a hand at the crowded squalor "– *this*."

"I think I've heard enough about Berlin, thanks very much."

Edith's home, when they found it, was a common lodging house, where you could stay for threepence a night. They had to tip the woman on the door, the deputy, a shilling to be allowed in.

Edith and her family inhabited two basement rooms. Here a black woman of about fifty held court over children of all ages, both black and white – there might have been a dozen, but they squirmed around so much it was hard for Giles to keep count. The walls were flaking and unpainted, and a kind of green mould was breaking through the ceiling. The only partitions were grimy blankets hung from ropes, and there was a stale stink of drying clothes, cooking and unwashed bodies.

And Edith was here, still in her cream uniform, but her hair was undone. She was shocked when Giles entered, and with a squeal she hurried out, primping her hair.

The black woman sighed. She was going through a child's hair, evidently searching for lice. "Don't you mind her, gentlemen. She'll come round. Does like to look nice always, like a china doll, that's what's wrong with her..." Her accent was strong and hard for Giles to place, a mixture perhaps of the African of only a generation back, and of the Liverpool area from where the family had recently come. She offered them tea, which they politely refused.

And as they waited for Edith their hostess told them something of herself.

Her name was Patience Wilcox, and she was Edith's mother. Edith's father, a white man from Liverpool, was only recently dead – killed, in fact, during the Jubilee Bridge construction, like a thousand others, working in a caisson that had cracked open. Not all these children were Patience's. Some of them belonged to the *other* family that shared these two rooms, two families living here without partition or boundary like animals in a pen. Patience was trying to encourage some of the children to sleep, while preparing others for work; all these little ones worked in factories or shops, all save the very smallest.

Patience herself was the daughter of an African, captured by slavers on the Gold Coast; she barely remembered him. After slavery was formally abolished in Britain in the 1820s, Liverpool, which had made its fortune from the slave trade, looked to a future as an imperial port. When the pioneering Liverpool & Manchester railway had failed following the notorious 1838 Olive Mount disaster, the industrial trade from Manchester was choked. In desperate times for the port, slaving returned, illicitly at first, and later legally when parliamentary bills set out various "exemptions" to the abolition act. The trade ceased at last in the 1860s after the American Civil War, and any slaves in Britain at the time were given their liberty. Freedom – but no work, not from the great land-owning aristocrats who dominated the region's economy. So Patience's family had come to London, which was big and hungry enough to offer them employment.

"Edith herself was born a slave." Patience cackled, opening a mouth with only a couple of stubby teeth. "Scrubs up well, doesn't she?"

As if on cue Edith returned. Giles and Ulrich stood. She was freshly washed and with her hair properly done up, her royal household uniform spick and span. "Giles. Thanks ever so for coming. I'm sorry to be so silly."

"It's all right. Your mother has been most gracious. Look, I've come because I thought we should talk. What you said about the race – and then the Trevi bomb going off like that –"

"It's Gemma! You know, my friend, you met her. I got it all from her. She just warned me to stay away from the Queen's Trevi, that was all. We are good pals, you know. She was only looking out for me. She made me promise not to tell, not even you! But I was shocked. I couldn't let you go ahead with the race, could I?" She looked at him with an intensity of affection that disturbed him. "Not if…"

"Not if what?" Giles crossed to her, took her hands, and tried to calm her. "Start at the beginning, Edith. It's all right. I'm sure we can sort this out."

"*Are* you sure? I'm not."

And she told him what her friend Gemma had told her, of the Jubilee Plot.

It was to be a threefold strike: the Irish assault on Westminster Abbey, the sabotage of the Queen's Trevi – and finally, Edith told him, her voice trembling, the most devastating assault of all, a detonation that would sever one of the long spans of the new Jubilee Bridge, just as the inaugural autocar race reached that point.

She whispered, "Oh, nobody expected all the bombs to work. But if just one did it might be enough. It"s all about striking back, you see. That's what Gemma told me. About showing you are strong."

"And how," Ulrich asked sternly, "does this Gemma know such things?"

Gemma Brady had family connections to the Home Rule campaigners who had attacked Westminster. But the Irish had links to other groups, anarchists, agitators for universal suffrage, campaigners against poverty, who together had worked out this spectacular multiple plot timed for a most symbolic moment, the Queen's own Jubilee.

Giles shook his head. "Do these fools imagine they will win their arguments by blowing up the Queen?"

"But what else are they to do, Giles? Call it an experiment in revolution! I've talked this through with Gemma and others. There are a lot of very clever people working below stairs, believe me! I've even been to a few meetings to hear for myself." But she hesitated; almost certainly any such meeting would be regarded as an illegal combination. "Look, for decades every step at reform in this country has been thwarted. The last attempt at parliamentary reform failed in 1832. The Chartists were prosecuted in 1838. Laws about factory inspections and the hours you can work a child were defeated or repealed in the 1840s. Efforts to repeal the Corn Laws were defeated in 1846, and the poor stayed hungry…"

This litany of history dismayed Giles, who knew little of these events; he found it slightly obsessive. And yet there was something admirable in this girl's self-taught understanding.

"It's amazing we haven't had revolts before, as they have in Europe. In 1848 –"

"You should have gone to the police," Ulrich said sternly.

"What, and get locked up as a conspirator myself? You know what the police are like – at least you do, Giles. And it's worse for a woman, believe me. And what if the agitators find out I've been talking to you, what if *they* come after me? Who will protect me then?"

Giles was moved, if astonished. "So you risked your life to save mine?"

Ulrich murmured, "Evidently she cares about you, Romillie. Can't imagine why."

Giles looked uneasily into his own soul. He had never thought of Edith in such terms at all – not at all. She was from a different category of society from him, and always would be.

How could he love such a girl? And how could he deal with the prospect that such a girl loved him?

Ulrich said, "We must set off if we are to be back in time."

Edith stared at Giles. "You won't give me away –"

"Of course not," Giles said, distressed she thought him capable of it.

"And, oh, say you won't race! You can find some way to cry off. Say you're ill. Or get the race cancelled, or at least postponed… There must be a way."

But Giles recoiled from the very thought. He glanced at Ulrich, and saw in the German's eyes that he understood.

*Giles wanted to race.* At this moment he cared nothing for Chartists or angry disenfranchised Irishmen. Even when he looked at the children crowding around Patience Wilcox, he felt this way. Tomorrow I will find out all about the history of electoral reform, he promised his Lord. For today, let me race.

But did he have the courage to see that resolution through?

Six o'clock approached, as measured by clocks set to Paris time – England had no universal standard time of its own, for it had no national rail system that required it.

Giles climbed into his Boulton coal-gas autocar alongside the other racers in their American Selden designs and German four-stroke petrol-engines, and Ulrich in his Daimler. It was a magnificent setting, the gleaming autocars lined up across the clean new roadway, the bridge set straight before him in bold, intimidating perspective, and the bright blue sky of a June evening over it all. The morning scare had much reduced the crowd, but the few spectators remaining were being rewarded with a cold collation, and beer for the men and tea for the women and children. And, it was said, the Prince of Wales was still here, braving out the panic, determined to open the bridge and start the race.

It would all have seemed perfect, the culmination of Giles's young life so far, if not for the doubt that still churned in his stomach.

He still had not finally decided if he should race. Even if Edith were correct about the bomb being placed on the bridge, there was no reason to suppose it would work as planned; the Jubilee Plot conspirators had failed twice today already – but still, if he raced he would be gambling with his life.

Or he could tell his father or the police all he had learned from Edith. If he did so, he would be safe, come what may. But he would show his father he had been dabbling with the wrong sort of girl. A floozy was one thing, but a girl with a brain and exposure to radical ideas was quite wrong for him. And the race would surely be stopped; he would lose his only chance.

And, worst of all, he would show himself to his father to be a coward: to be unwilling to take the ultimate risk in search of glory. It made it worse that Ulrich sat patiently waiting for the start, as aware of the risk as Giles was.

He still had come to no final decision minutes before the off, when his father walked up and clambered into the passenger seat beside him.

"Don't mind me stowing away, do you?"

Giles, astonished, could only reply, "Not at all, Father."

"I thought we should chat." Sir Joshua ran a finger along the leather surround of the dashboard. "Look, boy – do you understand what you're doing here? Do you understand *why* you're here?"

"What do you mean?"

Sir Joshua shifted in his seat to look at his son. "Just this. We're an old lot, we Romillies. For centuries we got our money and power from land, the oldest asset of all. But that all started to change in my father's time – your grandpapa's, God rest his soul. Suddenly there was industry everywhere; suddenly there was trade; suddenly there were these absurdly wealthy fellows in grimy northern cities making demands for parliamentary representation. And then that wretched man Stephenson started throwing down his railway lines.

"Well, your grandpapa and others of like mind had soon had enough. Once they had rid of Grey and his Reform Bill, they decided to deal with Stephenson and his crew. We were all for transport, it was obvious the old canals and roads weren't sufficient, but railways were far too – ugh! – *democratic*. Grandpapa told me of one of his workers who spent his pennies on a train ride to the coast. Do you know what it does to a man, to see the sea for the first time? Fills his head full of longings that can't be fulfilled. No, the railways had to go. Of course the argument mightn't have been won if not for the Olive Mount disaster."

In that notorious catastrophe, a cutting close to the Liverpool terminus of Stephenson's Liverpool & Manchester line had collapsed, crushing two packed passenger trains and killing hundreds – including Stephenson himself. The collapse was supposedly caused by poor excavation and vibration from the trains themselves.

Giles said, "Nobody wanted to ride the railway after that. I remember Grandpapa saying so."

Sir Joshua smiled. "Fortuitous, wasn't it? And good riddance to ruddy Stephenson, of course."

*Fortuitous.* Suddenly Giles saw what his father was telling him. The Jubilee Plot wasn't the only conspiracy he was learning about today.

"After that we Romillies didn't look back. We made a fortune during the Crimean War, when we poured buses and wagons into the conflict, and bought the lot back afterwards, along with an army of trained veteran drivers, the beginnings of a new industry of motor-driven hauliers. The recent war with the Ottomans was almost as profitable."

"I never really understood why we had to fight the Ottomans..."

"Oil," Sir Joshua said firmly. "That's all. The oil under the provinces we took, Baghdad, Basra, and Mosul. Oh, don't look so shocked! All the experts assure me that petrol technology is the way of the future. That doesn't mean to say the race can't be won by coal gas, today..."

Engines were throttled. Giles looked around. A box had been set up at one side of the road; a number of men surrounded a portly figure in a military uniform who must be the Prince of Wales. A white flag was raised: one minute to the start. Giles tested his throttle and choke, and squeezed the foot bulb that controlled the flow of gas. The engine hummed sweetly. He glanced across at Ulrich, who looked back at him sombrely.

Sir Joshua sat back in his seat, fixed a harness across his chest, and adjusted goggles before his eyes. "So you do understand what's happening here, do you, Giles? This new bridge, this race, this very autocar, they all represent the England *we* have built, we and others of our class. And now at this moment of national celebration the eyes of empire and the world are on us – on *you*. That is why what you are about to do is so important..."

The flag remained poised. Only seconds remained for Giles to make his choice.

It all swirled around in his head.

Above all, he found, *he still wanted to race*, that was the iron frame of his thinking. Even if it cost him Edith – even if there were other costs, and for some reason he thought uneasily of the hollow faces of Edith's brothers and sisters – even if it cost him his life, he had to race. And even if he were weighed down by his father's baleful presence, and the autocar by his weight, he would win.

He made his decision.

The flag fell. He engaged the engine. The Boulton shot forward.

He had travelled perhaps half a mile before he realised that his was the only vehicle that had started. The rest remained lined up on the grid.

Sheepishly he turned the autocar around and drove it back to the start.

"You arranged this," he said to his father.

"Surely that's obvious! Oh, don't worry, the bridge has been made safe. I set up this little trial with the race starter. Prince Edward himself thought it was all rather a lark!"

"So you know. About the Jubilee Plot, the bomb, Edith –"

"Of course I know. The police picked up that silly Brady girl even before you sneaked away from me in the crowd. Well, you were followed. The police should have collected Edith Wilcox by now."

"She wasn't involved," Giles said hotly. "She only knew what Gemma told her."

"That"s what she told *you*. But even if so, she didn't report it as she should have done, did she?

"As for you, I saw an ideal opportunity to test you, boy. I merely wanted to see if you had the courage, the sheer blind bloody-minded guts to hurl yourself into a race for glory, even if there was a good chance you would kill yourself in the process – and me, by God! And that was precisely what you did." He patted Giles's shoulder. "Good boy! You are a Romillie after all."

Giles reversed the autocar back into its starting place. The other drivers applauded him ironically. He glanced across at Ulrich, who shrugged at him and grinned. "I see you shared this plot with Zuba."

"Oh, yes. I didn't want *him* babbling about potential bombs. He was happy to go along with it. He too wants to win. And he sees a better chance of doing so without you in the race."

Giles frowned. "What do you mean, without me? I could win this yet."

"No." Sir Joshua leaned past him and opened his door. "Out you get."

"What?"

Sir Joshua's face became thunderous. "You kept the truth from me, boy! And, worse, you *hesitated*. You should have hauled the girl by her ear down to a police station, or brought her to me. *I* make family decisions, not you; when faced with a dilemma you come to me, you do not act alone. You need to learn a lesson."

"And this is the lesson?"

Sir Joshua grinned. "Certainly. To watch me take the glory that should have been yours. Never mind! There might be another chance for you when Victoria reaches her Diamond Jubilee in ten years" time. Out you hop. Shoo, shoo!"

So Giles got out of the autocar, pulled off his goggles, gloves and cap, and walked away, off the bridge. The spectators smirked and giggled. Everybody else seemed to have been in on his father's joke, save him.

There was a roar of engines. The spectators cheered. So the race was underway. Giles didn't bother turning around.

His father had set him a test he believed Giles had passed. Giles wasn't so sure, not any more. Perhaps, in fact, he had failed.

He thought of Edith, who had winked at him boldly when he was on the roof of the bandstand – Edith the freed slave and her mother and her toiling siblings – Edith who had tried to save his life, and had paid for it with her own liberty. He didn't even know if he loved Edith. He had never posed the question to himself before today. But now he wondered if he deserved such loyalty, such love. Perhaps that was the next test he would have to pass.

And as for her 'experiment in revolution' – well, now that she seemed to have provoked a revolution in his own heart, perhaps other tests lay ahead. A role in such a revolution for the heir of a family who had grown so rich while so many others had stayed so poor might be difficult to find...

But first he must find *her*. He looked around for a policeman, to ask him where Edith might be held, and how he could see her.

# Wilson at Woking

Ken MacLeod

The Greek chick in the leathers had roared up on a Harley, her pretty blonde pal on the pillion carrying a bow and arrows. The girls were both minor royalty, and the buxom brunette had some military rank – honorary, of course, and not much excuse for being there, but I suppose HMG has to keep the colonels happy. The Greek and Portuguese military attachés were off on the far left, looking at the burning town through binoculars. Jerzy Kornel, from the Czechoslovak Embassy, was the only foreigner there I recognised. I waved and headed towards him.

Wilson stood in the centre of the trench, on a short stepladder that enabled him to peer over the top of the sandbags. Instantly recognisable with his trademark Gannex coat and Dunhill pipe, he talked to the Chief of Staff, Lord Montgomery, in a low voice just loud enough to carry to the microphones of the BBC and ITV crews who crouched a few yards away. I caught a snatch of it as I scurried past, head down:

"Alamein," he was saying, flattering the old poser, who (typically) was standing one step higher on his own stepladder, "I frankly don't see anything the RAF can't handle."

"But, Prime Minister, my chaps are ready at a moment's notice to..."

Close by, a likewise earnest and public exchange was going on between a Brigadier and a white-haired scientist, eccentric in Carnaby Street Edwardian rig. I overheard some remark from the latter about sticky-tape across windows as a precaution against nuclear blast.

It was all for the benefit of the masses glued to the box. Morale boosting, very much needed after the images of the refugee columns streaming towards London, and the heat-rays flickering from the gigantic, half-buried cylinders on Horsell Common. So far, the word 'Martians' hadn't passed any official lips, but that hadn't stopped speculation, some of it even wilder.

I picked my way past the tangled cables of the TV OBUs. Jerzy wore a black velvet smoking-jacket over the olive-green shirt and trousers of a Czechoslovak People's Army uniform. He held out a cigarette pack and tapped.

"Light up an Embassy." Grinning, he flicked his Ronson for me then gave me what was for him a serious look. His voice was barely audible above the thud of the Beeb's generator, and the distant roar of the Vulcans circling below the horizon.

"Do you think it's the Russians?"

"Harold was on the red phone first thing," I said, as if I'd been at his elbow rather than having heard the rumour third-hand. "He's positive it's not. Word from the top. Straight from the Kremlin's onion domes, old boy."

"He trusts Brezhnev," said Jerzy, more sourly than seemed appropriate.

"Well, naturally," I said. "These two go all the way back to Helm's Deep."

I didn't need to allude to the other battles of the Second World War in which Wilson, Brezhnev, and Kennedy – the Big Three, as my father's generation called them – had forged their unbreakable alliance, shoulder to shoulder against the Weimar Germans' cyborg hordes and genetically engineered slave races.

"They've had their differences since."

I laughed. "The PM likes to say that when you've faced down the National Union of Boilermakers..."

Jerzy shrugged one shoulder. "Spare me. So who is it?"

A heat-ray scorched the air overhead, setting alight a gorse-bush half a mile behind us.

"That," I said, "is what you might call the burning question."

My presence at what later came to be called the Battle of Woking was pure chance, though no more so than the presence of most of those who'd turned up for what was as much a media circus as a national emergency. How a research assistant for the Fabian Society found himself working in 10 Downing Street is not worth recounting here – such sudden preferments were part and parcel of the Wilson style of government, aiming to circumvent the senior civil servants, conservative to a man. So it was that I found myself in the cramped back seat of a black Morris Minor at the tail end of the cavalcade of official cars that trundled out of Central London and sped down the M3 and M25 that fine May morning.

The three cylinders had arrived the night before, and the Fighting Machines had begun to lay waste to Woking almost as soon as the first lid had slowly unscrewed and toppled to the grass. The Astronomer Royal, Sir Patrick Moore, had rushed to the midnight emergency meeting of Wilson's notorious 'kitchen Cabinet' with what he claimed were photographs from a few weeks earlier of mysterious flashes on the planet Mars. They'd been wired from the Royal Observatory near Edinburgh, in North Britain. To the untrained eye the plates showed little more than a cracked sphere, with notable imperfections in resolution, but Sir Patrick assured us that he'd identified the source of the flashes as a major confluence of canals, and probable population centre, located as it was in the midst of a particularly lush area of Martian vegetation.

"This lush vegetation of yours," said Harold, stabbing at the blurry, over-enlarged photo with the stem of his pipe, "seems to have vanished from the latest picture."

"Precisely!" cried Sir Patrick, eyebrows twitching like the wings of a demented hen. "The fields have been stripped bare to supply the expedition! This is the last throw of a dying race, gentlemen! We are in serious danger!"

"Well then," Harold growled, "it's about bloody time we went out and had a look."

It had taken the redoubtable Marcia Falkender to talk him into at least waiting until the troops had surrounded the area. Which, over the remaining hours of the night, the Surrey Regiment – known since the Peninsular War as Sharpe's Rifles – had very competently done. Though not without cost; a Fighting Machine and a Chieftain tank were a terrifyingly even match. A direct hit from one could destroy the other. After a few such exchanges, each side had pulled back – the Fighting Machines to the cylinders, the troops and tanks to hastily-constructed trenches and berms. Hence the current stand-off.

It couldn't last. Aerial photography had revealed that some

process of manufacture – of more Fighting Machines, presumably – was going on inside the cylinders, but the heat rays had shot down too many brave pilots for even the RAF to dare to attempt to discern anything further. Beyond the heat-rays' reach, the Vulcans circled, awaiting the dreadful order to expend their hydrogen bombs – after, I could only hope, everyone had fled the area, and all the windows of London had been secured with sticky tape.

Jerzy stubbed out his cigarette on the side of the trench.

"No," he said. "The burning question isn't who they are. The burning question is what they have against gorse bushes."

I laughed.

"I'm serious," he said. "Their first targets – after the foolish gawpers – were the trees on the Common, and in the town's gardens and parks. They'll aim the heat-rays at a tank or plane in the open, but not at tanks behind sand-bags. Now they're burning the bushes. Why?"

"To create a conflagration, obviously, and the cover of smoke." I coughed, not from the gasper. "A tactic they're succeeding in."

"They could aim at cars or houses, which are far more inflammable. Instead, they attack vegetation."

Vegetation... something about that nagged at my mind.

"They stripped vegetation from around their launch sites –" I began, then belatedly shut up.

"'They'?" Jerzy quirked an eyebrow. "Ah, so you do know who they are!"

"It's speculative," I said.

"So? Tell me!"

I told him of Moore's claims. To my surprise, he didn't scoff. Instead, he leaned forward and spoke quietly.

"This all makes sense now," he murmured. "The Russians landed a space probe on Mars last month."

I yelped. "My God, man! Why don't we know of this?"

"They intended to keep it quiet until all the results were in, then announce it with much fanfare at the Party congress in October." He shrugged. "You know the Russians. Everything's for propaganda advantage."

"How do *you* know about it?" I asked.

Jerzy tapped the side of his nose. "Here is a Czech riddle: are the Russians our friends, or our brothers?"

I shook my head.

"Our brothers! You *choose* your friends."

I laughed politely. "But what's the connection between the Russian probe and – this?"

"The Russian probe," said Jerzy, "was atomic-powered. Who knows what damage it may have done? This" – he waved his arm around at the scene – "is more than a return visit. It's retaliation."

A sudden commotion interrupted us – yells, screams, a distant thud of artillery. Whirling around, and recklessly stretching to see over the lip of the trench, I saw Fighting Machines swarm from the cylinders like newly-hatched flies from carrion. Their previous striding motion had been replaced by a remarkable, rapid bobbing-and-weaving: they simply *dodged* the tanks' shells. I ducked hard and fast as the heat-ray barrage intensified overhead into a grid of fire.

Everyone in the trench had likewise crouched, or thrown themselves flat in the mud. We all cowered, even Lord Montgomery. All – except Wilson. He stood one step higher on the ladder, pipe in one hand and a bulky walkie-talkie clutched in the other.

"Now, Tony!" I heard him shout. "Now!"

From all around us, a sound arose that overwhelmed the noises of the distant jets, the shelling, the generator, the screams. It was the most fearsome racket I'd ever heard in my life. I looked up, just in time to be blasted head over heels by a ferocious down-draught from something enormous that passed about six feet above the top of the trench.

I picked myself up, and – inspired perhaps by Wilson's still unflinching demeanour – lunged to the front of the trench and hauled myself up to peer over. Dozens of grey-painted, armour-plated hovercraft, each about half the size of a house, were hurtling from all directions around the Common. They moved so fast that they were in among the Fighting Machines in seconds. Their prows sliced at the tripods' legs, knocking them down like ninepins.

But as I watched, I saw Fighting Machines that had been knocked down struggle to their feet. Their heat-rays still slashed the sky. Whenever a ray hit one of the hovercraft, it left a visible scorch from which smoke drifted. I could just make out the red-hot craters left in the hulls of these land ironclads. No ray had penetrated yet, but it could be only a matter of moments before the Martians improved their aim and learned to repeat their shots.

Then I saw an astonishing thing. I don't think anyone else did: only Wilson was cool enough, and I unhinged enough, to be looking. A few tens of yards away, the leather-clad Greek girl hoisted her slender friend – foot in cupped hands – right on to the edge of the trench. There the blonde stood, clad only in her flimsy minidress, and shot off in rapid succession a score or two of arrows from the quiver on her shoulder.

Each arrow flew unerringly to some joint or other in a Fighting Machine. And one by one, the terrible tripods toppled, not to rise again. The whole thing was over in about a minute. A silence fell, broken only by a mournful hooting from the felled machines, and a moment later by the roar of a departing motorcycle.

The day afterwards, it turned out that Brezhnev had taken the opportunity of the distraction to move Russian armoured divisions into Prague. Jerzy was beside himself. I took him to Number 10, in breach of all protocol.

Wilson picked up the red phone.

"Leonid," he snarled, "*get your tanks off my lawn*!"

And, incredibly, Brezhnev agreed.

There's little further to add. Except this: Wilson always attributed the victory to himself and to Tony Benn's armoured atomic hovercraft, which had melted the Martian invaders in the white heat of the technological revolution. He knew as well as I did that this wasn't true. But that's how it went into the history books – and we all know about them.

"The history books will be kind to me," Wilson used to chuckle. "I know, because I'll write them."

And, of course, he did.

Note: *this story is dedicated to that small, happy percentage of my compatriots who (according to a recent survey) believe that the Prime Minister of Great Britain during the Second World War was Harold Wilson; that the Battle of Helm's Deep, the War of the Worlds, Xena, and Richard Sharpe were real historical events and persons; and that the Battle of the Bulge, William Wallace, Adolf Hitler, and the Cold War were not.* – Ken MacLeod.

# The Killing Fields

Kim Lakin-Smith

The 1974 Triumph Stag V8 prowled the country roads, oiled black angles flickering against the night like a mirage. Regan gripped the leather steering wheel and glanced behind her. Curled up on the back seat under a worn blanket, the kid slept, her head awkwardly positioned on the makeshift pillow of an AK-47 assault rifle. She was snoring.

They hadn't hit a road block for the last fifty miles. Just as well, since they'd run out of currency as far back as Birmingham, Regan mused, downshifting the gears and easing off the accelerator to coast into a hairpin bend. But while she doubted any self-respecting road hog would bed down in such a desolate spot, it never paid to be complacent. Not when thy neighbour would sooner sell your ass to the highest bidder as help you out, particularly if it guaranteed a dozen extra food stamps or a tankful of bioethanol. Not when the 2020 civil war had seen every major city in England shorn back to its seedy underbelly, like stains on an otherwise green and pleasant land. Not when they were navigating a land of single-track roads, tangled hedgerows and night-shrouded middle distance, and Regan's foremost thought was *too quiet by far.*

"Are we there yet?"

Regan stared at the melancholy girl reflected in the rear-view mirror. "We're definitely *somewhere.*"

All raisin eyes and bed-head, the kid slung the gun aside and poured herself over the handbrake into the front seat. "Got anything to eat?"

Reaching sideways, Regan punched the glove box. She located a scrunched up brown paper bag and handed it over. "Couple of boiled eggs you filched off that farmer's wife this morning."

The kid grabbed the bag. Rooting around inside, she retrieved an egg, tapped it on the dash and started prising off the shell. "Nice lady," she said a minute later, her voice thickened by a mouthful of egg.

"Who?" shot Regan. She reined in the Stag as they approached a signpost.

"Mrs Jacobs. She pinched my cheeks." The kid rubbed at her face as if shining up the memory.

*Another half a mile.* Regan kept the vehicle at a sedate pace as the road turned into a dirt track. "Guess she thought you were just a kid."

"I *am* just a kid."

"Might look like one, but you've as much in common with the average eleven year old as I have with a nun," said Regan flatly. "Pinched your cheeks." She shook her head, bemused by the kid's idealised version of events and keeping stum about the truth, which was that while Mrs Jacobs had acted mother hen, her husband had followed Regan to the tithe barn where the Stag was garaged.

Bolting the door, Mr Jacobs had fixed her with rheumy, thread-veined eyes. "Wife says sorry but we can't let you leave without some dispensation."

Regan raised the bonnet of the Stag, leant into the engine and drew out the dipstick. She swiped the rod with a rag. "We traded a day's labour for provisions," she reminded him without emotion. "It was your wife who suggested we kip in the hayloft. I'll just load up the goods we rightfully purchased then me and the kid'll hit the road."

"Except I can't let you do that. It's the wife, see. Says the car's worth eight gallons of bioethanol on the open market. So I'm going to have to *insist*."

Regan glanced back over a shoulder to see the man reach for a pitch-fork. She replaced the rod, unhooked the arm of the bonnet rest and let the hood fall. "You're not getting my car."

The farmer moved towards her. He tried out a nasty smile. "What if I let you keep the car and you pay me in kind for my wife's hospitality. Nice girl like you has got to know a trick or two."

"I sure do," she drawled and eased back against the bonnet. Mr Jacob's smile broadened. Bending at the waist, she reached between her legs and ripped two CZ-75 handguns from their tape holsters under the Stag's front bumper. She tossed the guns up into the air, snatched at each with the opposite hand, cocked the clips and aimed twin barrels at the man's forehead. "I can juggle," she said dryly.

Later, when the farmer was duck-taped to the rusty, cobwebbed tines of an old ripper, trousers round his ankles, and Regan had refastened the handguns under the bumper, slung back the bolt and eased open both sides of the creaking barn door, she leant in by his ear. "And I'm not a nice girl." The pitchfork pierced the dirt an inch short of his groin.

"These are *bloody* tasty."

Regan became aware of the half-devoured boiled egg being wafted under her nose and forced her mind back to the present.

She cut her eye at the girl. "Don't swear." Turning in between part-hinged, dilapidated gates, she took it steady on a minefield of earth clods and potholes.

"I can fire guns but I can't swear?" The kid crammed the remnants of egg into her mouth.

The red haze of the beet farm's first warning lamp bled into the Stag's headlights. Regan felt a familiar sense of foreboding. "You don't have to swear to stay alive," she muttered.

Two types of farm existed post-civil war. There was the conventional sort devoted to agriculture and raising livestock, with produce quotas pooled and reassigned by the government, and which remained a relatively tranquil way to make a living. And then there was the beet farm, its acreage seeded with the raw plant stuff used to make bioethanol, and, as such, reduced to a rabid war zone by gang violence, mafia-owned cartels, and vigilantism. Given its rural location in the Shropshire Hills, the welsh-stone farmhouse could have been mistaken for the former, were it not for the bullet-pocked sheet steel coating the front door or the iron mesh at the gable windows either side of the porch. A sense that visitors were anything but welcome was reinforced by the hostile blaze of motion-triggered halogen bulbs and the warning bursts from a pair of wall-mounted flame throwers.

"Who's there?" demanded a voice sandpapered free of sentiment.

"The Scarecrow." Arms draping the open, driver-side door of the Stag, Regan tossed back her head, gulped to activate the resonator chip embedded in her throat then rapidly exhaled. The sound that issued from her lips was a reverberating caw, just bearable to the ear and synthetic. She closed her mouth suddenly. The noise cut off.

Regan waited as bolts shifted back, chains rippled, and, in a series of halting jars, the door worked open. A figure filled the doorway, chest panelled like a mutant armadillo, legs elephantine in voluminous canvas combats, feet encased in twenty hole bovver boots, and hair that stretched beyond the waist.

"Chase the red dragon out of my arse, if it ain't the original Scarecrow. Malkin as we'd call you in these parts, but who's splitting hairs?" Harrison stepped into the light, piggy eyes blinking. He stuck out a hand. Regan swung the car door to and strode over. Their hands sealed.

"Regan. I'd say thanks for dropping by, but we both know it was the scent of money got you hooked."

Regan cocked her head at the dark fields. "Grapevine says you've got yourself some rats."

"A proper pest problem this year. They're holed up at old man Robinson's o'er the hill. He pegged it last June."

"What breed?"

"Pirates."

"Shit." Regan raked a fist over her shaved head. If there was ever a breed of raiders guaranteed to kick up a stink, it was pirates. While their peers were employed by a handful of the world's elite crime syndicates – south-east Asian triads, Russian Bratva, a clan of the Naples' Camorra, and a few significant others – pirates were gang-led, targeting a different beet farm every harvest and with zero scope for negotiation.

"Numbers?" Her mind raced ahead, checking off hardware and small firearms stored under a false lining in the boot of the Stag.

"Crew of about eight or nine. Haven't had a run-in yet but I've seen the freaks cruising out by Claw Pond. Couple of choppers, a quad, dune buggy, dirt bikes, a Baja bug. Stilt walkers too."

"Just your common old garden variety of crop pirates then."

"Reckon so, except…" Harrison indicated Regan's bee-stung mouth – or as she interpreted it, the lethal voice box stitched inside her throat. "This crowd have got themselves a bona fide Captain Hook."

Regan dragged the back of a hand across her lips as if she'd been slugged in the mouth. Captain Hook was slang for a bandit touting the hardware to deflect a Scarecrow's infrasonic scream. She spat into the dirt. "Harvest starts…"

"First light tomorrow. I pulled the specimen beet on Thursday. Got the thumbs up from the lab today for sugar content."

"I'd best get an early night then. Half my money up front." She put out a hand.

The farmer rooted around beneath his breastplate. He drew out an envelope. Regan reached for the cash, but he held onto the envelope a second. "Where's that pretty little girl of yours?" His piggy eyes interrogated the Stag's back seat. "You've never gone and hid her in the boot again?"

"Not mine." Regan ripped the envelope from his fingers and stashed it inside her cropped leather. Stalking over to the car, she popped the boot and slung up the lid. The kid rolled out in a tangle of assault rife, daisy-shaped sunglasses and skinny limbs. She landed crouched with her gun trained on Harrison's breastbone. "Not pretty," Regan added darkly.

Mist ghosted the soft panorama of patchwork fields and drystone walls. Astride the icy metal gate, Regan swiped her stun baton to and fro like a homicidal majorette. She put her lips together and blew. A reedy whistle echoed off her cold surroundings. It was a human sound, but Regan recognised the nuances in the crackle of static on her tongue, and the small rush of air through very fine, steel vocal chords.

"Warming up?"

Regan stared up at a colourless sky. "I told you to stay back at the farm."

The girl scooted up alongside Regan, the gate clanging noisily with the extra vibrations. "Didn't want to. That farmer gives me the willies."

"Harrison? He's a harmless old coot."

"Folk said the same about Pol Pot."

Regan stared at the youngster.

"What? I went to school once. Once," repeated the girl, hiding her face to chase an itch at her ankle. Then she froze.

"Yeah, I hear it." Regan jerked her head left then right. She sniffed. The strange sweet smell of burning bioethanol filled her nostrils. "Coming in from the south. Stack of them. Going to scoot now?"

The gate reverberated. The girl had gone.

Regan waited with an even throb of a heartbeat, aware of the silverware in her throat. She cooed devilishly.

Claw Pond was an excellent spot to pick a fight. Not so much a pond as a dip in the ground, it was a dust bowl in the summer, glacier in winter, and a mud track all the weeks in-between. In its present frosted state, it was also the spot to house a nine row, self-propelled Beet Harvester. The pirates had raided more than the farmhouse at old man Robinson's, Regan concluded, pressing her mouth to the lock. The vibrations which emanated from her throat worked the pins and released the lock. Opening the door, she swung up inside and crouched – it would pay her to observe the gang. To know a man was to kill him.

Inside the minute, the grid beneath her feet shook with the noise of them. In great scooping waves of sound, they descended. Regan gauged the gang from behind the cover of grimed glass. Harrison was right in his estimation. Nine pirates, sand sharks judging by their weathered leathers and sun-dirtied skin. It was unusual for sand sharks to desert the beaches of the south-west and Wales, and their hijacking of anything the sea cared to deliver up: pleasure craft, fishing trawlers, and the solitary swimmer. But the beet farms were rich pickings. Regan's upper lip curled. Every other piece of scum in the UK believed himself man enough to have a go.

"Saddle her up." The command came from a man who looked as if he had been torn out of the earth and left to mulch down amongst his own bones. His hair was a tangled yellow mane. His leathers were dirty brown, and cracked or patched at the joints. He was short and muscular, and his dirt bike pep-pepped under him.

"You sure the Scarecrow ain't here already, Samson?" This from a large man in the bug, a pirate who was over-fleshed at the throat so that his head seemed to float above his shoulders.

"Not sure of anything when it comes to the Scarecrow, but we've got ourselves a Hook. Only question is, are any of you pussies man enough to stick it in her?"

Regan patted herself reflexively, feeling for the bone handle of the buffalo skinner poking out of its smooth leather sheaf on one hip, the checkered grip of the holstered P-32 semi-automatic on the other. She could see the Hook, or at least its harpoon cannon mounted between the handlebars of the yellow-maned rider's dirt bike. If discharged, the canon fired a miniature magnetised disc designed to home in on her throat, slice flesh and disable her sonic scream.

So the man in brown was its Captain. Regan felt the ghost of something like revulsion. She'd keep him in her sights; it'd be good to see him die. All she had to do was get the rest of the pirates within a ten metre radius then start screaming.

"I'll do the first shift on the harvester." The voice was young, a boy not yet comfortable in his adult skin. A second dirt bike was silenced. She heard footsteps and the scrabble of rubber sole on metal. Vehicles idled in the background. The voices of walking dead men melded. To Regan, the cab of the harvester was hot as hell and airless suddenly. *Now it starts.*

Opening the cab door, he saw her, startlement etched on his face as she slid in the knife…she'd learnt the rough way in the past that it did not pay to negotiate with pirates. He died in her arms like the child he had longed to be. Regan shook the body off.

It was a few minutes before the dead pirate was missed. Regan knew she had the Captain spooked when he sent his next weakest soldier, a thin girl, all hips and lips, with a shock of lemon-coloured hair. She rode in on her quad, a wide-axled black wasp. Dismounting, she sidled up onto the Harvester and reached for the cab door; Regan kicked it out into her face.

The girl ricocheted back. She fell badly. Regan heard bone snap. Staring up at her, the female pirate's features shrunk in upon themselves. "Scarecrow!" she hollered before swallowing a bullet.

Regan launched herself out of the harvester, tucked in her elbows and sprinted.

First to react were the stilt walkers, gangly and muscular on their clanking, pneumatic metal limbs. They moved towards her in enrapture, like insects siphoning off her juices.

It was the crackle of electricity which made her risk a glance backwards. The stiltwalkers reached for her with long, rubber batons tipped with coiled metal. Regan felt the flush of extra adrenalin. Her taser was a toy next to those mothers.

"Run Scarecrow run," teased the tall boys in their hoodies and graffitied board shorts. Regan sprinted harder. Her flight had been intended as a ruse to lure all of the pirates into pursuit. Now the stakes had been upped. On impulse, she slid to the ground as she ran, drew the P-32, used the propulsion to roll onto her back and peeled off a couple of shots. One stiltwalker crumpled, his baton falling onto the earth, rolling, and completing a 360 degree radial before shocking its owner. The other daddy-long-legs plunged his coil against her arm.

A tight rip of pain shot through her. Regan fought the need to gag. Air flooded between her parted lips, lit up the antechamber of her throat with its chords, flesh and resonator, and she sang then, a string of metal notes designed to ground her. The pain vanished. The stiltwalker stabbed her again with the cry of "Shoot her now, Samson, while she's out!" Her song had also drained his baton of its charge; the stiltwalker used it as a battering ram while kicking out at her with his mechanical legs.

Steam released in great wet bursts. Pistons shunted hard against her face. Amongst the blur of flesh and metal, Regan made out a face. She smashed out with a fist and felt the pull of skin beneath her knuckles. The stiltwalker buckled back. Regan threw aside the now useless P-32; she would have needed to return the handgun to its memofibre holster to shield the weapon against her song. Ripping her taser from a sheath inside her leather, she jacked back up onto her feet and lunged at the stiltwalker's face. Spasming, he collapsed to one side as the roar of what Regan knew had to be the choppers dirtied up the morning air.

Her game was off. Only three dead and she was way out in the open. With the rest of the pirates outside of the ten metre radius that she required to unleash the full, lethal capacity of her sonic scream, she was a sitting duck.

Regan squinted at the Captain sat astride his dirt bike and resting forward, his elbows on the handlebars. Her skin prickled. He was playing with her. But she was on fire with the thrill of the fight. She could deflect their bullets and knives; all she had to do was give a little whistle. Meanwhile, they'd got the Hook, which meant that she would just have to have eyes in the back of her head.

With the choppers circling her like tremendous metal dragonflies, Regan tore her gaze left and right. The men astride the hogs wore tight black leathers, mirrored aviators and tie-dye bandanas, their features indistinguishable. Identical twins, she realised, pondering the best route to take them out. A couple of metres away, her opponents were at too close range to draw, aim and fire the borrowed AK-47 assault rifle from the sling at her back. The P-32 handgun abandoned, Regan wielded the stun baton in one hand, the buffalo skinner in the other. If the hogs' riders tried to take a pop at her, she'd lock up their guns' mechanisms with a single note.

But these riders toted a Sai sword apiece. They also seemed less concerned with bringing her down as baiting her.

"Hey girlie. Bet she doesn't get many takers with that throat full of metal."

"Going by appearances, I'd say she's a man-hater. What'd you reckon, Billy? Think the dyke's gonna cry?"

Regan was kneeling down. Utilising the blade as a mirror, she kept the Captain in view. The twin pirates struck her as innately stupid; if she could just sprint past their blades and head for the Captain, she was pretty sure they'd follow, and then she would have the full crew inside the crucial radius.

"I thought Scarecrows were meant to be tough, Billy."

"That's what I heard too, Brad. Whereas this girlie seems sloppy."

"Things aren't always what they seem." Kicking off an icy tree stump that she'd crouched down to conceal, Regan spun herself into a high round house kick, the boot of one foot ricocheting off the left cheekbone of one of the twins. The rider skidded, just managing to right the chopper before he collided with a massive oak. Regan landed, feet splayed, fists tight to her sides, and still clenching her weapons.

The second twin whipped open the throttle of his hog and charged for her. *Beautifully stupid.* Regan took to her heels and ran. With the subterranean pulse of the pursuing choppers at her back, she zigzagged in and out of the branches and brambles at the field's edges. And she could run, Regan reminded herself, feeling the air thick as syrup in her lungs. She'd been running all of her life and she was damn good at it.

Heading for the Harvester and its fresh dead, Regan ducked as one twin drove his Sai at her neck. She didn't want to unseat him, but draw both men back to the killing ground. The incessant swish and stab of the blade was distracting however; she clucked on a mouthful of air, pursed her lips and threw a slicing note at the pirate's hand. He dropped the Sai as if the double-pronged handle was liquid metal.

She stared hard ahead – the Captain hadn't changed position. Neither had his men. The Baja bug idled. Throaty rumbles spattered from the dune buggy's exhaust. And while the chopper rider who had pursued her closest slowed to a crawl as they returned to the basin of Claw Pond, it was the other twin who was most noticeable by his absence.

Regan glanced over a shoulder. No sign. Then she felt the blade plunge in. In seconds, the hot wetness of her own blood greased the inside of her jacket. An inch to the left and the Sai would have punctured a lung; Regan knew her own physiology like a studied map. She tore her shoulder aside before the pirate had a chance to rip out the sword and retry for her heart. *How'd he got up so close?* She risked a sideways glance. He'd abandoned his chopper for her first victim's dirt bike, its sound a more subtle wheeze of noise that had been lost to the revs of the nearing vehicles.

Too late Regan realised that she had taken her eye off the Captain. She heard a cicada-like whirl of sound before feeling a pure, clean bite of pain as the Hook sliced in. Blood ran from her throat, draining between her breasts, becoming cold at her stomach…Regan faltered as she ran. Through a blur, she saw the Captain unfold from the sight of the harpoon at the rear of his dirt bike. She was just aware of a great gust of noise tumbling towards her, the war cry of human voices and engines.

"Shot you down, Scarecrow! Now let's really hear you scream," she heard the Captain demand.

Regan tried for the rifle at her back, but couldn't rip it from its holster. Craning her jaw in a futile bid to drink in the vital air to sound her scream, Regan tried to rip the Hook out. The disc was slippery with blood; she cut her fingers on its razor edge. Through a film of pale, fading consciousness, she saw the pirates closing in, led by their Captain and with their swords and guns drawn. *Get up and fight,* she screamed internally.

Sound pummelled in her ears like fast flowing water. She reeled. The pulse grew stronger, deep, reverberative and lushly mechanical... Regan's eyes shot wide. A dragon in gleaming black body armour smashed through the metal gate to the right of Claw Pond. Regan felt the transfiguring glow of victory as the Stag crashed head on into the soft meat of the Captain's body and carried him high on its bumper before he ricocheted forward and was flayed beneath the wheels. The Stag ripped a path through the beets; Regan fastened her grip hard on the Hook and disgorged it from her throat. She discarded the disc carelessly, like a handful of soil returned to the land, and looked up.

The remaining crop pirates had frozen in mid-stride, their mouths slack, eyes greased and reflecting the figure of the resurrected Scarecrow.

Regan stretched out her arms. Had the girl driven the Stag out of range, Regan imagined that she would have had to crash it, having very little control over the beast of a vehicle and straining to reach the pedals. Her pause was brief. Letting her head fall gently back, feeling the wound at her throat weep, Regan made her voice heard.

Harrison had cleared a good part of the first field by noon. She'd helped him remove the bodies. The girl she'd found inside the shadowed ribs of one of Harrison's unused hay barns. Having ripped clean through the barn door, the Stag had come to rest against a wall of aged hay bales. The girl was alive, forehead blooded at impact. The Stag was intact bar some new scars to the paintwork.

Having patched up her throat, Regan pocketed the remainder of her payment, refuelled the Stag with a full, complementary tank of bioethanol, and pilfered enough of Harrison's larder to last them to the Scottish border. She paused then, resting a foot against a back wheel of the Stag, arms crossed, and surveyed the beet fields, the hardy leaf set in rows and unobtrusive on the landscape. A subtle ache pulsed in her throat.

Where was the girl? How long did it take to clean up a bruised forehead?

Regan eased away from the Stag. She crossed the yard, stepped up onto the porch of the farmhouse and was reaching for the pocked steel door when the kid came crashing out.

"Filthy bastard!" snapped the girl. She glanced back at the doorway and the figure of the farmer now filling it. Harrison was nursing a stained cheek where the girl's fist had connected. He breathed in gulps, eyes wary as they settled on Regan.

Stepping backwards, the Scarecrow drew slowly off the porch.

"I told you not to swear. Get in the car."

She listened for the slam of the passenger-seat door.

"It'll be your turn again in five years, Harrison." Her gaze was steady. "Girl will be all grown up then. Her aim gets better all of the time. Time comes we're knocking at your door again, I'd suggest you watch your ass."

She left the farmer behind, his piggy eyes at her back as she slid into the driver seat of the Stag, told the girl to buckle up, revved the engine and pulled off down the dirt track.

# Having the Time of His Life

Ian Watson

"To be inside some total strangers' house – in their absence! – with a good-looking fellow such as you would excite me a lot," the red-headed woman confided to Andrew after they'd been talking for little more than five minutes. "The idea turns me on like nothing else."

Was this her party trick? Did she tempt men to commit a minor crime in the hope of scoring with her? *Steal me a scarf from that shop and I'm yours*, that sort of thing? Did fellows fall for this, then find out that she was only a tease? Or did they discover *otherwise*?

"Are you proposing we should break in to some place… to make love?"

Of course he'd spotted the redhead as soon as he arrived at the party, but she'd been bantering with some fellow, then with some other man. Had she made the same suggestion to them too?

"Hi, I'm Gwen, who are you?" she'd accosted Andrew presently. She was quite gorgeous: those long red curls, cherubic lips, dark smouldery eyes, full figure in an Indian cotton dress of green and gold sewn with tiny mirrors, high-heeled brown leather boots which brought her to Andrew's height, bright bangles on her wrists, chunky rings on her fingers. She was exotic, provocative. And predatory? Or just capricious?

He'd told her he was a geologist, did analyses of oil company surveys.

"Is that *boring*?" she'd asked with a sly smile.

"Oh no," he'd riposted, "I get my rocks off. I love thinking about rocks. A rock isn't just for Christmas, it's for a billion years."

He'd just divorced after four years, as he soon mentioned to Gwen. Alice's elder sister, who influenced her unduly, had become enraptured by an American Creation Science evangelist. Alice herself duly became sceptical of Andrew's billion-year-old rocks. Maybe sceptical wasn't quite the right word, suggesting as it did rationality rather than credulity. As Andrew saw it, his wife had succumbed to wicked delusions, egged on by that bloody sister of hers. From then on, communion of mind was impossible. The situation became intolerable.

In turn Gwen confided that she had gypsy blood. Did this suggest that magic lurked in her? Magic seemed preferable to fundamentalist lunacy, certainly more fun.

Gwen pursed her lips as if about to plant a kiss, then echoed, "Break in? No no, that's so unsubtle. You get into the home of a stranger by pretending to want to buy it! An estate agent unlocks the door for you."

"And then he or she escorts you round." Andrew was puzzled. "Where's the privacy?"

He visualised himself tumbling Gwen on to a stranger's bed while an estate agent stood by voyeuristically. This seemed highly implausible. He imagined Gwen inviting the estate agent to participate. This might happen in a porn video. In reality rather less often than once in a blue moon.

"So it's all a fantasy of yours. Fair enough!"

"No, I've done it several times. The trick is getting the timing right."

"What, you ask the estate agent to wait downstairs for a few minutes to let us get the feel of the house – as it were!"

"Not exactly."

"In that case, are you a hypnotist?" *Gypsy Gwen the Mesmeriser. See yourself on video doing things you knew nothing about!*

"Hmm," she said. "Seeing is believing, so they say..."

"Not in the case of my ex. For her, belief is – was – like blindness to the Rocky Mountains, Mount Everest, the whole mountain of knowledge."

"But I say *being there* is beyond belief."

"Being where?"

"In the house of total strangers. The witness cannot believe it or see it."

"Sounds like Zen to me."

Around the twin-island of themselves the party ebbed and flowed, bobbing tides of Burgundy goblets, champagne flutes, chilled bottles of various Belgian beers in two huge connected rooms. The party nibbles could have been by Fabergé. A CD of Jazz played. Lights were dim. What an exorbitant house-warming this was, but then the house was worth a million. Of the hosts, the wife appeared quiet and shy, the husband much more outgoing. He seemed to have invited everyone they'd ever met, and by extension everyone's acquaintances.

Gwen added, "So often these days home owners aren't at home when a would-be purchaser comes. That's since it became illegal to tell lies about nuisance neighbours or whatever – it's safer to be absent during a viewing, and the estate agent doesn't know about those things." Now she sounded practical, not fantastical.

"I still don't get it," said Andrew.

"Trust me!" she said. "Shall we make an appointment to view somewhere?"

"Maybe. Why not?"

"I'll choose. A lot of web sites have virtual tours. Rotating videocam on a tripod in the middle of various rooms. I can suss out a good place in advance. Give me your mobile number?"

Like many people, he didn't know it by heart. "Do you have a mob with you?"

A ringed hand plunged into a narrow pocket of that mirrored dress.

"I'll phone you," he said. "You capture the number. Oh, but only if you can tell me yours."

"I can!" Practical, again. She recited her digits as he keyed them in to his mob.

Her ring tone was the *Ride of the Valkyries*. A few people looked round, but Gwen immediately killed the tone. What did the *Ride of the Valkyries* suggest about her?

"There. Done." She snapped the slim handset shut. How weird to phone one another when they were both standing face to face. Was this a new technological way of relating in a world of alienation – or was it an *enhanced* symbolic means of communicating, almost ritualistic?

"Me, I like pre-lunch for viewing. Can you take a couple of hours off from oil surveys?"

"I think I can manage that."

It might seem slightly strange to the estate agent, Gwen had said to Andrew on the phone, for a supposed couple to arrive in two separate cars. She suggested meeting late Wednesday morning in a village pub which Andrew had never been to, The Black Bull, for a pre-viewing drink; then she would drive him onward while his own car stayed in the pub car park.

"Why don't I drive you in mine?" he'd asked.

She'd laughed. "How manly. But I know where I'm going. The vendors are away for a week, so it seems. Keys with the agent. Ideal."

He doubted that it would seem odd for a couple to arrive from opposite directions, supposing that both persons had day jobs. Evidently Gwen wished to feel in control.

In the pub she chose red wine, a Pinotage, so he did likewise. She was dressed as before. A bit Bohemian for a viewing? No, her clothes suggested purchasing power.

When they sat, he remarked, "Pinotage used to be regarded as a mediocre grape but it's come on great guns in recent years."

Gwen ignored this show of amateur expertise. "You can teach yourself time distortion," she said, "using self-hypnosis. Set a metronome going at 60 beats per minute, or use a clock that ticks the seconds loudly enough. Say to yourself, 'All's well. I'm full of confidence. I can accomplish whatever I want. I'm in no hurry. I've plenty of time to do this. The beats or ticks are getting further apart.' And they do. Breath deeply and rhythmically. You can get each tick to seem two minutes apart, four minutes apart. Objectively a dream may only last a minute, but subjectively it seems to last for hours. This can happen while you're conscious too. Learn to speed-read a book in a few minutes and forget nothing. Prepare kinesthetic body movements for gymnastics or martial arts."

"Do you teach this time distortion trick?" he asked.

"No, obviously I live by stealing." A joke?

"Do you do martial arts?" It was as well to know.

She nudged him mischievously. "I rather prefer erotic arts. Time to go. Drink up. It's six miles."

Was he supposed to have acquired *time distortion* from her quick summary? Again she was way ahead of him, as though he was her toy for today. *Relax*, he told himself. *I'm full of confidence.*

And of disbelief too.

The house was mock-Tudor, an ocean of gravel and giant terracotta urns in front, high hedges at the sides. The blond estate agent, Robert, was in his twenties, a flamboyant fruit salad of a tie contrasting his grey suit.

Presently: "And this is the master bedroom, fully en suite…" On the king-size bed, a lilac duvet garlanded with irises. As Robert walked across thick fawn carpeting towards the integral bathroom, Gwen caught hold of Andrew and kissed him passionately, at the very same time stroking his crotch, quickly causing what that *would* cause, even unzipping his swelling to free it. Robert had paused in mid-stride – at any instant he would turn!

*You're crazy*, Andrew would have hissed at Gwen except for her pressing lips and tongue.

"You're aware," she said in amazement, stepping back to stare into his eyes.

"Aware?"

"You can speak!" She seemed flabbergasted.

"Of course I can speak," he whispered, staring distractedly past her at Robert – who was still paused in mid-stride like a statue, if statues wore suits. The house wasn't anywhere near traffic, but Andrew now became aware of a silence that seemed total. He could hear no external noise at all: no bird-call nor bark of a distant dog nor hum of an aeroplane.

"Oh my god, you can share. You're part of my bubble!"

"Your bubble?"

"Of fast-time. You're my twin, Andrew, my *twin*." She moved further away, staring at him in wonder and fascination. "What if I leave the room – how far does the bubble extend? No, right now we must celebrate! Mustn't lose excitement – excitement speeds time." She sounded like an erotic Einstein. "Be careful with *things*. But not with me." Already she was loosening her dress. "Things have inertia."

And while Robert continued to stand in mid-stride, gorgeous nude Gwen hurried past him and lugged a luxurious bath towel which she wrestled open to lay upon the lilac duvet, fighting it into position. And on that surface which only yielded very slowly to their weight, they celebrated each other's bodies, which were so pliable and amenable and also so intense, until they both cried out.

"Incredible," she exclaimed moments later. "Now be quick, get dressed."

Clothes on, towel to bathroom, tug the duvet straight; and lo, Robert moved again.

Gwen squirmed briefly and smirked.

"Little leak," she confided ever so softly to Andrew, and squeezed his hand.

As Gwen drove Andrew back towards The Black Bull in her Toyota Celica, she rejoiced.

"Oh I've been waiting for you! To be able to share – other men, they're oblivious. This is *magical.* At last, at last, you darling man."

The question bubbled from him: "How did you discover this amazing talent?"

"A cousin of mine, Mark. So handsome. I was sixteen, he was a bit older. Midnight mass on Christmas Eve, candle-lit, enough to read by but deep shadows too, the place packed with so many people. He manoeuvred me behind a screen, *just a couple of minutes, a Christmas kiss and cuddle, no one'll notice.* And the miracle happened, though Mark didn't know. *Silent* Night suddenly! So exciting, the sense of power, the freedom from rules in that place of commandments."

Evidently the incident had imprinted her with a strange and special fetishism, reinforced by seeking similar incidents.

"I couldn't come by any other means. In time I began to yearn for someone to share this gift with. You never suspected you have it?"

Her great gift. Andrew shook his head. "I was never in a situation… Has *nobody* else had an inkling? Surely you must have made a mistake some time or miscalculated?"

"I can hold the moment long enough till things are back to normal. Bit like holding off a pee. The pressure builds. I haven't tried to extend fast-time beyond what I sensed I could. Maybe with *you* we can extend for longer."

"I'd have liked to hold you afterwards."

"Maybe next time. We mustn't pass out from using up all the oxygen. I'm sure other men and some onlookers have picked up subliminally, judging by how they look afterwards – confused, flushed – yet if so it can't be believed, it's a momentary hallucination in their minds. Imagine running a film in superfast-forward, too fast for the eye to see. Something happens, but what?"

How should he phrase this? "You actually *used* those other men?"

"I'm quite strong. But what's in my hands, or within any part of me, is also part of the bubble."

"You had to wrestle with that bath towel."

"Inertia trouble, because I wasn't holding most of it."

"I see." He tried to visualize her riding upon a recumbent man placed on a bed, the motionless man's stiff penis within her. "Your man wouldn't ejaculate, would he? Time's at a standstill inside him. Smart thinking this time, that towel."

"No, time's normal. I can't pause the universe – it's *me* who speeds up. And *you're* my man now, my beloved Andrew."

"You said at the party that you live by stealing. Is that true? You speed up and steal?"

Such a smile she gave him.

"But," he asked, "don't you need to be sexually excited first?"

"So I choose a suitable bystander, someone close to the thing I want. Right now I want you again."

She took both hands off the steering wheel. For a few seconds the red Toyota sped onward. As he braced himself against being hurled forward on impact he knew that he was reacting far too late, yet in fact nothing happened except for the provoking touch of her left hand.

"A question of timing," she murmured, there in the seemingly paused car with him. A Toyota Celica is spacious in front.

She was like a zany superheroine in an erotic comic book. Fastwoman.

"I suppose," he asked, "you won't come to my place to sleep with me? Nor vice versa?"

"Of course not. There's only one way *I* come."

A field of sheep passed by, relatively speaking.

"Have you ever tried the normal alternative?"

"Don't be so ordinary! Would you disdain my wonderful gift? Which," she added, "is also *yours*."

"So how come I never found out about it till now? And why did you say those things about self-hypnosis?"

"Those things I said are true. Obviously I investigated everything that might be connected with my gift. Well, not so *obviously* perhaps. A lot of people are seriously lacking in curiosity. But I'm not. I've experimented. I've played with my gift to try to discover all its secrets. The first time I did it in a speeding car, *that* took a lot of curiosity and trust in myself."

"Hmm. I can imagine."

"You don't want to think about previous men? Jealous, are you?" Her eyes were bright. "Don't worry about that, not now that I've met you at last!"

"And me, you." His response did not sound quite sufficient. "You're *wonderful*," he added, as a church passed by and she slowed for a small village.

"But not entirely unique, not any more. We met by destiny, not coincidence, Andrew. A different kind of attraction from the usual one. Like two rare birds homing on a nesting place from far away. In our case, homing upon one another. You're so innocent, but I'll teach you. Life can be so special if only you know how."

"That's why you almost left the bedroom, to find how far this might stretch between us – out of curiosity."

"We'll discover another time. Telling a man about self-hypnosis is a useful cover story for when nothing seems to have happened. A man can be embarrassed, frustrated, angry maybe."

"So you won't normally arrange to meet the same man twice."

By now they were nearing the village of The Black Bull. Another church steeple loomed beyond a copse of saplings. Flapping low through the sky, Andrew spied a heron, raider of fishponds.

"So," he said, "you can't be having sex all that often. And there are only so many estate agents."

"I move on," she told him. "So must you, unless you don't mind driving for long distances."

He felt himself being drawn into… what, exactly? Gwen was making enormous assumptions, as though she had a perfect right to. Maybe she did have the right. Andrew hungered to learn more about this miracle.

"I suppose you're worrying about those oil surveys. Don't. I can steal millions, if need be."

Steal funds, for him to become a kept man? Like some mistress maintained in a nice house or luxury flat, which wouldn't even be a love nest. Undoubtedly he and Gwen could never live together – that might dilute the magic.

So how would he occupy himself all the rest of his time?

Rocks were his passion. His *other* passion. He could get his rocks off on rocks without needing to be employed. Now wouldn't that be lovely? He might write a book about rocks. *The Clock of Rocks.* Rocks were like a clock in that they told the time: fifty million BC, a hundred million BC, a thousand million.

They drew in to the car park of The Black Bull, where his grey BMW waited, bought quite cheaply at auction a few years ago, repossessed from its former owner.

"May I buy you lunch?" he offered.

The pub's lounge bar contained only one other couple, thus he and Gwen could talk quietly and privately till gammon steaks arrived. A limited edition print hung on the wall near them, of a russet fox seeking prey amidst long dry golden grass.

"I'd be a kept man, kept for pleasure always with a deadline. Finite pleasure, as it were."

Teasingly: "Oh wouldn't you say *infinite* pleasure?"

"Then of a sudden: *quick, get dressed.*"

"That's all part of the thrill, dearest twin. Ours will always be an adventure."

"Are you going to tell me where you live? Or must arrangements always be by phone?" When she hesitated, he plunged onward: "Your parents, sisters, brothers, *cousins*? What do they think you do in life?"

She laid a hand upon his thigh. "I could do it here, you know."

A plump young woman wearing torn jeans and a busty folk festival t-shirt came from the kitchen with two plates.

"But right now I'm famished," said Gwen.

As was he, he realised.

Of course, she was utterly addictive, perhaps all the more so because their love-making was always so brief, like an explosion for each of them. Andrew found himself day-dreaming intensely about each explosion. In fact, each explosion was almost identical except for the varied décor of the surroundings, and a new estate agent statue, male or female as the case may be, and Gwen's choice of clothing to discard. These explosions punctuated his existence like successive bullet holes fired unerringly into the heart of the same target. They served as full stops to long mundane sentences consisting of several days between seeing Gwen; but, being all the same, the explosions seemed to abolish the intervening days, to reset Andrew always to the same moment. Soon he felt that he was living outside of ordinary time, and that there was only one short span of real time which signified… the out-of-time when ordinary reality appeared to pause. Maybe this was a new take on infinity, or perhaps on eternity, something which mystics aspired to apprehend, although mystics didn't generally seek this ecstatic state *by way of* intense pleasure. Maybe some Indians did. What were they called, Tantrics? He didn't really know.

"Have you ever taken LSD?" Gwen asked him once, on the phone. She was trimming their ordinary encounters in the flesh to the minimum. No more pub lunches.

"No," he said. "Do you want us to take LSD to heighten the experience?"

"If you'd taken LSD," she replied, "you'd know *that* isn't at all practical. No, I asked because I took LSD a couple of times out of curiosity, and then I stopped because LSD is very time-consuming, but then a few years later I took a tab again – and the experience joined up seamlessly and timelessly with the previous trip, just as if I'd *come home* from far away to find everything exactly the same as before."

Yes, he thought, the explosions were like that. They joined up. Whenever he and Gwen joined together.

At the same time, his ordinary world was being… extracted, sucked away.

Their phone conversations lengthened in proportion *as he did not see her*, those tumbling red curls, dark smouldering eyes, cherubic lips, and all her other more intimate graces; did not see her until those timeless moments when they came hotly together when she was more like a tangible vision than a person, and also less like a vision because touch rapidly brought him too entangledly close to her to see her entirely.

Thus it didn't seem at all out of the ordinary for him to sell his maisonette and follow her to a city a hundred miles away. For the ordinary was extracted from his life.

And he did start writing *The Clock of Rocks* to pass the days in between explosions. A year went by, which signified little on the clock of rocks. On his own he tried to pause time, heeding the techniques she'd mentioned; yet he couldn't succeed. Cheques would arrive in the post, his share of her thefts, so she said.

"I want to see *more* of you," he complained, as if suddenly jerked awake from a trance.

"But less is more, darling twin, don't you see?"

"I don't even know what you do most of the time."

"Don't worry, there's nobody else but you. I'm busy stealing."

Stealing, yes. In a sense she had stolen him, and hidden him away from life.

"I don't know enough about you!"

Her cousin Mark, Midnight Mass on Christmas Eve once upon a time, a few other things which could conceivably be inventions.

"You know me intimately," she said. "More than any other man has ever known."

"Do you have any old photos you could send me?"

"I don't carry baggage with me."

"Can't we just have a drink together some time like ordinary lovers?"

She was silent for a while, then said, "You want to be ordinary? Rather than extraordinary? Maybe *ordinary*'s better for you than standing upon a high peak."

Sensing danger, he joked, "I've stood upon high peaks. I'm a geologist, remember."

*Had* been a geologist. Still was, thanks to *The Clock of Rocks*, which was going slowly. Maybe he was trying to write it too elegantly, too perfectly, too obsessively.

"Cut me some slack," he begged.

"Just what do you mean by that, Andrew?"

"I mean please give me a break. Stop keeping me away from you."

"Cut me some slack means *relax and get off my back*, back off and take it easy. You don't mean that. I'm never on your back. Though, do *you* want to be on my back next time, like a doggy? So do I give you a hard time? Oh yes, every time!"

She was too quick for him! Actually, he thought, her first response sounded as though she had a computer switched on while she was talking to him, in case she might need instantly to websearch the definition of something he said which she didn't follow, as though she was not quite of this world but certainly knew how to use the tools of this world. As it were. No, she was too fast in her response to do a websearch – unless she had accelerated herself… and he hadn't noticed the pause because he wasn't physically with her. They had of course carried out the experiment of him moving away during accelerated time, him hurrying downstairs in he forgot which house. The range didn't seem limited to her immediate vicinity, yet there wasn't time to protract the test further. Her excitement might fade. He wouldn't want her to make use of the statue to hand.

"All right," she conceded. "Just this once." And named place and time, three the following afternoon at a pub near the market square which shouldn't be crowded then.

The pub would need numerous customers to become crowded. It was a converted cinema in Art Deco style, expensively restored. Egyptian papyrus columns to either side. The ex-auditorium sloped, not down to stage and screen, but now to a very long bar. Several descending railed levels replaced the former rows of seats, like the decks of a liner except that the theme wasn't marine but cinematographic. Among many vintage posters now adorning the walls, Andrew noticed one for *Brief Encounter*, that poignant repressed love affair conducted in a railway tea-room in the intervals between the unconsummating lovers regularly catching different trains; yet that was merely a coincidence. A spaghetti western soundtrack was playing.

Gwen was dressed exactly as at the party long ago, and to be able to ravish her only with his eyes for minutes on end was a delight as well as, admittedly, a mounting frustration. At the bar he'd bought two of what she chose to drink, red wine, in fact a Pinotage which he quickly realised was a repetition of their only previous drink together. When they sat at a table on the otherwise deserted midway deck and he set down her glass, she immediately drained at least a third from it in one long swallow.

"A succubus," she informed him from out of the blue, "is a strong and clever creature who rebelled against God and was expelled from Paradise. Which doesn't make her evil, just differently motivated. She didn't wish to be controlled by God. She prefers to do the controlling. That pleases her. Especially when she visits a man in bed and makes love to him whilst he's unable to resist. Not exactly paralysed – that wouldn't do! – but while his will is somewhat suspended. Joyfully, deliriously, she extracts his semen, or shall we say the vitality or whatnot, from him. That is the food of her soul."

"Why are you telling me this, Gwen?"

"As if it isn't obvious!" Gwen tossed her curly red mane. She leaned closer, and her perfume intoxicated Andrew. "I'm a succubus, although a complicated one. And immortal."

"You're making this up. To add *frisson*."

"As if any were needed."

"You didn't get kicked out of Paradise thousands of years ago."

"Or even longer ago."

"The clock of rocks say *no* to that."

"All depends what you mean by Paradise. A previous state, let us say."

"State, as in condition of existence, or as in ancient country? Like, say, Atlantis?"

She mused, running a finger sensuously along her lower lip, then back along her upper, as though miming secrecy; or alternatively, disclosure.

She chuckled, a rich throaty sound. "*The Succubus of Atlantis*, what an intriguing title for a book. Does it beat *The Clock of Rocks*? Or maybe *The Succuba of Atlantis*." Saying which, slowly she sucked on her index finger till it disappeared entirely inside her mouth. Then her finger popped back out and pointed moistly at Andrew. "Succubus, Succuba, which is better? Anyway, both words come from the Greek, meaning to lie upon someone. I thought of that when you said 'get off my back,' or my front, as the case may be."

"No, *you* used that phrase."

"Did I? Whatever. It arose between us." Her eyes gleamed. "But it didn't separate us. No, it plugged us together. Here and now."

Whereas she seemed determined to speak in teasing riddles, Andrew felt a mounting urge to simplify their, well, intercourse; here in this ex-cinema with the lights up.

Which, of course, was possible, if he forsook his wish for once to spend an ordinary time with her. Was what she was saying designed to provoke him? Under Andrew's shoe, the newish dark red carpetting didn't feel too toughly utilitarian.

"Atlantis, or somewhere else entirely," she added.

"Why do we only *plug together* in houses up for sale, Gwen?"

"Because they have beds? Besides, it turns me on."

"We could fuck anywhere in public. In the bed section of a department store, just for instance. In a four-poster bed in a stately home, while the guide and other tourists stand like statues."

"There's no atmosphere…" She broke off.

"But stately homes reek of history."

She shook her head, as if confused for once.

"You mean," he pursued, "they have no atmosphere *for you*? Because no one uses those beds now? And a department store would seem – I don't know, featureless? – because nobody has *yet* used the beds? You get a sense of real people living in a home –"

A shiver seemed to run through her.

"– with real possessions, there in the homes of others, even though the owners are planning to move out? I've no idea where your home is, Gwen. You always keep me at a distance."

She stared at him wildly.

"Because I seem to love you," she said. "But I need to protect myself." Tears welled in her dark brown eyes, trickled down her cheeks. Quickly she raised her wine glass and drained it, as though she was about to depart suddenly.

Andrew laid a hand upon her bangled wrist, to prevent this.

"Protect yourself *from me*?" he queried. "You're in control of everything that happens. Where. When. How."

"I'd seem less exciting. If a woman is in control, a man will die for her. If she surrenders control, she becomes less desirable."

"That's absurd. I'm utterly addicted to you, Gwen. This addiction controls my life. I'm only now realising how much so, because the rules seemed to make sense before. But they don't. If we lived together –"

"In an ordinary way! We can't. Why are you different from all the rest of men, Andrew? Never in all my," but she didn't specify. "You must be a freak, no I don't mean *freakish*, quite the contrary. Although I suppose you'll grow old."

"Do you mean that *you don't* grow old?"

"Although you mightn't grow old, not if you're able," and she whispered, "*to steal the lives of others.*"

The way she had already stolen his life from him? Or at least the way she had narrowed the course of his life into an obsessive channel in exchange for explosive regular treats.

A quartet of young fellows in stupid t-shirts, close-cropped heads, assorted tattoos, came bantering noisily down the left side of the auditorium. Drunk already; bent on getting drunker. One of them stared sidelong at Gwen before his mates pushed him onward towards the bar.

"On a winter's night," said Gwen, "the little matchgirl stares greedily in through a windowpane at a family sitting for supper. She feasts her eyes. She lights matches in the darkness. *Flare, flare*, lovely. It excites her so. She warms her hands and thrills at the flame. The family don't notice this. They can't turn their heads."

"But surely," said Andrew, attuned to her rather than puzzled, "that means you want a more ordinary life."

"In between the matchgirl and the ordinary life is a pane of unbreakable glass."

"At least until you met me at last, out of all men?"

"Why are you different? I have to keep you different! But not –" She wiped her cheeks with the back of her hand, then licked the dampness from a knuckle, like, he thought, an animal craving salt.

After some apparent hassle, the young drunks had negotiated bottles of Corona lager and were mounting the stairs again, bumping into one another. The barman must have baulked at filling glasses with lager – too easy to spill. Yet he wasn't going to pass up trade. This place was probably thronged at nights with youth getting pissed. Would there be bouncers by night, though none now, therefore the barman hadn't wanted to invite trouble?

The chap who had previously figured on Gwen nudged his mates into her area, and Andrew's. Now she was a magnet for them, a lantern for four rather large moths. Not that they were likely to do more than hang around nearby, displaying themselves noisily, as if she might be impressed by their capers and stupid jokes, but right now Andrew was engaged in what seemed the most urgent conversation of his life, even if it was filled with enigmas. For this to be intruded on by idiots! *No closer, you twats! Stop there!*

They stopped. Absolutely stopped. Everything stopped. The background music went silent.

Gwen's eyes gleamed. Her free hand flew to her green and gold dress – it was as though she were trained to start sex in such circumstances, greedily, almost as an automatic reflex. At the same time terror, or amazement, stayed her hand.

"I didn't will this! *What have you done?*"

He still held her other hand by the wrist, and said:

"You can't be a succubus because that's mythological."

"Factual. A sacred whore of Ishtar in Babylon."

"You mentioned Paradise, not Babylon."

"The first woman, created for Adam's pleasure. Before Eve. But she didn't want to lie on her back for him. Rebellious type. So she escaped, even though angels chased her. Actually she adored having sex; that was her nature. Just, she didn't care for pompous Adam. She didn't like being imposed upon."

"Hang on. She adored sex, but *who else* was available back then?"

"She escaped by accelerating herself. That's the flip side of stopping time. Time flew by for her. Angels and ordinary people couldn't see her unless she chose to be seen. And touched. After a while things stopped being mythological and she was inside reality."

"You mean you can be in mythology, and then reality kicks in?"

"The universe is constantly being recreated at every moment – so said some Arab. Of a sudden, the universe can have a history going back billions of years. It gets its clock of rocks. It's like a baby universe suddenly inflating to huge, with its own new set of rules. Realistic rules instead of mythological ones." She grinned crazily. "I'm a remnant of mythology, from when mythology was real."

And still the huge cinema-pub was silent, its customers unmoving. Could they only move again if he and Gwen had an orgasm together, a big bang of re-creation?

"Maybe," she said, "I caused this universe we're in. Maybe I'm the Creatress."

She was insane. Had to be.

And yet she could make time stop.

Except in his case.

And now he too could stop time. At least while he was close to Gwen, whatever her real name might be. Touching her.

Why himself, out of all men whom she had met, ever since – if she were to be believed – at least as early as Babylonian times? Statistically it was highly unlikely that any single individual would be struck by a meteorite plunging to earth, just for example. But when a population numbers billions, this must happen now and then.

It came to him that he'd been acquiring power during their copulations – or was it on account of the obsessed intervals in between?

She fed on real lives because she was a myth. She fed on the imprint of real lives upon places.

Slowly he released her. Slowly he stood and backed away. Five paces, ten. She gazed after him, fully able to follow, at least so it seemed, but not doing so; *studying*.

Andrew turned and trod the broad steps up to the next level. Ruth's head swung to keep him in sight. Down at the bar he noticed a glass being filled by the motionless barman seemingly forever.

He ascended further, to the top, to the foyer, and waved at Gwen almost limply.

She waved back likewise. She might stifle if she stayed where she was! Was she holding her breath now, awaiting, trying not to make a ripple in what he was doing? Like someone underwater, not moving more than she must, to conserve the oxygen in her blood.

When would he feel the onset of the pressure which she had likened to one's bladder filling up? Or might this never come, seeing as the two of them hadn't exploded together? Surely, surely the pressure must arrive soon. Imagine an elastic band stretching and stretching. By now he could no longer see her, where she sat.

The foyer, street beyond, wide-open doors through which cinema-goers had flooded once. Imagine a reel of film snapping in a projector, flickering bright whiteness replacing the motion picture.

Surely the world must renormalise. Surely he was building up strain by outpacing ordinary time. Imagine two tectonic plates caught against each other in their movement past one another, for a period. Then they must pull apart.

On the right side of the foyer was an Art Deco mural from the glory days of this cinema. Art Deco, plagiarised from Douanier Rousseau. Lush vegetation, giant flowers.

*Ruth was there in the mural, in the middle distance!*

A nude figure, her back to the spectator – how well he knew that tumble of long red curls, the full curves of her buttocks!

Had the mural been there when he first came in? Preoccupied, he hadn't noticed. If it had been there, had it been *thus*?

A painted jaguar peered from riotous shrubs; a painted serpent also looked out. As Andrew watched, the naked redhead began visibly to *walk away* within the mural. Quickly away, now half hidden by bushes, now gone.

Andrew launched himself at the mural, and collided, brought to a thumping halt, banging his nose. Audible suddenly from the street: the sound of traffic, voices. He swung round, hand to his nose, to see a taxi passing outside, and two teenagers walking by, the bloke with his hand proprietorially in his girl's rear pocket.

Of course he ran back into the ex-cinema. In vain. Ruth was nowhere to be seen. And it came to Andrew that, whatever her feelings were for him, she had succumbed to a more powerful attraction. She had gone home at last, after haunting so many other homes.

"Don't worry about a thing," Andrew whispered to the red-haired escort, as they followed the estate agent into the master bedroom. She was from Ireland, a Dublin accent perhaps. Stephanie might or might not be her real name.

When the estate agent, who was middle-aged, tubby, and suited, turned towards the en suite bathroom, Andrew caught hold of Stephanie and fondled her breasts, thrusting her towards the bed.

"Don't be so *crazy*," Stephanie hissed, teetering, as he began to unzip her dress.

The tubby suited man turned and gaped at them, incredulous. His face reddened. "Bloody hell," he exclaimed.

"And why you weeping now?" the redhead demanded of Andrew. "What did you expect?"

Outside, a dog barked and barked.

# The Dog Hypnotist

Tricia Sullivan

Wild barking sounded from the rear of the premises as Jane got out of Mrs. Poleax's Volvo and slammed the door. She looked up at the sign that hung out over the A267.

*CANINE HYPNOTHERAPY*

In the back of the estate car, behind the wire mesh, Xena was fogging up the windows and beating her tail against the glass. Every so often the intensity of her whining broke in her throat and a series of incongruous little puppy barks burst out of her bear-sized body. Drool everywhere, of course.

Jane went round to open the door. Xena turned in the car and it pitched from side to side. Jane took a deep breath, got her thumb into position on the sonic stunner and checked that the discipline spray bottle was working properly, just in case. She set her jaw.

As Jane lifted the hatchback, all seven stones of Xena came shooting for the aperture. Jane grabbed for the lead and there was a cartoonish struggle of limbs, fur, dust, and hot canine breath. Jane shouted a good deal. As Xena careered across the gravel turnaround area, Jane managed to steer her towards the front door of the large house. Holding the car keys in her teeth, she slapped the doorbell button once before Xena dragged her into the rhododendrons.

The door opened and a willowy blonde stood there, notebook computer held up in the air, out of jumping range of Xena.

Xena, oddly enough, ran up to the woman and promptly sat down just as she'd been taught in obedience school. Jealousy stabbed at Jane. She rubbed her shoulder. One of these days Xena would dislocate it.

"Come in, come in," the woman sang. "I'm Clarice; we spoke on the phone."

She led them down a homely corridor lined with pictures of dogs. Jane glimpsed a tall grey poodle at the end of the hall, but it disappeared into the kitchen as they approached.

"Here we are," said Clarice, opening a side door. The consultation room reminded Jane of a cardboard box she had once customized for a wild turtle she'd tried to keep as a pet. The tiny, bare room was tiled and it had hundreds of small holes punched in the walls. There were no pictures on the walls, no posters, no windows.

Xena ducked between Jane's legs and forced herself into the room first in a flurry of stray hairs and saliva. She set about sniffing the air vents and making small, belly-deep 'woofs' under her breath. Jane looked for a place to sit down and found none.

"Now, then," Clarice said. "How can we help? You sounded quite distraught on the phone."

Jane launched into a description of Xena's many behavioural problems. She was aware that she sounded weak and hysterical, especially because Xena was now lying quietly on the floor licking her front paws meditatively.

"My fiancé wants to get rid of her," she finished. "But I can't rehome her. I promised a dying woman I'd take care of her. I used to walk Xena for her, you see. She was too frail."

Jane didn't mention the terms of the will. It was too embarrassing. All of Mrs. Poleax's considerable fortune had been left to Xena, with the stipulation that Jane should be her caretaker. Jane had expected this to be a pretty cushy job, but it was one thing to be Xena's dogwalker and another thing to own her.

*"This whole thing has got out of hand,"* Trevor had complained just before he'd left for the airport. She wasn't completely certain he'd been joking when he'd threatened, *"You'd better sort it out by the time I get back, or I'll be calling the bloody taxidermist."*

"Have you tried homeopathy? Aromatherapy?"

"Mmm-hmm."

"What about boot camp?"

Jane sighed. The Marky-Dog biscuits had left a permanent aroma in all her pockets. She smelled like a pet shop; Trevor complained about that, too.

"That didn't work at all. I know I'm supposed to be pack leader, but…Xena is very strong-willed."

"I understand. We get a lot of this. How did you hear about us? Referral?"

"Actually, I found one of your cards when I was cleaning Xena's bed."

"Really? I thought this dog looked familiar. I'm just going to check our files."

Jane and Xena waited while Clarice consulted her notebook.

"Ah, here you are. Actually, Mrs. Poleax brought Xena here some time ago because Xena was sleeping in Mrs. Poleax's bed and not letting Mrs. Poleax in!"

They both laughed, a little giddily.

"So, yes, you've got a dominant dog there. But our records show the problem was solved with one session. It may be that she just needs a refresher. You know. With a new owner. So. Any questions before we get started?"

Jane glanced around the stuffy little room.

"What are the holes for?"

"Dogs use smell to communicate. So we are helping to focus Xena's attention by using subtle smells. Grover is actually in the next room all the time."

"Grover? Oh, I thought you were the hypnotist."

Clarice smiled. "You can meet him at the end."

"You mean…he doesn't need to actually see Xena?"

"They don't need to see each other, no. We're nearly finished. We've been doing the work the whole time we've been talking."

"Wow," said Jane. "That was fast."

She glanced at her watch and saw that she had been chatting with Clarice for over twenty minutes.

"My head," she sighed. "Trevor says I'd lose it if it weren't attached to my neck. I have the worst sense of time."

Clarice laughed. "My sister's just the same. But if you always knew what time it was, you wouldn't need a watch, would you?"

"Speaking of time. How long will this therapy take? Trevor's away on business for three weeks. I've promised him an improvement when he comes back."

"Oh, you're done."

"Just like that?"

"Yes, indeed. Come on, Xena can have a play with the other dogs before you go."

They went out into the garden, which had wood chippings instead of lawn. A huge canine obstacle course had been set up, and there were dog toys lying about on the ground. Four other dogs cavorted and, soon after Xena bounded amongst them, the grey poodle emerged from the kitchen door's dog flap. The others seemed to defer to him. Even Xena.

When it was time to go, Jane called Xena. And Xena came.

"It's a miracle!" Jane cried. "Xena, sit."

Xena sat. She also barked, rolled over, walked to heel, and lay down.

Clarice smiled.

"I think you'll find that everything will be different now."

It was. Jane felt as though a weight had been lifted from her shoulders. It was such a relief to have Xena behaving so well. Jane thought of all the time she'd spent cleaning muddy pawprints off walls and hoovering up splinters of chewed-up furniture; now she was free of all that. She bought a needlepoint kit of a beautiful Alsatian and set to work on it when Xena was passed out on Mrs. Poleax's white Italian sofa in the evenings.

It would look nice in Mrs. Poleax's study, amongst all the other pictures of Xena.

"Trevor, she's completely changed," Jane reported over the phone. "I really think it's going to work out."

"You still want to sell our house?"

"Why keep two houses? I'm Xena's caretaker, and this is Xena's home."

"Call me crazy," Trevor said. "I just think it's weird, living in a house owned by a dog."

"Don't be silly. I'll see you soon. You want sorting out and I'm just the woman to do it."

"Ooh, you little vixen. I can't wait. Get yourself some sexy underwear."

Jane smiled.

Life was so much more fun now that she needn't worry about Xena. Jane found she was overcoming her natural shyness. At the park, instead of blushing and apologizing every time she and Xena encountered other walkers, she stuck up for herself. A man pushing twins in a buggy got the sharp end of Jane's tongue when he harassed Xena.

"You should teach your kids not to throw their toys!" Jane snapped, and Xena backed her up with a low, protective growl when the man started to get stroppy. He retreated, muttering darkly.

Xena took the Dora the Explorer doll home and ate it. Jane couldn't suppress a vicarious smirk.

Before Xena had gone to the dog hypnotist, Jane's dreams had been clandestine, muddy affairs. She had never understood them. Now they beamed through her sleep like high-definition TV. She dreamed every night of a different world, a world where dogs drove cars and pushed supermarket trolleys. Dogs sat in boardrooms and dogs, as in some cheesy pool-hall painting, played poker and smoked cigars.

Dogs were fed complex *hors d'oeuvres* by wealthy old ladies.

"You know, Xena," Jane said, watching Xena clean the cat box by eating the poo. "Wouldn't it be great if all dogs learned to behave like you? Think how happy people would be. And how happy the dogs would be. You're happy, aren't you darling?"

And Xena planted her paws on Jane's chest and licked her face thoroughly.

"I think," Jane said, "that I should spread the word."

Xena gazed soulfully into Jane's eyes.

"I should study canine hypnotherapy. I wonder if they offer certifications?"

She phoned up Clarice.

"I get this question all the time," Clarice said. "We're looking to set up a national network of affiliates."

"Wow."

Jane could hear Clarice's dogs howling in the background.

"How many dogs do you have now?" Jane asked loudly.

"Seven. It's great fun round here. We party all the time. You should bring Xena – she'd love it."

Jane looked at Xena, who had her paws on the kitchen counter, trying to reach the raw chicken Jane had been defrosting. The cat looked on warily, from the top of the fridge. He'd been spending most of his time there lately.

"Yeah, I bet she would. She's very sociable."

"Does she round up other dogs at the park?"

"How did you know that? And she charms everyone. People offer to buy her, but I tell them no way, she's not for sale. She's too special."

"Aren't dogs great?"

"They really are. Clarice, I've got to go. I'm afraid she's going to choke on a bone, she's got a whole chicken in her mouth."

"Whoops! Talk to you later!"

Trevor wasn't in love with the idea.

"It sounds bizarre," he said on the phone from Singapore. "Xena's got it a little too easy, doesn't she? That dog lives the life of Riley, and now she's got you turning into some dog freak. You never used to be like that."

"I'm not a dog freak," said Jane, offended. "And let's not forget we are enjoying spending Mrs. Poleax's money, Trev."

"I wonder if Mrs. Poleax was always such a dog lover," Trevor muttered.

"Of course she was," Jane said. "She once told me that Xena was the only thing giving her life meaning."

Trevor said nothing.

The canine hypnotherapy certification courses were especially wonderful because Xena got to attend them. Jane and Clarice had their meetings in Clarice's kitchen. Jane noticed that the grey poodle didn't go outside to play with the other dogs. He stayed by Clarice's feet, just as Xena tended to do whenever she and Jane were in the pub or some similar social situation. Showing off her good behaviour to the public.

"The first principle of behaviour modification," said Clarice, "is to remember that the problem doesn't lie with the dog. The problem nearly always begins with the human."

Jane glanced at Xena, who was playing tug-of-war with a border collie in the garden. She smiled.

Clarice added, "Like I always say to Grover, it's the humans we have to train. Not the dogs."

"Grover?" The name was familiar. "Didn't you say the hypnotist's name was Grover?"

Clarice gave her a blank look. "Did I? No, I couldn't have. I'm the hypnotist, of course. See?"

She pointed to her certificates, framed on the kitchen wall.

"Oh," said Jane. "I must have got mixed up."

The poodle caught her eye and came over to her, tail wagging. He sat down before her and cocked his head. Clarice gestured towards him.

"No, Grover is my dog, of course. He's very intelligent, but I wouldn't go so far as to call him a hypnotist." She laughed and stroked his ears.

Grover wagged, his eyes fixed on Jane.

"You're so cute," Jane murmured. She'd never much cared for poodles, but Grover had won her heart. She could vaguely hear Clarice going on in the background, but the time seemed to fly.

"I'm sorry," said Jane as they were leaving. "I'm not sure I took in everything you said. I guess it's been a long time since I was at school."

"Don't worry. This type of training works on a subconscious level. We don't have to remember it consciously, we just have to be able to use it. See you tomorrow."

At the end of the week, Jane was a board-certified canine hypnotherapist.

Once Jane had her certification, it didn't take long to set up the website. The actual road sign took a week, during which time Jane couldn't be bothered to eat or sleep much, she was so excited. She and Xena spent their time doing mail drops and handing out flyers in the town centre. It was hot work, and Jane would have liked to swim in Mrs. Poleax's pool at the end of the day. But she'd had to have it drained because Xena kept chasing the neighbour's cats into it.

A little sweat didn't matter, though. Finally Jane had found her place in the world. Her life had some meaning. She would bring happiness to dogs and their owners everywhere.

The feeling was like being in love. When the phone rang and Irina, the receptionist from the sign-makers, said, "Your sign is finished, Miss Whitcover," Jane almost couldn't speak. The elation was indescribable, and everything around her at that moment was limned with a sensory detail she wouldn't have believed possible.

The paper of the *Horsham Friday Ad* felt wonderfully soft as she turned the pages looking through the classifieds. With ink dusting her fingertips she phoned a landscaper and hired him to set up the post. She had him position it so that the sign would be instantly visible as drivers came round the bend from Hillier's Garden Centre.

*CANINE HYPNOTHERAPY*
*All breeds*
*Jane Whitcover, C.C.H.*

Jane got herself a mug of tea and stood on the bank with Xena, watching the cars go past the sign. Yes, it was very satisfying.

After a little while, Xena turned and trotted back towards the house. Jane followed.

That afternoon, the phone started to ring.

"...my dog eats the kitchen lino..."

"...can you stop him stealing food?"

"...pees on the kids' beds..."

"...won't stop barking..."

Jane's appointment book began to fill up. Every time the phone rang, Xena barked delightedly.

The last call came well after teatime.

"I'm at my wits' end," said a man's harried voice. "She's pulling out all her fur. She'll be bald soon. I've got her in an Elizabethan collar but she can't spend her entire life like that."

Jane pitched her voice low and soothing. "Not to worry," she said. "This is a very common neurosis. Completely curable."

"Really?"

"Mmm-hmm. Everything will be fine. For both of you."

Trevor came home the next evening. He must have been tired; he acted grumpy and complained about Jane's housekeeping. He made her change the sheets on the bed. And he wouldn't share his steak with Xena.

She made her best doggy-eyes at him, but he was unmoved.

"Maybe she needs to see the hypnotist with you," Jane suggested.

"No way. I'm not into that New Age shit. That's not my world."

So grumpy. Poor Trev. He didn't perk up until Jane showed him the lace teddy she'd bought at La Senza.

"I'm sticking the dog in the garden for the night," he said, over her protests. "It's a warm night, and she'll be fine. I'll even take her for a quick walk first, so she knows there are no hard feelings."

"I'll open a bottle of wine," Jane said as Trevor grabbed her bottom on his way out.

She heard the two of them go out through the garage. She ran the bath and undressed, wandering into the bedroom. Through the open window she could hear them going down the drive like a comedy act. Trevor was trying to get Xena into the walled Victorian garden beside the house.

"Get down, you stupid beast!" Trevor kept saying. There was a crash. "Shit, you broke the torch, you idiot. Hey! Come back!"

Jane bit her lip. She'd forgotten to tell Trevor that Xena had become used to thinking of the back garden as her wild play area. And she'd avoided mentioning the fact that the pool had been drained. It might have upset him.

She strained her ears. She couldn't hear anything.

After a few minutes, Xena's claws came clicking back up the drive. Jane looked out the window and saw that Xena was holding her lead in her own mouth.

"You clever thing," Jane said. "Where's Trev?"

But of course Xena didn't answer.

After all, she was only a dumb animal.

# The Crack Angel

Jon Courtenay Grimwood

The kid in the flat below is on the drums. Windows rattle, as he hammers his way from snare to hi-hat, ending in a crescendo of pedal work that shakes my windows. He's had three girlfriends in five months; two of them fashion models.

The new one sings with a band.

I want to ask what he's doing right that I'm doing wrong, but I know the answer, it's been years since I had cheekbones like his.

We're off Wardour Street. Opposite Doc Savage's Walk In Medical Clinic and next to Lester's Comic Shop. William Hogarth drank in our local, Jeffrey Barnard used to piss in the doorway, and Karl Marx bought his cigars in a shop round the corner. Using Engels' money, obviously.

These days the shop sells mobiles.

The Brazilian girl below our drum player is away for the week. Her father owns a slum above Rio. Someone's after her, she told me one drunken night. Three brandies and a fumble later, I still don't know if she meant the police or enemies of her father. Either way, I'm meant to warn her if strangers come snooping.

I live at the top. A poky little flat.

At ground level in our alley, next to Doc Savage's, is a vodka bar. Before it was a bar, it was a computer-repair shop, before that an internet cafe.

All three owned by a blond Russian. Vladimir has knife scars on both arms. The wounds are not defensive, they're invited. The kind you take when blocking a blade, because you intend to do worse damage in return.

Vlad's not someone you want to meet in a fight.

A knock at the door dismisses that thought. It's the kid with the drums. Although now he's clutching a five-string bass. He has it slung over his shoulder like a rifle, on a strap that mixes Cabalistic symbols with bad Egyptian and worse Greek.

"You've got a caller."

As he turns to go, I see a blonde standing behind him. She's tall and obviously not English. Almost nobody in Soho is, although I can pass for it.

"Mr Red?" she asks.

The boy with the guitar shoots me a grin.

"That's me," I say.

She checks the card she's holding. *Panama Red, Esq*. The card's black plastic, English on one side, Japanese on the other. Special deal from ProntoPrint on Dean Street. "You really a licensed PI?"

"Take your pick," I say.

A dozen PI certificates decorate the walls of my office. At least two are real, and one of them is actually mine. Of course, you can't use a Puerto Rican licence in London. But most of my clients don't know that.

"Why are you smiling?"

"Thinking about an old case," I tell her.

It's true. Five cases in seven years. The last one made me rich enough to take things easy for a while. Of course, that's rich in my language. To the Brazilian it's two handbags, a Burberry trench coat and one of those little Louis Vuiton cases with trolley wheels.

My *while* is up. And here comes a knock at my door. One step ahead of the bailiffs. Which is a lot better than one step behind.

The newcomer glances doubtfully around at my office. Since the window is broken and a Victorian gutter gurgles under a wooden window seat, I don't blame her. But my whiskey bottle is in the drawer, the cocaine is long gone and what's left of my dope is in the bottom of a North African vase.

"What's wrong?"

She wants to tell me it's none of my business. Only, if it's none of my business why is she here? At the top of five flights of stairs, looking all the better for being caught in the rain wearing a thin cotton blouse and no bra.

"Finished looking?"

A temper, tightly under control. Sounds like my kind of case.

Her jeans tight enough to have been spray-painted directly onto her buttocks. Since every other woman in London is wearing them loose these days, I know she's from out of town. Just how far out I have yet to discover...

"Bratislava," she says, in answer to my question.

One of the few places I've never been. If I remember rightly, someone chopped Czechoslovakia in half; one side got Prague, most of the money and five-star raves in the travel sections. The other got slums, Bratislava, and enough crumbling Soviet concrete to last a lifetime. If I was faking an identity, I'd chose Bratislava too.

After all, who's likely to check?

As I watch, she spreads fifty-pound notes across my desk. A great fan of them. She spreads an even bigger fan below. Two fifties make a hundred pounds, twenty make a thousand, a hundred make... She takes back the largest fan and leaves the other in place.

"I pay for good service," she says.

My grin must be too wide because her smile tightens. "Just listen, okay?"

Yeah, I can do that. Particularly on a slow day, when a drenched blonde climbs five flights of stairs to offer me money.

"You listening?" she asks.

Tapping a cigarillo from its packet, I offer her one. She doesn't smoke, so I sit in the side window, looking down on tourists in Wardour Street, and wondering if half-hanging out a window counts as not smoking in the office under the new regulations.

"Shoot," I tell her.

She needs me to find someone called Eloise. Apparently, Eloise is a crab-eating macaque; which turns out to be a kind of monkey.

When I ask if she's serious, she nods.

I'm happy enough to take her money. All the same, I need to know what she expects in return. For some reason this turns out to be a difficult question. So I ask her name and she tells me it isn't important. I don't push it. Any name she gives is likely to be as fake as the blondness of the hair spilling damply round her shoulders.

Mind you, who am I to talk?

*Panama Red* for God's sake. It wasn't even a good joke when the New Riders were singing about coke, dope, platform heels and spit curls. Takes me back to an age of innocence, though. When Russian gangs were a novelty. Now we've got Colombians, Chechens, and Vietnamese. The Triads are gone, along with their old-school manners.

"You're not listening," the blonde tells me.

"I'm listening," I say, watching a boy with spiky white hair and coffee-colour skin take up his position on a street corner. Five dead punters in three weeks. The killings began with his arrival and my guess is they'll stop when he leaves.

London's changing.

Hell, the whole world is changing. Most of the people out there have no idea how much or why. They still see it as a local problem. Sometime soon, someone's going to work out that the edges of all these little local problems join up. And they'll slam an exclusion zone round this century so fast it'll take the inhabitants a while to realise they've been shut down.

"So," she says. "You'll do it?"

For that amount of money I'll do anything.

I don't say this, obviously. My reputation is for difficult jobs undertaken discreetly. Like most things about me it's self-created; and self-promotion is fine, you just need to be careful not to believe your own publicity. "You want to meet tonight, at 11.30?" I say, feeding her back the only bit I've actually caught.

The blonde nods, and leaves.

She looks as good exiting my office as she did entering it. If a little drier.

In the last few years the area around Kings Cross station has gone upmarket. The Victorian back streets have been redeveloped. The worst of the old 1960s estates have been ripped down. The Met have moved a hardcore of crack addicts and muggers out of central London, making them someone else's problem.

You don't have to look far for the ghost of the old King's Cross, though.

A few hundred paces back from Euston Road, you'll find street walkers and pimps, petty dealers and thieves who have not yet come to the Met's attention.

The house I'm looking for is on the edge of this area.

Early Victorian. This means pale stucco pretending to be stone, rather than that rich brick red found ten minutes to the north. You can trace London's decline into senile obesity in a two dozen changes of girth and a dozen of building style.

It waits under an arch and round the dog-leg of an old mews.

All the houses in the street are empty. New bars cover the lower windows. All the doors are six panelled, freshly painted, with appropriate door knockers. Maltese dolphins, mostly. A gutter runs down the middle of lovingly-restored cobbles; mimicking the original, from when the mews were stabling a hundred years earlier.

Of course, I'm not looking at the cobbles, I'm concentrating on six figures who've just appeared behind me. Five burly men, and one blonde.

"Stay where you are," she says.

Since I'm standing in the porch of a Victorian mews, with walls to both sides, a door to my back and a woman holding an Uzi to the front, it's easy to obey. The Uzi looks new. Maybe she thinks a machine pistol is what it takes to fit in around here.

"Okay," she says. "Hand over the monkey."

"What?"

Not the reply she wants.

Picking myself up, I look round. The man who just punched me is rubbing his knuckles and grinning ruefully. Not sure why. It wasn't that hard.

"Where's the monkey?"

"How would I know?"

This time when he throws a punch, I'm waiting.

Sweeping my wrist, I block his fist, and the palm of my other hand strikes him under the chin, snapping back his head, and slamming his jaws together loud enough to echo off the walls around us.

Another man steps forward.

His punch never lands. Instead, my wrist blocks his punch, and as he jerks back his head to avoid a palm strike, my heel rakes his shin and grinds into his instep. His whimpering stops when I slam my elbow into the side of his head.

*Wax on/Wax off.*

You must have seen the film.

A third man steps back as I slip a gravity knife from my sleeve.

When the first man stands he's spitting teeth. The second stays down. As for the others, they look shocked; apart from the blonde, who smiles grimly. Maybe she wasn't expecting this takedown to be easy as she let them imagine.

"Enough." She raises the Uzi.

"You won't shoot," I say.

"Don't count on it..."

She nods towards my knife and I let it drop, with enough of a clatter to make one of the men twitch. A couple of the others help the fallen one to his feet.

"So," says the blonde. "Where's Eloise?"

I shrug.

"You've had a week and you've had my money. I want to know where the monkey is. And I want to know now."

"I've had less than a day."

It's her turn to look at me. Her face is in shadow, but the sodium glow around us yellows her hair to a tacky bleach job and throws her scowling face into cheap silhouette.

"A week," she says.

"Way less." Dipping my hand into my jacket, I drag a fat wedge of notes from my pocket and thrust them at her. "Here," I say. "Find your own fucking monkey."

She backs away as if the cash is contagious. When a man mutters, she rounds on him. Their argument is vicious, and though it takes place below my hearing, it lasts long enough for me to realise this is not the blonde I know.

A twin?

Someone made to look like her?

"Another twenty-four hours," she says. "That's how long you've got."

She swirls on her heels and stalks towards the mouth of the mews. The men trail behind her like shadows and they're gone before they reach the bend. As if someone pulls the slider on a special-effects desk.

The boy from the corner of Wardour Street smiles from under white hair. "Everything changes," he says.

I nod, non-committally.

"So why?" he asks. "Does it always remain the same?"

His own collar is turned up into sharp points. It looks better on him than it does on me. Both hands are bunched deep in his pockets and I wonder what they'd be holding if he removed them.

A knife?

Maybe a gun or a garrotte?

"I didn't kill those girls," he says. "Not my MO."

He grins as my eyes widen. Does a little shrug. "I know what you've been thinking. He has to be the one who killed the whores."

"You came looking to tell me this?"

Again, that little shrug. "Just passing through," he says. "I don't want there to be any mistakes about that." When he pulls his hand from his pocket it's holding a lighter, and I realise I've tapped a cigarillo from the packet I always carry. Smoke fills the air.

"Cuban," he says, sniffing heavily.

So I give him the packet.

We walk back together, not speaking but smoking companionably as the streets narrow and we enter Soho proper. I lose him somewhere around Flaxman Court, as he gives me a brief nod and slips behind a metal door that gapes wider to release music.

The ground floor to my building is also open.

Wind rifles the edges of a pizza menu. Cigarette ends show where someone's been breaking the law. A glossy magazine from an estate agent advertises apartments I can't afford and wouldn't want to even if I could.

I make my way upstairs in darkness. Silence from the Brazilian's flat. The drum-player's girlfriend is having an orgasm. A snatch of angry Russian rises through a window from the alley below. A creak from above stops me on the stairs.

My hinges, my door...

Very slowly, the door swings open.

So I wait and wait some more. All that happens is that wind nudges the door a little further. Neon shimmers from between curtains I left closed. A sash window is open enough to let someone in or out.

Assuming there wasn't a thirty foot drop to Wardour Street beyond.

England has rules about owning guns. That's why the one I own is taped inside a gas meter in the hall. It's got more tape wrapped round its handle, and stuck down the length of its trigger to stop me leaving prints. I don't know if that actually works, but it was good enough for Al Pacino in *The Godfather*...

The drum player and his girlfriend are now talking.

My muffled knock fetches them from their bed. A chain protects their door. Or rather it doesn't. I hope he realises that a single good kick would smash that chain and take the door off its hinges.

"What?" he demands. Then, seeing it's me and spotting the finger held to my lips, repeats his question in a whisper. Ending with, "Everything okay?"

"You hear anyone go past earlier?"

"No," he says. "I've been busy."

His preoccupation stands behind him wearing a tee shirt and nothing else. It's a very short and well-worn tee shirt. But then the night is hot, and neither of them were expecting me to call.

"Why?" she asks.

"Think I have burglars..."

"You have?" says the boy, and then does a double take. "You mean, you think they might still be there?"

The fact he insists on helping tells me how young he is. Gripping a steel baseball bat in one hand, he sets his jaw and prepares to lead the way up those stairs. Only giving way, reluctantly, when I tell him I'll go first.

My office is in chaos.

Papers from the filing cabinet litter my floor. They came with the flat and belong to a plumber who owned the cabinet before me. He left in a hurry, leaving his desk, an in-tray, and a cabinet full of old invoices.

Since *Been-round-for-twenty-years* was the look I wanted, they stayed.

"Red," says the boy.

Yeah, I heard the noise too.

He lets me take the bat from his fingers. Watching, slightly surprised, as I swing it in a figure of eight and roll it backwards across my wrist. It's close enough in balance to a pair of old Indian clubs I used to own.

Gripping the bat, I approach my bedroom door.

The creak as I open its handle is loud. But the sounds from inside don't stop. Drawers slam and cupboards keep opening and shutting. So I push the door with my foot and step inside, holding up the bat.

A snarl greets me. Bared yellow teeth and furious eyes.

Their owner takes a single step, bares her teeth again and grabs an ashtray stolen from Spearmint Rhino. It cracks plaster beside my head and hits the floor without breaking. So maybe it isn't glass after all.

As I advance, the figure backs away.

Hurls a lamp in my direction, and howls with fury as its flex brings the flying lamp to a sudden halt. And then the figure is gone. With a single leap to the window, a scrabble over my sill, and a jump that reaches a street light jutting from a cafe opposite.

"Fuck," says the boy. "What was that?"

That's the trouble with his generation. No one's bothered to teach them anything.

"It's a crab-eating macaque," I say. "What the fuck did you think it was?"

"That was a monkey?"

"Yeah," I say. "Her name's Eloise."

The drum player wants to come with me. His girl wants to go with him. I don't want either of them getting into trouble on my account. Takes longer than I'd like to make this clear. And when I leave they're both looking sullen and wearing the hurt in their eyes.

They'll get over it.

Kicking the outer door shut behind me, I find myself facing the boy with the bleached blonde hair and the turned-up collar. He's grinning.

"Went that way." He points to the roof above.

My scowl widens his grin. Should have known we were in the same business.

That's the thing about working in time management. No one trusts anyone. At one point, a few years back, twenty-five members over three departments turned out to have been watching each other for the best part of fifteen months.

I was one of them.

After that, I took early retirement. Since time-keeping is a job for life, my boss refused to believe I meant it until I went on holiday and forgot to come back. Hell, I liked the Renaissance. Wall to wall squalor, matched with high art, low politics, alcohol and a lot of naked flesh.

"So," I say. "How long 'til you graduate?"

His grin vanishes.

My guess is right. This is his final. Nail this and he has a job for life. Of course, and this is the good bit, it's a very long life and it's a very lucrative job. In my case, the kid with the drum kit would probably count it as several lifetimes.

"You want help or not?"

"No," I say. "But you can tag along if you want. And I promise not to tell your boss you were just here for the ride."

That's as good an offer as he's going to get. His nod says he knows that.

We split up, taking the area either side of Wardour Street. I meet the usual collection of drunks and druggies and wired-up kids looking for all-night bars. So I recommend a place in Chinatown to boys from the North. Tell a girl from the suburbs that community support are doing a sweep, and she should grab a night bus home. No one I ask has seen the monkey.

It says something for London these days that no one is surprised by my question. The kid with the blond hair has no success either.

"So what do we do now?" he says.

"Go home," I tell him.

"That's it? You're giving up?"

"No," I say. "I'm going where the monkey is."

His stare is sullen. But he bites down on his questions until he works out which one he really wants to ask. And I know that he knows – when he asks it – that he already knows the answer. That's how this stuff works.

"We're out here so the monkey can return to the flat?"

"You've got it."

Since he's younger than me he gets to climb the drainpipe and shut my bedroom window from without. Only, he's not to shut it straight away. I have him repeat the instructions back until I'm sure he's got them right.

And then, sliding myself inside, I creep up five flights of stairs to stop outside my door. The couple in the flat below are back in each-other's arms from the sound of it.

The stab at my heart is jealousy.

Unless it's regret. I can just remember when life was that simple and its cure so uncomplicated.

At the door I pause, turn the handle slowly and slip inside. The next thing I do is turn on the lights. On cue, the blond boy slams the window from outside. He has orders to hang on for grim death if that's what it takes to keep it closed.

As Eloise looks round, she bares her teeth at me.

But her heart's not in it.

Guess her real attention is on the blonde in the trench coat exiting my bedroom. "Nice work," she says. "I thought it was going to take you a week." She glances once round my office; raises her eyebrows at ten-year-old estimates for unblocking drains. "That's the worst cover story I've seen," she says. "Panama Red, international plumber."

"If I was a plumber I'd be called Aziz."

She looks puzzled.

"Have you needed a plumber or electrician recently?"

Of course she hasn't. The last one I used had a doctorate in anthropology from the University of Baghdad, charged me less than was decent to replace an entire fuse board, and swept up before he left. I'm still trying to remember what I did with his card.

"Didn't we run into each other earlier?" I ask.

She finds my question strange.

"So that wasn't you carrying an Uzi, backed by five bodyguards. And you didn't have your people do this..." I tap my lip which has dried to an unpleasant scab.

"I don't carry a gun," she says tartly.

"You don't believe in violence?"

"I don't need one."

The silence which follows lets me take that answer any way I like. She's considering my question. She doesn't like it any more than

I liked running into the five thugs and a woman who apparently wasn't her.

"Did they say what they wanted?"

"Yeah. They wanted Eloise..."

Her face tightens. She glances between me, Eloise and the boy with the spiky hair hanging from the window outside. He's got his ear to the glass, while he tries to hear what's going on. Probably wants to work out if I'm double-crossing him.

I'd be happy to tell him. If I only knew the answer to that myself.

"So," says the blond. "You hired some local backup?"

"He's official," I say. "Making his final run."

"Really?"

"Yeah, really."

She's lying about not owning a weapon. Although the one she drags from her pocket fires no projectile our friends in the flat downstairs would recognise. Sonic waves pass through glass and stop the heart of the boy clinging to the windowsill outside.

His fall alerts a drunken girl.

The girl's scream brings other drunks. Although it's three minutes before someone remembers to dial 999. And another five before a cop car howls its way along Shaftesbury Avenue and turns into Wardour Street.

Half the drunks scatter.

Someone should tell them that walking away is more effective.

In the time it takes the two officers to order the stragglers back from the body, I bolt my window on the inside and begin scooping up the contents of my filing cabinet, stuffing invoices randomly into files.

"Leave it," I say, when she moves to kill the lights. "We don't want to appear counter-intuitive."

She smiles at the old jargon, leaves the switch alone.

By the time I get back from tipping half a bottle of Californian Shiraz down the sink, she's taken off her trench coat and thrown it over the back of a chair. Ripping a couple of cigarettes in two, she stuffs the longer ends in her pocket and lights the stubs. She smokes both down to their filters before grinding them out on my ashtray.

Then she reaches for a glass and the half-empty bottle. The only time I saw Doc Savage on a professional basis, he told me alcohol would rot my brain. He was wrong. Seven years later I can still remember his warning perfectly.

As an afterthought, she offers a cigarette to Eloise.

The monkey reaches for my lighter.

By the time the ambulance pulls away and the police have made it to our level, we've finished the bottle and are curled up on the office sofa, the blonde's head on my shoulder, while the monkey sits on top of the filing cabinet finishing a second cigarette, a sardonic smile on her face.

"That's illegal," says the first officer through the door.

She's looking at Eloise, who sneers back, her yellow canines glistening in the light from my desk lamp.

"Are you sure?" I ask.

The officer stares at me.

"I mean, that the law applies to monkeys as well?"

They ask me what I know about the body on the pavement below. So I tell them I've seen the kid hanging around outside for a few days, maybe more. They ask how I know it's the kid, and I tell them that spiky bleached hair is unmissable anywhere.

Even with a recent blood wash.

The male officer glances at my companion, looks at the empty wine bottle, takes in her trench coat across the back of a chair, and the two buttons undone at the neck of her blouse and writes his own version of what we've been up to so far that night.

He has a round child-like face, under a tangle of dark hair still messy from where he pulled off his police cap. The female one hasn't bothered. She just stands there, swinging her foot like a sullen toddler, while sneering at my office furniture.

Before they go, they take our names and tell me someone will be along in the morning to talk to me again. So I ask for their names in return.

Don't want them. But it's always good for a wind-up.

As they turn for the door, they get a final question of their own. This time from my companion. "Did anyone else see anything?"

"We can't say," the woman tells us.

The man shakes his head.

"You do realise," I tell the blonde. "Someone's going round London pretending to be you?" My stare hardens. "Unless they are you, of course. And you're the fake...?"

She doesn't like the way this conversation is going.

It's not that I've got anything against clones. I just wish the law would insist on significant differences between the original and any copies. Apparently, the technique exists. But we don't demand visual markers for identical twins or triplets. So it would be discriminatory to demand it of clones. That's what I've heard, anyway.

"You're both working on the same thing," I say. "The question is, are you working for the same person?"

She wants to tell me, *No*. But she's begun to wonder.

What are the odds of two people like her ending up in a city like London on a night like this? Come to that, what are the chances of both of them looking for Eloise? Less than Zero. I reckon this one's job is to find me. And the other's job is...

She's looking at the trench coat I'm holding.

"We're going out," I say.

One arm goes through a sleeve. She's trying not to tangle with the second, when I lean forward to lift the sonic gun from her jeans pocket. It's a model I don't know, smaller than I remember, lightweight and strong. Makes me realise how long I've been away. Reminds me why I'm never going back.

"Bastard," she says, but there's something admiring in her voice.

Lots of people feel like they were born out of their time. I was. My father was an eighteenth-century diplomat. My mother was born six hundred years after that. I'm the result of what happens when a timekeeper breaks every rule going.

Both my parents were Londoners; so I live in their city, right between their time frames. Three hundred years before my mother was born, three hundred years after my father died. The Agency must have wept with joy when they saw me coming.

A rift runs through this city.

Always has.

My job is to police that rift. There's a long and fancy title that involves the words *consul*, *temporal* and *autonomous*... But I forget the order in which they appear. The short version is that I'm a crack angel.

You get lost in time, come and find me and I'll do my best to get you home. Doesn't matter how stupid you've been, I'll nod sympathetically, reissue your papers, find you missing body organs to replace ones you've lost, listen to your tearful confessions and breathe a sigh of relief when you're gone.

All I ask in between is to be left alone.

"You realise..." the blonde begins to say. I'd ask her name, but then I'd have to start caring about her.

"Yeah," I say. "Of course I realise."

Her clone, unless it's her original, is out there waiting. With an Uzi and five bodyguards who are probably still pissed that I punched them. And then there's Eloise.

The blonde looks at me when I say this.

Realisation dawning in her eyes.

*"Eloise is yours?"*

That's one way of putting it. The monkey and I came to an arrangement. It involved not killing each other. I don't bother telling her Eloise is a top-flight assassin. I imagine she knows this already.

The door of the Russian bar opens slowly. Vlad's standing to one side of the frame, hidden from sight. Tells me all I need to know about who he thinks might come calling.

"Vlad," I say. "I need a favour.'

His face appears.

"Who's that?" He jerks his head towards the blonde.

"Don't know her name."

Vlad nods, like that makes sense to him.

Probably does. His hand is out of sight, down to his side and hidden in shadow.

"What's the favour?"

"You're holding it..."

We settle on £750 for two Sig automatics, plus an extra two clips and a silencer for each weapon. £250 of this is deposit, rising to £350 if I bring both weapons back unused. Vlad takes my old gun in part exchange. Although I get the feeling he only agrees as a favour.

I give one of the Sigs to the blonde. She looks surprised when I give the other to the monkey. Vlad just grins. He thinks I'm mad anyway.

Dropping out the clip, Eloise checks it's full, slams it back into place and jams the other clip between her jaws. A second later she's gone. A rattle of drainpipe, a scratching of feet finding purchase, and then a creak from tiles above.

"Okay," I say. "This is how we're going to work it."

We wait, on a bench in Soho gardens for dawn to arrive. It does, but our enemies don't. So we head for Pat Vals in Old Compton Street for breakfast, drinking orange juice and coffee as we watch the street from a first-floor window.

The day vanishes in a series of coffees and glasses of wine, a pizza augmenting the croissants we had for breakfast. A blonde, alcohol, food that's vaguely edible... This would be a perfect day if not for the feeling that I'm being watched.

Shadows reveal themselves to be just that.

A hard-eyed man simply wants to know the way to Selfridges. A gang of tattooed rent boys turn out to be on a charity run. Morning slides into afternoon, and afternoon gives way to one of those London evenings when the sky is blue and lovers overspill the pavement cafes in Dean Street. But still I have that prickle at the back of my neck.

Maybe they're waiting for darkness?

The thought cheers me up enough to pull the blonde to her feet.

Outside my flat a police sign asks anyone with information about a suspicious death to call this number. Someone's leant it against the wall, out of people's way.

"The police came back," says the boy with the drums.

Behind him, his girlfriend nods. "They wanted to know where you were," she adds. "We said we didn't know."

I thank her and turn to go.

"Also..." The drum player hesitates, looks puzzled. His eyes flick towards the blonde and he shrugs, then nods to himself as if something is settled.

"It's okay," I say. "She found me."

"Yeah," he says. "Look, I'm sorry we weren't much help earlier..." He disappears into his flat to fetch her something. "You'll probably want this back, then."

The blonde smiles thinly, and we make our way upstairs.

"Why would she do that?"

She means, why did the other blonde come here? The answer is to unsettle us. We spend all day waiting for an enemy to strike. And when they don't, we discover they've been the one place we didn't expect them to go. Our base.

My flat is in chaos, but no more so than when I left.

A packet of cigarettes is missing from the kitchen. So it seems Eloise dropped back at some time or other.

"What now?" the blonde asks.

That's the question. I can't let them have Eloise. And I can't let the blonde have Eloise either. I'm sure she realises that by now. Eloise likes it here. She likes London, and she likes the twenty-first century, and she likes being retired.

I'm not going to let anyone mess that up for her.

Also we have a neat little sideline. There isn't a building in London she can't enter. Mostly through the roof, sometimes simply by scaling the sides. We steal back things that are stolen. You'd be surprised how many people would rather use us than go to the police. Or maybe you wouldn't.

As I'm thinking this, the blonde opens the package; the one she was supposed to have left for me with the boy downstairs. I know it's bad when she hands me a note in silence.

They have Eloise. They want a meeting.

If I don't agree, they're going to return Eloise bit by bit. Inside the package is the gun Vlad provided and a bloody tissue. I know what's inside the tissue before I unwrap it.

Eloise's trigger finger.

I call the number on the note and agree a meet. They say come alone, then call back a minute later to say bring the clone.

Outside the streets are crowded. Saturday in Soho. The offices are shut, but the bars and cafes and shops are open. I check to see if we're being followed. It's hard to tell but the prickle is gone from the back of my neck, so I guess not. "This is where we say goodbye," I tell the blonde.

She looks at me. Did I mention she had green eyes?

"They want both of us."

"Yeah," I say. "That's because they want to kill us both. Face it, the damn monkey's probably dead anyway. And I'm next in line. So bale out while you can."

"Why go yourself?" she says. "If you think she's dead."

"Because she might not be."

I make the rest of the journey alone, jostled by the crowds and wrapped in a loneliness too cheap to call existential. Soho gives way to Charing Cross Road, and I cut behind Centre Point, heading through Bloomsbury towards a jumble of streets just south of Kings Cross.

The mews is where I left it.

And as I step under the arch, I feel prickling begin on the back of my neck. It matches the ice in my heart and the ache in my gut. *Dumb fucking monkey.*

A noise makes me turn. Another makes me turn again. Four grinning men and a blonde. She doesn't bother with the grin. She simply sneers. "Who thought it would be this easy?"

Although her sneer slips when she realises I've come alone.

"Where is she?"

When I shrug, the woman clicks her fingers.

The fifth man appears from a house, dragging Eloise on a lead. Her right hand is crudely bandaged and blood mats her chest below a busted mouth. She stops fighting against her leash the moment our gazes meet. Her shoulders slump and the look she gives me is resigned. Not sure what she expected me to do that didn't involve us meeting like this.

"My clone," says the woman. "Where is she?"

"No idea."

As the man rips the bandage from Eloise's hand and reaches into his pocket for a pair of secateurs, Eloise screams. Her second scream is louder and longer. It echoes in my head, even after I hit the cobbles.

That's where I end up after going for her attacker.

Blood drips from my fingers when I take my hand from the back of my head. Clubbed with the butt of someone's pistol. Eloise has backed away from her tormentor as far as her lead will allow. She's sucking on a bloody finger stump. A nod from the woman has him drag Eloise close again.

Two of the other bodyguards lift me to my feet. One of them finds the sonic weapon. He whistles, passes it to the woman, who scowls.

"Where did you get this?"

"From an old client."

Eloise screams before her tormenter can even reach for her wrist.

*"Told you,"* I say. *"From a client."* My voice sounds desperate.

"We're still only on the first hand," says the woman. "After that, we've got the other hand, her toes, ears, nose, eyes, nipples... How much screaming can you stand?"

*"I don't know where the clone is."*

"I do," says a voice behind us. Think ice, make it colder.

As one, the bodyguards swivel.

A bullet takes the nearest through his forehead, blows his brains into the face of his boss. She's lucky that shards of bones miss her. The man behind isn't so lucky. Egg white runs from where his right eye used to be. Opening his mouth to scream, he swallows a bullet instead. Vertebrae exit from the back of his neck.

Swift as lightning, Eloise grabs secateurs-man by his wrist.

I'm still wondering how she'll fight with two fingers gone, when she levers herself up his body, digs her toes into his groin and rips. He's just begun howling when she bites out his throat and spits gristle onto the cobbles.

It gets messy after that.

Rupturing the elbow of the nearest bodyguard, I slam both my fists into his back, knee him in the temple and stamp on his spine when he goes down. His pistol skids away across the cobbles.

As I go after it, the woman draws the sonic weapon.

Eloise goes for the last bodyguard, and a muffled boom slams my blonde into a wall hard enough to roll her eyes up in her head. As the woman turns her gun on me, Eloise snaps the bodyguard's neck with a single twist and drops to the dirt.

"Catch," I say.

God know how she catches the pistol I kick. But Eloise does, and her shot takes the woman between her eyes.

Exactly between her eyes. You could take out a ruler and measure it. There are three things you need to know about that monkey. She's the best assassin you'll ever meet. She can find her way into any locked room. And she's ambidextrous. The woman should have cut off both trigger fingers to be certain.

There wasn't time to get grafts for Eloise, so these days she makes do with five digits on one hand and three digits on the other. She's getting good at throwing a dagger with either. Eloise likes our new home. The blonde's name is Lucretia. She tells me that shortly after she regains consciousness, and I offer her same deal I offered Eloise when we met.

Neither of us tries to kill the other without warning them first.

Over the years I've pieced most of the story together. Eloise's owner wanted her back. Lucretia was to find me. I was to find Eloise. The woman who was Lucretia's original was to kill me and Lucretia, then return with Eloise. Her bad luck was that Eloise and I had already introduced ourselves.

Lucretia refuses to believe this was luck.

She looks for evidence of a greater conspiracy; sulks that I won't let her into my deeper secrets. Although there are no secrets for her to enter, and she never sulks for long.

Life here is too interesting.

We have a little palazzo overlooking the square. And rumours of our skills are beginning to circulate. They're quiet rumours. As befits a city where the right word in the right ear can make you rich; while the wrong word, or the wrong ear, can find your body floating in the nearby river or lost from sunlight in one of our new duke's dungeons.

Milan in the 1450s is an interesting place. Interesting enough to make up for me deserting my post in London. It's a city in flux; the way London was. No one's quite sure of the new rules, everyone getting used to things changing. I know what will happen, of course. Francesco Sforza and his family will rule Milan for the next hundred years; to be replaced by the Spaniards, the Austrians and the French.

In the meantime, it's as good a place as any for a man, a woman and a monkey. Particularly if they have certain talents.

# Keep Smiling With Great Minutes

M John Harrison

Volsie came out of me in a room at the Les Halles Citadines, from somewhere near the top of my left leg. It was hot and soft, a lot of discrete masses like grapes, or the inflationary universes of the new cosmology. I got hold of it in my hands and struggled with it and pushed most of it back in. I had just that moment arrived – it was my first time in Paris – so I let the rest sink into the carpet and went straight out. I didn't think much of it. That was my mistake.

Père Lachaise cemetery, the Metro gate: a lunatic, bearded and dreadlocked, spun round and round at the top of the steps, raising his arms to bless all us tourists as we entered, while he recited an endless list of the fallen. "All those who failed to find the ashes of Max Ernst," I heard him say, "in the columbarium in the year 2006. All those who failed to kiss the tomb of Oscar Wilde. All those who wandered about looking for Colette but found only Jim Morrison. All those who went to the wrong place." It was hardcore rant, rich with the sheer physical sweat of a world being held together for our benefit, with our unknowing souls and dormant sense of the relations between the spiritual and the spatial. "All those," he concluded, as if only now testing the pivot of his argument, "who *gave up*, but later found a monument to the death commando at Buna Monowitz work camp, and couldn't for once think of anything cheap to say (being instead silent).

"This song," he told us, "is respectfully dedicated to all those who refused to sign the truce because it was written in the wrong colour ink."

Too late I understood that he was Volsie too, and so we wandered together in and out of the little unkempt tollbooths and wrought iron urinals of the many dead, up and down between the cobbled levels, dirt paths and exposed tree roots in the sunshine.

"What are you on?" I said.

"You'll find out," Volsie said. "See that man there?"

I said I saw him.

"Stepped on a grave this morning. Dead within the year."

He looked ordinary enough to me. He looked like an American.

"Which grave was it?" I said. "Out of interest."

"Someone called Darjou, 1757 to 1843. But see the expression on his face ? Dead before August."

I was puzzled by that: by what it meant for me. I went back to my Citadines apartment with its chic, nervous little kitchen and the special bed from under which a second bed slides suddenly and bangs your ankle. I listened all evening to the quiet yelps of laughter from down in the central courtyard.

You ask how it is that Volsie manifests as an episode of psychic piles one moment, a madman in a famous cemetery the next. You ask what its voice sounds like. Volsie will come out of you soon. It might be in the form of the oyster, it might be in the form of the pearl; it might come out of your mouth in the form of the Teratoma of Entitlement, a ball of dry Victorian-looking gristle, horsehair and compacted papier-mâché complete with a single eye from a species on the extinction list. You won't ask questions after that. Answers will be the last thing you want. If you didn't have bad teeth before, you will now. That cough will soon appear to be the worst thing that ever happened to you; the glaze of the eye – the passive eye of a dead seal, the button eye from a French teddy bear bought years ago by some old friend of the family – will encode all the information you need.

Next morning proceeded with fine rain. Paris rain, not enough to stop anyone going out but enough to soak them piss wet through in half an hour. I walked around. I began by crossing the river a few times, going the same way each time, over by the Pont des Arts and back across the Ile-de-la-Cité, looking down at the tents of the homeless pitched along the bank. I took to the Seine on a sightseeing boat and watched the rain run down the curved viewing glass. I saw

Concorde Square, I saw the Alexander III bridge, "the most luxurious bridge in Paris"; I saw the Eiffel Tower lurch abruptly out of its own fog. Arches of blue and yellow plastic flowers ran the whole length of the boat inside; also lines of fake lamp posts with dim lights behind bright orange glass. Right down the middle of the boat. What do you say about something like that? I didn't get it. I debarked cold, and had to have a calvados in a cafe near the Musée d'Orsay.

Volsie came out of me while I was there.

This time it came out from a bit higher, somewhere around the upper bowel, and slithered into my lap.

"I know how you feel," it said. "You feel like an outsider, as if you ought to be living in a tent near the Pont-Neuf." I felt soaked. I felt odd to be sitting with all those purple grapelike universes inflated over my thighs as warm as a pet dog. "Not one of your contemporary lifestyle-choice outsiders either," Volsie said. "Just some old bloke who can't fit in." There are those who believe Volsie is synonymous with death. Others associate him with any journey by train. He was with me in Paris and he was with me on the return journey, where he gurned up and down the aisles of the Eurostar in the guise of a food steward.

"All those," he said, "who ate Ghent ham and Westland salad, all those who ate macaroon au chocolat noir. You never look me in the eye, but I piss in your mouth while you sleep and you taste it when you wake. Oh, don't thank me, it's what I do." He pushed his face into the face of the woman sitting next to me across the aisle. She was reading the *Sunday Times*. "Watch this," he said to me over his shoulder, before passing his face right through the paper and into hers: "They fall asleep like children, clutching their mobile phones." The *Sunday Times*, he said, was a red top for people who thought they were special. He said, as if it was connected, "All that counts is the individual moment of suffering." He said that everything else was ideology, hypocrisy, lies, claim and counter-claim, bullying and self-serving and pretending to be the victim: everything else was the financial news. "The only time people are human any more," he said, "is in the moment of having their humanity taken away from them by other human beings. Being killed revalues your life, it's a way of choosing dignity. Another thing," he said, "I never saw a nuclear explosion I didn't enjoy. You think that's all over? Think again."

He showed me his own phone, black, rubber-coated, the size of a fox. By then we were in Waterloo.

"This is my stop," I said.

Volsie walked me as far as the Dali statue. Then he got smaller and smaller across the polished concourse floor and went spinning into the crowd, like a dropped coin of small denomination no one bothers to pick up any more, off towards the Embankment. He was going to the Tate Modern. After that he was off to Clapham to undermine a reading group. I thought I'd got rid of him but I hadn't. The next time I saw him was three weeks later, in the Pret A Manger on Cranbourne Street W1. He was a thin man about sixty years old with cheeks hollowed by a fanaticism like the desert wind etc etc, and he was eating the All Day Breakfast with Free Range Mayo. He watched the women going to and fro along the pavement outside, up and down the kerbs, waiting at the junctions. It was Thursday lunchtime. After a while he put the All Day Breakfast down with an impatient sigh.

"You think you see the real world," he said to me.

"Pardon?"

"You heard. You think you see the real world. But you don't."

I had a bite of my sandwich. He watched me with satisfaction, as if he was eating it himself. "Good," he said. "Good!"

"There's a world, then?" I said. "Somewhere round here?"

"A world, but not the real one. The real one would –" He shrugged. "I don't say what the real one would do to you," he concluded.

"How could I see the real one?"

He shrugged. "It's easier than you'd think," he said. His watery blue eyes measured me. "In your case," he said, "I wouldn't recommend it."

"Thanks," I said.

"Some are strong enough. Some aren't."

"I'm going to a get a pecan slice," I said.

"Get me one, too," Volsie said.

When I came back with the pecan slices he was looking out of the window again. I didn't want to disturb him so I drank my mocha and unwrapped my pecan slice, which I ate in silence. After a while, he smiled to himself.

"Ask me another question," he said, still looking out of the window.

I woke up this morning from the same old dream.

New Year's Eve, I'm at someone's house. It's in Warwickshire. Snow falls on and off all evening. Every so often someone opens the curtains and reports, "It's wet. It won't settle." Then at half past twelve, adults and children alike, everyone puts on their coat and boots and they run out into the village street. One three year old, rather bemused, wears her little Boden parka over her pyjamas. In the orange lamplight every snowflake rushes down to meet its own shadow. The sky shakes with fireworks from some other party, red, greeny-silver and a strange heavy blue, a blue too dark to be seen yet visible anyway just for this one night. Two inches of snow are on the ground. The parents can't believe it; the children easily can. Christmas at last! They dance in the hallowed empty street. They throw snow at one another. I watch from the window with a woman I have just been introduced to, like me she's up from London to see friends. We kneel on the leather sofa with our champagne glasses, looking out, saying things like, "This is amazing!" and, "Isn't this amazing?" We don't know each other. We don't even like each other much. But we can't stop smiling and saying, "This never happens!" and, "I mean you couldn't wish for more."

You can't wish for more than snow falling after midnight in the lamplight at the start of a new year, to structure the children's expectations, remain as a memory, magic their lives forever.

After that everyone goes safely home wrapped up in a suit of initials, SUV, BMW.

At the end of any dream Volsie comes out of you whether you welcome it or not. It flops down your leg or swells up under your arm. You find yourself at the foot of the stairs still half asleep. Volsie is half outside you, you are still all the way inside it. It is a condition. It is a space or state. You don't have any further queries when you understand that. What a sight you've become. You look even worse without clothes than with them, some old desert man or woman with long hair and half-focused eyes, emaciated or running to fat, with spectacles or without, still reeling about under the impact of having once been born. It's never any less than that. Some of us are just shocked and appalled to find ourselves alive. It keeps echoing on. For me that's the meaning of it, anyway; for you, perhaps, it'll be something else. There are those who equate Volsie with the conceptual motor of the empty heart, those who know him as lovely food and drink. They are not right but they are not wrong either.

Every time I travel into central London by tube, Volsie comes out and looks at the debt-servicing ads. He looks at the ad which tells you everything is possible. He looks at the ad that reassures you, *Fly Business and be as cosseted, as protected, as the handsome, lone, powerful-looking wild animals in a conservation park*, as if you are under threat when it is you that threatens everything else. "The strangest thing," he says in a kind of gentle wonder, "is to live in a time like this, both bland and rotten."

He says, "'Keep smiling with great minutes'."

# Living with the Dead

Molly Brown

I went to the park today, and for the first time in five years, Alice looked at me as if she knew me.

Alice used to be my best friend. We were in the same class at school. We used to do each other's hair and borrow each other's clothes until one night when we were both sixteen, and everything changed.

The details don't matter now. All you need to know is that we were at a party in a basement, and we both snorted something that we thought was cocaine, but it wasn't.

The next thing I remember is waking up in the hospital with everyone telling me it was a miracle I was alive because the other girl was dead.

There'd been a story in the local paper a couple of months earlier about a guy who'd collapsed in the park. He was declared dead on arrival at the hospital and was taken to the hospital mortuary. A few hours later, he woke up.

No one thought much about it at the time, everyone just assumed he'd been mistakenly declared dead when he was actually in a coma. These things happen. Not often – and never before in the kind of place where nobody dies without the whole town knowing about it – but they happen. The man hadn't spoken once since waking; they said he just stared into space.

I remember they interviewed some expert on the news who used a lot of big words just to say: sometimes it's like that when you wake up from a coma.

Alice had been dead a little over twenty-four hours when she opened her eyes. Like the guy before her, she never spoke or reacted to anyone or anything; she just seemed to stare into the distance as if she were looking at something no one else could see.

A few weeks later they sent her home, saying there was nothing they could do.

I wasn't that well myself – as everyone kept reminding me, I was lucky to be alive – but I went to visit Alice every day. We would sit in her room with me talking and her staring straight ahead as if I wasn't there. And every day as I left, her mother would beg me to come back again tomorrow: "You're her best friend. Keep talking to her; maybe you can bring her back."

When a forty-nine-year-old man named Sam Jenkins woke up the morning after he'd died of a heart attack, people finally began to suspect that something strange was going on. This man was definitely dead, the doctors insisted. They were being especially careful about who they declared dead these days; Sam Jenkins had been repeatedly checked – and double-checked – for any signs of life, and his body had been cold when they finally allowed it to be taken to the mortuary. Like the previous two people to wake in the hospital mortuary, Sam Jenkins never spoke. Unlike the other two, Sam Jenkins had risen naked from his mortuary slab, walked home without being noticed (it was four a.m. and the streets were empty), and got into bed beside his wife.

By the time Rosemary Harold died of cancer, they'd decided the problem must be something to do with the mortuary, so they kept her body upstairs. But this didn't make any difference; Rosemary was awake the next day.

Then everyone thought maybe it was something to do with dying in the hospital, so – as much as possible – people started dying at home. Once again, it made no difference; they all opened their eyes within twenty-four hours.

People eventually came to the conclusion that the problem was the town – as far as anyone knew, this wasn't happening anywhere else – so the next time someone died, the body was immediately shipped to another state. But the guy still woke up. The other state wouldn't allow him to stay – they said it was not their taxpayers' responsibility to support another state's walking dead – so he was brought back here.

Soon the dead fell into a routine of spending their afternoons in the park. You'd see them there from one o'clock every day, sometimes sitting on benches with their faces tilted up to the sun, other times just standing in a kind of loose formation. And every day at dusk they would go their separate ways, returning to the homes they'd known in life.

Some, like Alice, were obviously cared for by the living. Alice's mother always made sure that her clothes were clean and her hair was combed.

But others were not so comfortable with their dead. On finding her husband in bed with her, Sam Jenkins' widow had at first moved into the spare room, but having a dead man in the house soon became too much for her and she changed the locks, with the result that her dead husband spent his nights standing on the front lawn. It was around this time that I first heard the word 'zombie' being used.

The first thing that happens when the dead start waking is not that they go on a rampage like you see in the movies, it's that you find out all your insurance policies are worthless. Sam Jenkins had a life insurance policy with his wife as the beneficiary, but the insurance company refused to pay out because they said Sam didn't meet their definition of dead.

Then Alice's mother got a huge bill from the hospital because her daughter – being officially deceased – was no longer covered by her health insurance.

The second thing that happens is property values plummet. Sam Jenkins' widow, unable to pay the mortgage, tried putting the house up for sale. But nobody wants to buy a house with a dead man standing on the lawn. Even if – like Sam's widow – you try to make the dead man a selling point by explaining he deters burglars.

The third thing that happens is church attendances rise. The fourth thing is they fall again as everyone comes to the conclusion there's no point in worrying about the afterlife if you're only going to spend it hanging around the park.

The fifth thing is all the jobs go, as businesses tend to prefer locations where the dead stay dead.

The next thing that happens is the town itself begins to die as everyone who can get away gets as far away as possible, until the only people left are the dead and those few who refuse to abandon them.

Sometimes I go to the park and watch the dead together. Despite being all different ages and backgrounds, they seem at ease in each other's company.

The silence of the dead when faced with the living can seem awkward, but when the dead are together, their silence is a comfortable one, their blank faces not so much vacant as serene. And though their faces are far from expressive, I was there one day as a newly-deceased came to join them for the first time, and I am sure I saw recognition in their eyes.

Five years ago, there were more than three thousand people in this town. Now there are less than three hundred. As the town's living population continues to move away, more of the dead are being left to fend for themselves.

With no one to dress them or comb their hair, some of them were getting into quite a state until a woman named Hilary Frentzen stepped in. The first thing Hilary did was to get a shelter built so the dead would have somewhere to get out of the rain. Then she set up a charitable foundation to collect donations of food and clothing, which she distributes in the park.

The dead *do* eat, just not a lot. Every day Hilary hands out slices of day-old bread donated by supermarkets, and watches as the dead take one or two bites and then scatter the rest on the ground for the pigeons. Of course the pigeons – being dead themselves since the town council poisoned them all a couple of years ago – are no more interested in the bread than they are. Not even the insects are that interested since the park was sprayed, so every day before she leaves, Hilary picks up the leftovers.

She's tried giving them vegetables, but the dead won't touch them. If you ask her, she'll tell you that no matter how hard she tries, she cannot get the dead to eat broccoli.

Once, as an experiment, Hilary bought a dozen chocolate cakes and took them to the park. The dead didn't leave a single crumb behind. She told me she can't afford to do that every day, but now once every month or so, she'll buy them some chocolate cakes as a special treat. (Even dead wasps perk up at the smell of chocolate, which is another reason she doesn't bring it too often.) Hilary used to get very annoyed when tourists turned up with portable sound systems playing *Thriller* at full blast, or shouting: "They don't want bread, they want brainzzz!" but that kind of thing has been happening less and less since the state barricaded the highway and put up all of those 'Quarantine' signs.

And there's hardly been a single crime since the day a guy who was stripping the lead off a dead person's roof slipped and fell, breaking his neck. He's been in the park ever since, walking sideways with his head twisted over one shoulder.

I don't think the dead feel any pain. When I used to visit Alice in her room, I'd always ask her: "Do you feel any pain? Do you feel anything?"

But she'd never answer.

Then one day as we sat with me talking and her staring into space, I picked up a pin and jabbed it, hard, into her arm.

She moved her head slightly, just enough to look down at the pin.

"You felt that, didn't you?" I said. "Does it hurt?"

She went back to staring into space.

When she stood up to leave for the park, the pin was still protruding from her arm.

I reached up and pulled it out; she didn't notice.

The dead don't seem to age, either. Eating only a few bites of bread a day – plus one piece of chocolate cake a month – they've all lost a bit of weight, but otherwise they haven't changed. I'd kind of expected their hair to keep growing, but that doesn't seem to be the case. Which is probably just as well because the dead's hair is invariably a mess. Someone living always has to comb it for them because for some reason they will not do it themselves.

The one exception to this is Rosemary Harold, who died without a single hair on her body – not even an eyelash – because she'd been in the middle of chemotherapy.

Alice is one of the few dead people in the park who hasn't been reduced to wearing hand-me-downs thanks to her mother, who still buys her new clothes when she needs them.

The first couple of years, she used to take her to the mall, which wasn't easy because the sales people didn't like serving the dead and wouldn't let her try anything on, and there was one guard who'd obviously seen *Dawn of the Dead* on television and would always follow them around, scowling, from the minute they arrived. But Alice's mother persevered because she said it was the one time Alice actually seemed to know where she was and why she was there. She even claimed Alice would invariably head straight for the most expensive thing in the shop, just like she did when she was alive.

Not that it matters now the mall is shut.

At one time this town had five churches, four cafes, six bars, two auto dealerships, three banks, two primary schools, a high school, a motel, a funeral parlour, and a meat-packing plant (which closed the day after a calf's head on a shelf in the freezer room was seen blinking). All of them are boarded up now. So are most of the houses.

The streets are full of abandoned dogs and cats. It's the live ones you've got to watch out for, because they're nervous.

My next door neighbour adopted a dead dog. When I asked her why, she said, "Why not? He's no trouble and he doesn't bark."

Five years ago, they said it was a miracle I was still alive. Three weeks ago they told me the miracle was coming to an end; my organs were shutting down one by one. All because of one stupid thing I did one night when I saw sixteen.

People told me my only hope was to get out of this town before I died. They told me it only happens here; if I die somewhere else, I won't wake up. I won't end up with those zombies in the park.

I'm sure all those people were right, but I knew something they didn't know. I've been going to the same doctor since I was a kid – he's the only doctor in town these days – and the last time I saw him, he said he was going to tell me a secret.

Remember I told you about when it all first started, and how they shipped a man's body to another state to see if he would wake up, and he did?

It turns out my doctor was sent along to accompany the body. He was there when the man woke up, and he'd asked him: "What was it like being dead? Do you remember any of it?"

And to his amazement, the man had answered him.

"He spoke?" I said.

My doctor nodded. "Only that one time, and never again. Considering what he said, I thought it best to keep quiet about it."

"What did he say?"

"All you need to know is: there are a lot worse places a person could end up," my doctor said as I left his office that last time, "than in the park."

I went to the park today and saw a dead man sitting on a bench with Hilary Frentzen combing his hair.

What is it about the dead that they refuse to comb their own hair? For five years I had been telling myself that I would be the exception. I would be the one who speaks, who dresses herself, who eats vegetables, who continues to do simple things like comb her own hair... but with every moment that passed, these things seemed less and less important.

The next thing I knew, I was standing face to face with Alice. And for the first time in five years, she looked at me as if she knew me.

# Next to Godliness

## Brian Stableford

As the cab drove away Adam looked down, checking his clothing carefully from the bottom up. The black moccasins, charcoal-grey slacks and chocolate-brown sweater seemed supremely casual — which was exactly how they were supposed to look. They seemed slightly loose, but that was a carefully-contrived surface effect; like all smart clothes, they clung fast to his own skin. He took out a pocket mirror in order to make sure that his hairpiece was on its best behaviour, spruced up the petals of the scarlet roses he was carrying and finished up by taking one last look at the label on the bottle of wine expertly clutched in the same hand, to reassure himself yet again that it was the '98 and not the '99.

The gate didn't creak and the path to the Millers' front door was entirely free of weeds. The smart WELCOME mat was spotless. The stained glass panels in the front door depicted characters from Greek mythology: Tantalus and Sisyphus to the left and the right, Ixion upraised in the centre. The door chime was as mellow as a concert grand.

"Adam!" said Nick, responding to the signal with wonderful alacrity. "It's great to see you again. Come into the kitchen for a moment and say hello to Eve."

Adam was ushered through the hallway and into the kitchen, where he presented Eve with the roses and Nick with the wine, swiftly fulfilling the true purpose of his abrupt summons to Eve's inner sanctum by admiring the astonishing cleanliness of the cooking area.

Even while cooking a four-course dinner for six, Eve Miller was in total control; there was not a drop of spatter anywhere on the gleaming tiles, dumb as they were, not a crumb or a flake on the polished work-surfaces. The crockery for the later courses was stacked with military precision; the knives, ladles and spatulas assembled in wall-racks were gleaming so brightly they might have been chrome-plated. Eve was wearing a frilly apron that was as dead as a doornail, but the blood-red dress she was wearing underneath was vibrant with artificial life.

Nick, like Adam, was conscientiously clad in drab plumage; a superficial glance might have rated them as nearly alike as two peas in a pod, although Adam saw things very differently. He always had, even before the divorce from Lilith, but his new circumstances had sharpened his regrets considerably. Reducing the dosage of his patches might have helped with that particular problem, but that kind of retreat was unthinkable for a man of Adam's stripe.

The door chime resounded again, impossibly mellow, and Nick rushed off to admit Seth and Ruth Wright, leaving Adam alone with Eve. That hadn't been in Nick's script, but Eve had known Adam far too long ever to be flustered by his presence. She gave him a swift peck on the cheek and whispered: "How are you holding up?"

"Pretty well," Adam replied, but he couldn't help a reflexive twitch of the right hand towards the left bicep, where his patch was. Eve pretended not to notice. Her fake ruffled sleeves were amply long enough to conceal her own patch. The day was not far off, Adam knew, when the work of patches would be fully integrated into the smartness of clothing, but the time was not quite yet. Lilith was still working on the problem, but she was unlikely to win the race to the crucial breakthrough.

Nick hustled Seth and Ruth into the kitchen. There was a further handover of flowers and wine, efficiently executed given the crowding. Adam was relieved to note that Seth had brought silver carnations and Chilean wine. Seth and Ruth were both solicitors; he was a specialist in company law while she was in criminal – another marriage made in Heaven, but one more likely to survive infernal corrosion. Legal minds always tended, in Adam's slightly churlish estimation, to be somewhat lacking in the aesthetic department, although legal stomachs certainly seemed to enjoy fine food. Adam was proud of his own aesthetic sensibilities, even though he was a scientist through and through. He was always prepared to argue that there was as much aesthetics as logic in bioscience, especially its creative aspects.

At least, Adam thought, neither Seth nor Ruth would be inclined to spend all night explaining to him how badly the divorce settlement had been mismanaged by his solicitor. He greeted them both politely, but with a certain reserve. They were among Nick's newer acquaintances – of which he had made a great many since becoming a successful corporate analyst, assessing the potential of takeover targets for a mysterious cabal of private equity investors – but they had already achieved a remarkable closeness, to Eve as well as Nick.

The Millers' sitting-room was as spick and span as the kitchen, though not as conspicuously polished. There was not a speck of dust on the carpet, nor a thread of lint on the sofa, nor the remotest ghost of a cobweb in the corners of the ceiling. Adam, determined not to be consigned to the sofa with an empty space yawning beside him, beat Seth to the armchair without seeming to make a race of it.

Nick was busy with the cocktail-shaker when the chime sounded again; politeness demanded that he pass the shaker to Adam, who was the older friend, and Adam stood up to pour, allowing him to turn his back to the door when it eventually opened after the obligatory sidestep kitchenwards. Nick would, in any case, have introduced the newcomer to the couple first, leaving Adam for last.

"And this is my old friend Adam Goldsmith," Nick finished, as Adam handed round the chartreuse-tinted cocktails. "He lectures in biotechnology at the Uni – the old one, not the new one. Adam, this is my new friend Judith Apter. She's a web developer."

There was something about the combination of a female Christian name and the term 'web developer' that made Adam think 'black widow', but Judith Apter wasn't dressed in black and he had no reason to think that she was a widow. The miracles of cosmetic somatic engineering made it impossible to judge anyone's age simply by looking at them, but there was something about Judith's smile suggestive of authentic innocence. Her purple sleeves came all the way down to her wrists. There wasn't the slightest hint of a bulge, but Adam guessed readily enough that she'd be wearing a patch the size of a five-pound coin, just like his own. Even if she were merely making up the numbers, there had to be something at stake between her and Nick, business-wise. She had to be feeling the stress of opportunity and expectation, and must have taken extra precautions in the interests of maintaining focus and incentive.

"What sort of biotech do you do?" Judith asked, politely.

"Mostly artificial," Adam replied. "Some microbial, some textile. What sort of web development do *you* do?"

"The usual cocktail of commissions – two-thirds ads, one-third edutainment."

"Are you doing some work for Nick?"

"Consultancy for one of his takeovers. You?"

"We've never worked together," Adam said. "We used to play together, when we were young – back at the dawn of time." He looked away, slightly discomfited. At the dawn of time, according to *Genesis*, Adam and Eve had been happy in the garden, until Old Nick had come along in serpentine guise – but Adam had had another wife before then, if you believed the Apocrypha: a non-conformist Lilith who would doubtless have insisted on baring her arms to demonstrate her independence, her 'ownership of her emotions', her 'responsibility for her own telic intensity'. Adam felt an urgent necessity to change the subject.

Fortunately, Judith did it for him. "Are the Wrights old friends too?" she asked.

Seth Wright, having left his wife to entertain Nick, immediately elbowed his way into the conversation. "I only met Nick a few months ago," he volunteered. "We came into the Propriotech takeover from different directions and joined forces to manage the leverage. We've become thick as thieves, though – we live within walking distance, although we'd never dream of actually walking. Adam was somewhere in the Propriotech battle-line too, although I didn't meet him at the time – he made a small killing when the buyout went through."

"*Killing*'s a corporate lawyer's term," Adam said. "He means that one of my patents was among the assets that got stripped."

"*Stripped* isn't a corporate lawyer's term," Seth quipped, "and my lovely wife has far more to say about killing than I do. She sometimes defends killers of the literal kind – paratelic killers, of course. There's no point defending telic murderers – no arguments to be made in mitigation."

"Patches aren't supposed to encourage violence, let alone murder," Judith observed, gauchely – making it obvious that she really was as young as she looked.

What she said was true, of course – PIA patches were only supposed to encourage *socially acceptable* telic behaviour, although they couldn't forbid natural telic behaviour, or its association with inappropriate neural rewards. The sin that Judith had committed was an error of judgment rather than fact. Discussions of that particular topic were already passé, quite worn out.

"Adam's a bioscientist," Seth observed, dismissively. "He can give you all the technical details, if you're really interested."

"Actually," Adam said, "the problem with designing patches to promote telic violence is economic rather than technical. There's no substantial black market in them. Patches promoting paratelic violence, on the other hand, are always in demand."

"I thought that was a tabloid myth," Judith said.

"Just because it's a tabloid myth," Seth put in, beating Adam to the punch, "doesn't mean that it's untrue."

Nick ushered them into the dining-room then, and promptly disappeared into the kitchen, from which he returned bearing bowls of asparagus soup, a basket of French bread and a bottle of Chardonnay in a portable cooler. Eve emerged in his wake, bearing more soup-bowls, a second bread-basket and Adam's bottle of '98 Bordeaux. There were no place-cards on the oval table, but Nick and Eve cleverly maneuvered all of the guests into their carefully-allotted seats. Adam was set between Eve and Judith, directly opposite Ruth.

The soup, as was only to be expected, was divine. Seth was the first to spill a stray drop on the tablecloth, but the smart cloth swallowed it with alacrity. Adam could not suppress a pang of regret as he looked at the place where it had vanished; in a kinder world, that might have been one of his patents, worth a great deal more than the one that had brought him such a derisory windfall in the Propriotech takeover. It might even have been a shared patent, cementing his Heaven-made marriage and protecting it against disaster – but Lilith had refused to take advantage of the technology that could have facilitated their partnership.

"It's obscene," Lilith had said when the first PIA applicators came on to the market, eighteen months after the first TGAD applicators. Until then, TGAD patches had been called 'pleasure patches' by their users and detractors alike, but as soon as the new antithesis was established the popular parlance shifted. TGAD stood for Third Generation Anti-Depressant but PIA wasn't so stubbornly descriptive; it stood for Pride in Achievement. From that day onwards, the rival product-categories were known as Pride and Joy, at least among the users who loved Joy. Those who preferred Pride eventually came to favour a sterner terminology; it was they who had taken up the telic/paratelic dichotomy.

"It's inevitable," Adam had assured his wife, as the mild philosophical debate turned into their fiercest and most enduring quarrel.

Adam argued that people had been using drugs to control their moods for millennia, ever since the primal discovery of the intoxicating effects of fermented grains and the hallucinogenic effects of certain fungi. Organic chemistry had made that kind of artificial intervention far more sophisticated, eventually leading to the invention of the first and second generation anti-depressants. What was inevitable was that genomic augmentation would lead to a further order of sophistication, ensuring not only that people would never have to feel miserable again if they didn't want to, but that they could actually employ artificial happiness as a carrot to encourage them in productive endeavour.

"The problem with TGADs," he had said, "is that they just make people feel good, with no regard to circumstances. They're just the latest opium of the people, blotting out the misery of poverty and failure with blunt neurochemical instruments. They take away incentives, facilitating bliss in ignorance. PIAs are different. PIAs accommodate the fundamental principle that feeling good – happiness, joy, pleasure, and so on – ought to be *earned*, as a reward for some task completed, some artistry attained. PIAs enhance the neural pathways that connect the pleasure areas in the brain with purposive action, with physical and intellectual accomplishment. They guarantee that people can take an entirely proper delight in the results of their creativity, and an entirely appropriate pleasure in the products of their labour. TGADs drag their users down, forging a society of modern lotus-eaters, but PIAs lift their users up, reopening the road to Utopia."

"That's foolishly optimistic, Adam," Lilith had riposted. "These things have more in common with the old nicotine patches than mere appearance. They're peddling poison; while pretending to help us free ourselves from addiction, they're actually feeding and enhancing it. We've grown used to thinking of TGAD reliance as the ultimate addiction, but that's because we couldn't see PIA coming. All PIAs offer is the opportunity to become happier workaholics. When you talk about enhancing the neural pathways connecting to the pleasure areas in the brain, you mean that it will intensify the rewards associated with the pathways that are already there, not that it will encourage the development of new pathways. In fact, it will discourage the development of new pathways, preventing the further elaboration and sophistication of an individual's spectrum of rewards. PIA isn't a road-map to Utopia; it's a recipe for a society of obsessive-compulsive freaks who rejoice in their obsessive-compulsiveness."

And the argument had rumbled on, while Adam experimented with various kinds of PIA patch, until he found the one best suited to his particular vocation, while Lilith had worn the shortest sleeves she could find – in dead and living clothes alike – to show the world that her arms and mind were clean. That kind of cleanliness, in her perverted opinion, really had been next to godliness – but the conventional kind had fallen increasingly under the responsibility of Adam, who had become more and more intent on keeping a tidy house, as well as a tidy appearance and a tidy mind.

He should have realised five years before it actually came about that the break-up was inevitable, but he had loved his wife, just as she had loved him, after her fashion. That was one thing the patches seemed impotent to affect; all the telically-focused bioscience in the world had not yet succeeded in manufacturing a reliable love-potion, nor in finding a cure for love-sickness for those of a contrary disposition.

After the soup, following tradition, came the fish course. "The sole's magnificent, Eve," Adam said. "Done to perfection."

"Thanks," Eve said. "It's difficult to judge the frying time, especially when you're doing six at a time in a mammoth pan, but if you can get the butter to the right temperature..."

"Eve's a genius in the kitchen," Nick put in.

"Not just in the kitchen," Eve supplied, blushing slightly as she realised that the remark might be taken for a *double entendre.* She had only intended to claim further expertise as a mother. Samuel – who was two years old now and not, technically speaking, a baby any longer – hadn't uttered a sound thus far, and probably wouldn't.

*There, but for fortune*, Adam thought, allowing himself another twinge of regret as he pretended not to notice the delicate pink flush that had stained Eve's pale porcelain cheeks. He knew, though, that there had been more than one kind of fortune involved in Eve's decision to abandon her career in accountancy to concentrate on household management. Nick made more money than all four of his guests put together.

When Eve and Nick got up to clear the plates for a second time, Adam asked Judith whether her edutainment work ever involved her with the university.

"Not really," she said. "It's mostly aimed at younger age-groups. I'm not much of a talking head farmer, more an infrastructure planner. What sort of web resources do you use in your teaching?"

"I don't do that much teaching, to be honest," Adam admitted. "Lecturer's just a title. I have postgrad students, but they're really my research assistants. Basically, I'm a lab rat." He added one more mental click to the tally of things that he and Judith didn't have in common, and assumed that she was doing the same.

Ruth leaned forward across the table then, addressing them both in a quasi-confidential manner: "I really envy Eve. I know the domestic goddess thing is supposed to be old-fashioned, but it can't ever go out of style, and she's so utterly perfect in the role. Seth does more than his share, bless him, but we just can't find the time to keep the house as tidy as this, let alone entertain."

"Eve's an artist," Adam said. "Even when she was training to be an accountant, she was an artist. Whatever she does, she does with an unmatchable flair."

In spite of all the food-bearing skills they had developed, it still required all Nick and Eve's collective effort to carry in the silver platter bearing the roasted suckling pig, neatly encircled by a chain of roast potatoes, topped and tailed with conical heaps of diced carrot and broccoli florets. They had to make a second trip to bring the plates, which they had left behind in order to give their guests an adequate interval to admire the meat.

Once the plates had been distributed, Nick began to carve. The chorus of murmurous admiration went on for a long time, renewed when Eve brought out the sauceboat. Adam, in his capacity as oldest friend, helped out by pouring more wine, making sure that he got a particularly opulent glassful of the '98 – which he then had to gulp, in order to pretend that he'd been more scrupulous in his division. Nobody seemed to notice, except Eve, who didn't seem to mind.

Adam observed that Eve waited until everyone else had started eating before she picked up her fork; even then, she took up her wine-glass in her other hand instead of her knife, in order to have a few more moments to watch her guests' reactions.

Their reactions would have been effusive in any case, but Adam's was perfectly sincere. The pork was superb, the sauce ambrosial. He saw Eve smile as she put her wine-glass down to take up her knife, and knew that for her, that had been the critical point of the whole evening. Adam smiled discreetly sideways, to signal his recognition of Eve's contentment, and gave her a near-imperceptible nod. That brought an extra twitch of broadness to her smile, which she maintained while she cut the meat on her plate, added a moderate complement of sauce-steeped vegetables and slowly brought the fork to her mouth, savouring every instant of expectation. Adam was still staring at her as her head snapped back, and then jerked forward. The mouthful of food was blasted out again, scattering its glutinous fragments in every direction before they cascaded down upon the tablecloth and her guests' plates.

Ruth screamed. Seth's jaw dropped. Adam couldn't see Judith's reaction because he had already turned his back on her as he leapt to his feet, but he saw Nick's. Nick was utterly horrified, and for one fleeting moment the expression on his face was pure wrath: anger that his dinner party had been spoiled, and that his carefully-laid plans had *gone wrong*. By the time the anger was replaced by concern, Eve had fallen to the floor, jerking uncontrollably.

Adam knelt down beside her, supporting her head and forcing the edge of his napkin into her mouth to make sure that she couldn't bite through her tongue. "Phone an ambulance, Seth!" he said, trying not to shout. "Tell them it's a type-two NA seizure. Ruth, get me a cushion from the sitting-room. Judith, get these chairs out of the way and help me pull her clear of the table-legs. She'll be okay, as long as she doesn't damage herself." The last assurance was not entirely honest. As a bioscientist, Adam he knew perfectly well that the world had not yet seen the worst of type-two seizures, and that no one had any idea as yet of the full scope of the damage they might do.

When Eve was clear of any hard surfaces, laid on her side with Adam and the cushion both supporting her head, everyone became preternaturally still, as if they could somehow force motionlessness on the victim of the fit by means of their own contrived inertia.

"Call a cab, Judith," Adam said, when the silence became unbearable. "Nick can ride with Eve in the ambulance; Seth, you and I can follow with Judith. Ruth will have to stay here, with Samuel." When Ruth opened her mouth to object he added: "Samuel knows you, probably better than me. I need to go with Eve."

Nick was becoming hysterical, in spite of Adam's brief reassurance that all would be well. The future possibilities opening before his vivid imagination were putting his earlier horror to shame. For a moment or two, Adam thought that he might have a second seizure victim on his hands. Ruth grabbed hold of Nick and hugged him, babbling that it would all be okay, that type two seizures were never fatal. *Hardly ever* would have been more accurate, but it wasn't an occasion for accuracy.

By the time the ambulance arrived Eve had passed into a quieter phase of unconsciousness and Adam felt sure in his own mind that she really would be okay. He gave a curt report to the senior paramedic, then stood aside as Eve was loaded on to a stretcher and borne away. The cab that Judith had called was already waiting; it followed in the ambulance's slipstream all the way to the hospital, with Adam, Seth and Judith wedged in together on the back seat.

Once they reached the hospital, there was nothing to do but surrender control to the staff and wait. Adam knew that the waiting would be hard; telics always found waiting hard, especially in the wake of something going wrong. Open-ended waiting was the worst of all. Pleasure in Achievement was all very well, until achievement was frustrated – as Adam had had abundant opportunity to discover during and after the divorce. He left the job of calming Nick to Seth, who seemed both willing and able to take it on, while he sat down, uncomfortably aware that all the colour must have drained from his cheeks, and that his distress must be clearly visible.

Judith sat down beside him, awkwardly tense. "Are you all right, Adam?" she asked, in a low voice – as if she feared that the question, or its answer, might somehow upset Nick if he were to overhear it.

"Fine," Adam lied. "It gave us all a fright, I dare say – but she'll be fine now. It won't take the doctor long to give her the all clear."

"I've seen it on the news," Judith said, "but never for real. They're adamant that the patches don't cause it, but that can't really be true, can it? As Seth says, just because something's a tabloid myth doesn't mean it's a lie."

"PIA patches don't cause the seizures," Adam told her. "They just open up the possibility. That kind of neural amplification can happen naturally, but it rarely did before PIA. It's far easier nowadays to die of happiness – or at least to go into literal fits of ecstasy – than it ever was before."

"It can't be the pleasure that does it," Judith objected, again displaying her naivety. "Paratelics don't have fits like that."

"No, they don't," Adam admitted, dully. "The new epilepsy is strictly a middle class disease. It's not the pitch of the joy so much as the tautness of the obsession. Thank God Lilith's not here – the conflict of emotions would probably tear her apart."

"What conflict of emotions?" Judith asked, keeping her voice strictly neutral. She obviously knew that Lilith was the name of Adam's ex-wife.

"She's known Eve for as long as I have," Adam said. "She'd be heartbroken – but, Lilith being Lilith, she wouldn't be able to hold back a surge of triumph. She'd see this as proof that she was right."

"She's a dissenter," Judith observed. It was a comment, not a question.

"Is that what we're calling refuseniks these days? She's clean; she doesn't use patches. Never has, never will – and I really do mean *never*."

"That's why you divorced," Judith said, maintaining her tentative tone.

"Irreconcilable differences," Adam replied. "When they say mixed marriages don't work they usually mean telics and paratelics, but that can sometimes be a winning combination. Refuseniks and paratelics can get along too, if the rest of the chemistry's right. I loved Lilith and she loved me, but there's no hope for a marriage between a telic and a... dissenter. Didn't Nick tell you to avoid the subject of Lilith when he invited you along to balance the numbers at the party?"

"Of course they did," Judith said. "What does she do for a living?"

"Industrial biotech. Textiles."

"And she doesn't feel the pressure to compete? She doesn't feel she's losing out to her PIA-enhanced peers?" Judith's voice had suddenly become more intense, and Adam guessed that she was not disobeying Nick's orders just for the hell of it.

"No," Adam said, shortly. "She insists that they're the ones who are losing out. There's none so blind as those who will not see."

"I wouldn't dare to try," Judith told him, confirming his conclusion, "but when you see something like that..."

"There's no need to worry," Adam told her, not meaning it kindly. "There's no reason to expect anything like that to happen to you. You're not Eve."

Judith looked at him sharply, but Adam judged that she hadn't taken offence, or even been aware that she might have done. Judith wasn't wondering what Eve had that she didn't; she was wondering how Adam had ended up with Lilith instead of Eve, if he felt as intensely about Eve as he seemed to do. That was something Adam had no intention of explaining.

Nick interrupted them then. He was still exceedingly fretful, even by the standards of a telic forced to wait. "She is going to be all right, isn't she?" he said, to Adam.

"She'll be fine," Adam assured him. "It's just nature's way of telling her to take it a little bit easier. She's bright enough to heed the warning."

"It's not that easy, though, is it?" Nick said.

"Yes it is," Adam told him. "It really is."

The reason why Adam and Lilith had ended up together, instead of Adam and Eve – if there really had been a reason, rather than a mere freak of circumstance – was that Adam and Lilith had had the potential to change the world, whereas Adam and Eve would only have changed one another.

Adam and Eve might have been – *would* have been, Adam now felt sure – the happier couple, but Adam and Lilith had planned to be collaborators as well as eternal lovers. They were both bioscientists, and their specialities had an obvious overlap in the economically significant field of smart clothing. If only they had been able to sustain an adequate level of domestic harmony, they might have worked together as closely, and as productively, as Pierre had Marie Curie – but they hadn't. The patent applications they might have formulated and filed together had never come to term, and they had missed out on their due share of the big boom. They had had their separate successes, but those had been minor compared to what they might have done together.

Adam knew that he ought to phone Lilith, to tell her what had happened to Eve. But for a whim of circumstance, it might have been her they'd invited to dinner tonight, along with some unattached Byronic hunk who cherished his satanic gloom far too much ever to surrender to the joys of PIA… except that it wasn't a whim of circumstance at all. There was no way Eve Miller would ever tolerate a refusenik at her dinner table, even one she had known since childhood. Lilith knew that too, and the knowledge would only add to the awful confusion of her emotions when she heard the news.

It was better, Adam decided, not to phone her. Instead, he rehearsed the argument in his mind that he would have been forced to put to her, to prove to her that Eve's misfortune wasn't conclusive evidence that she was right about the awful iniquity of PIA patches.

"The problem," he would have told her, "isn't the enhancement of pleasure in achievement. The problem is the complexity of the enhanced neural pathways that are set up. It's a matter of focus. Common-or-garden workaholics like me and Nick, or Seth and Ruth, can narrow the scope of our potential achievements, so our neural pathways, as enhanced by the patches, are simple and direct –

motorways of the mind. Common-or-garden mothers can do the same – but Eve is an artist, who brings an unmatchable flair to *everything*. She could never be content to concentrate on motherhood. She's given up her own career, but she hasn't given up her involvement in Nick's, and she hasn't given up her determination to maintain a social life. She's tried to maintain too many strings to her bow. The enhanced pathways she's built in her brain, with the aid of PIA, are too complicated and intricately tangled. All she needs to do is slow down, take things a little easier, lower her standards a little."

Unfortunately, Adam had known Lilith for far too long not to be able to synthesize the arguments she would have constructed in opposition to his. "That's exactly what I've been telling you all along," she would have retorted. "PIAs are creating a culture of obsession. They help people with unhealthy tendencies to become even more unhealthy, even more manically focused on their petty specialisms. To a mentally healthy person – a *well-rounded* person like Eve – they're a curse, leading to neural overload and mental breakdown. How can she slow down, take things easier and *lower her standards a little* while she's addicted to her PIA cocktail of choice?"

"PIAs aren't addicted," Adam replied, reflexively.

"Not *physiologically* addictive," his Lilith-anima countered, "but in psychological terms, they're as addictive as anything can be. Who can't get hung up and strung out on *success*? Who can resist the temptation to *excel?* We have to resist it, Adam. We have to retain mastery of our own motivation."

"But we could have had success," Adam objected, plaintively. "We could have *made a killing*. We could have done our bit to change the world."

"Are you all right, Adam?" Judith asked, yet again.

Adam woke up with a start. He became aware that the fingers of his right hand had been plucking at his left arm – not, he realised, to test the patch beneath the fleshcloth but to tease the garment itself, the living clothing to whose evolution he and Lilith might have made a crucial contribution, if only they had not been torn apart by a difference of opinion.

"Yes," he said. "I'm fine."

"Eve's awake," Judith told him. Nick popped his head out just now to say that you can go in to see her if you want. Seth and I waved at her from the doorway.

Adam looked around and saw that Seth was in the far corner of the waiting room, muttering into his phone while staring at his wristwatch: the perfect image of Telic Man. He was presumably bringing Ruth up to date, and assuring her that they would soon be back on schedule.

Adam stood up, and went in to see Eve. The room she was in was very clean, but Adam couldn't believe that it seemed clean to Eve. To her, it must seem gloomy, dingy and dangerous. She was desperate to be out of it and home, but she had the obligatory fluid drip attached to her arm and a whole battery of electrodes clustered on her skull, feeding data to an EEG. The doctor had doubtless set a deadline for the completion of his enquiries, but the waiting would be agony for the patient.

Nick was sitting on the right-hand side of the bed holding Eve's right hand. Adam brought a chair up to the other side.

"You gave us a fright," Adam observed, as Eve's anxious blue eyes met his.

"I ruined the dinner," she said, tearfully.

"The dinner was fabulous," Adam told her. "You know as well as I do that no further mouthful can ever match up to the first. It was a kindness to interrupt us, really. Imagine the emphasis your performance lent to the memory of that perfect moment. It was a masterstroke – a pure *coup-de-théâtre*."

Eve smiled.

"I wish I could bullshit like that," Nick said. "Why did you ever become a scientist, when you could have worked for the tabloids?"

"I wanted to change the world," Adam said, rising above the insult. "I still might."

"You never got dessert," Eve lamented, losing her smile again. "You didn't even get to finish the '98 Bordeaux."

"It's a full-bodied claret," Adam said. "It'll be all the better for a chance to breathe."

"You ought to have decanted it," Eve immediately said to Nick. "We really must try harder to get things right."

"Not according to Adam," Nick retorted, a trifle spitefully. "Slow down, take it easy, lower our standards – that's his advice. Did the doctor say anything?"

"The same, but not as succinctly. Is Samuel all right?"

"Ruth's with him," Nick assured her. "He'll be fine. You'd better go now, Adam – it's getting late, and you must have things to do tomorrow. You might take Judith home – this isn't really her concern."

"What must she think of us?" Eve wondered, aloud. "Do you like Judith, Adam?"

"Yes," said Adam, dutifully. "She's very nice – brought a perfect balance to the party."

"I picked her," Nick said, proudly.

"And you're right about my seeing her home," Adam said. "Be sure and take the doctor's advice, Eve. You don't have to be perfect in *every* respect, and you're already perfect in more ways than any normal human being could ever hope to be."

"You really ought to phone Lilith," Nick suggested, maliciously. "She'd want to know what happened wouldn't she?"

"I'll phone tomorrow," Adam said, still looking into Eve's eyes, knowing that she would understand that he intended to phone *her*, not Lilith. "It was the single greatest mouthful of roast pork I've ever tasted, or ever hope to taste."

"I know," said Eve, softly. "It blew my mind."

Adam and Judith arranged themselves in the back seat of the cab, careful to leave a symbolic margin between them. He was glad that they seemed to be in agreement on the issue, although there hadn't been much doubt about it. It would have been embarrassing if one of them had been interested, while the other wasn't, but the catastrophic interruption of the party would have put paid to any chance either one of them might have had of forming such an interest.

"One thing I've never understood," Judith said, by way of making conversation, as the cab set off in the direction of her home, "is why patches work so well in helping people to work harder and more effectively, but don't seem to have any effect at all on personal relationships. You'd expect them to reward success in marriage just as much as success at work, wouldn't you?"

"No," Adam told her, slipping into his lecturing mode now that he was sure that he and she were ships that would pass in the night without a flicker of remorse. "The whole point about PIAs is that they assist *telic* behaviour. They can only increase the pleasure derived from the completion of goal-orientated tasks."

"You're saying that marriages – romantic relationships in general – aren't goal-orientated? But TGADs don't affect them either."

"Of course not. TGADs are their own reward – that's the essence of paratelic experience."

"I don't believe that relationships are paratelic," Judith said, flatly. "They're not just things to be enjoyed for the sake of the experience. They *are* goal-orientated. At least, they can be. They *should* be."

"I thought so once," Adam admitted. "I changed my mind."

"Bitter experience?"

"More careful theoretical analysis, and the lessons of objective empirical observation. If romantic relationships were as telic as mythmongers sometimes pretend, there really would be PIAs that function as love potions. There aren't."

"There aren't any that enhance the rewards of telic violence," she observed, "but you wouldn't rule out that possibility on theoretical grounds when we were talking earlier."

"There's no substantial pressure of demand on that particular innovation," Adam reminded her, "in spite of the potential military interest. The demand for love potions, on the other hand, is potentially immense – and so are the potential commercial rewards."

*What a terrible thing it would be*, he heard Lilith whisper, in the depths of his mind, *if we could choose who to love, and who would love us, and make our choices stick with the aid of drug-induced reinforcement.*

*Would it?* Adam wondered, silently. *Would it, really?*

"I don't think that you can rule out the possibility," Judith insisted. "We can't know today what we might discover tomorrow. The world is changing more rapidly now than ever before, and we have no idea where it might end up."

"The road to Utopia isn't closed," Adam said. "It's just that there aren't very many of us capable of following the map."

The cab drew to a halt. Judith got out. Adam didn't bother to get out with her; he already knew that she wasn't going to invite him in. He leaned over to say: "I'm sorry the evening was such a disaster."

"It wasn't," she said. "I've never seen a house so perfect, and a meal so perfectly planned and executed. It was quite an inspiration, in its way. I'm sorry for Eve, of course – but I hope I'll have the opportunity again. Perhaps they'll invite us both." She tried to sound enthusiastic, but couldn't.

The cab got under way again. Adam's flat was only five minutes away. As he paid the driver he was struck by a gust of cold wind, whose suddenness overwhelmed the compensatory capacity of his smart sweater. He shivered. The patch on his left arm made itself felt, although the heat it seemed to generate was illusory. As the cab drew away, Adam paused to scratch his arm. He resolved not to use such a heavy dose the next time he went out.

*The problem with being wired to obtain superabundant pleasure from success*, he thought, framing the words as carefully as he would have done had Judith still been there, *is that when one can't succeed, in spite of one's best efforts, life becomes very difficult.*

As he walked up the stone steps to his front door, he heard someone in one of the other flats laughing excitedly. *Bloody paratelics*, he thought, uncharitably. *It's all so very easy for them.*

Lilith, he felt sure, would not have laughed at him, any more than Eve would. She had loved him, after her fashion.

# Mellowing Grey

Dave Hutchinson

Rain is pelting down outside, hailing the side of Moll O'Connor's shed like handfuls of gravel fired from a cannon. Water finds all the little holes and cracks and drip-drips down inside. Some of it lands in a scattered landscape of battered cookware, aluminium pots and pans, casserole dishes, chipped mugs, Pyrex ovenware, arranged across the floor. Most of it misses and just runs across the floor.

Moll O'Connor doesn't mind the rain. Rain is good. Recently some of the arseholes from the village have started coming up here at night and throwing stones at the side of her shed and shouting things and she's been reduced to lying wide awake in her sleeping bag, knowing that one day the stones and shouted obscenities will become petrol bombs thrown through her window, knowing there's nothing she can do about it but leave, knowing she isn't going to do that because she's lived in this village all her life. Recognising the voices of some of the arseholes because she went to school with them, or with their parents.

But arseholes seem to be sensitive to the weather. The rain keeps them at home, so a good cloudburst usually means she can sleep soundly. Although not tonight, because she has things to do tonight.

The rain makes it difficult to do what she needs to do. She's scavenged dozens of bits of candles from households in the area, some of them not much more than stubs, and she's placed them around the inside of the shed in locations which seem less likely to be inundated than others, but the rain keeps getting in and putting them out. She's been going around the shed half the night replacing extinguished candles, and she's more or less reached the point where she's had enough, where this has become *much* more trouble than it's worth, so she stomps over to the warped Welsh dresser she found on the local tip last year, and she opens one of the doors and takes out a bundle wrapped in an old Laura Ashley curtain.

She carries the bundle over to the middle of the floor, where she has laid a big sheet of paper begged from the butcher's shop. It's the driest place in the shed, but there are still spots and splashes on the paper and she hopes it'll do. She kneels beside the paper and unwraps the bundle.

It's a badger's skull. She found it last Autumn during one of her regular scavenging expeditions. It was just lying on the rubbish-strewn flagstones of the Abbey, among the piles of leaves and old fast-food cartons and discarded mattresses and used condoms. She was lurching along, poking at likely-looking piles of refuse with her stick, when she found this black and white head looking up at her, snipped cleanly from the body as if with a pair of bolt cutters and crawling with maggots. Impossible to tell what did it, although there have been stories of an owl the size of a Rottweiler living in the ruins. She's not so sure; it'd take a hell of a bird to bite off a badger's head and carry its body away.

But things like this are important to Moll. She manoeuvred the head into an old Tesco's carrier bag and took it back to her hut by the railway embankment and buried it, and for the past year she's been resisting the temptation to dig it up and see how Nature has been taking its course. Until yesterday, when she went outside with her spade and reclaimed her prize, picked clean, jaw disarticulated.

She'd already lit a bonfire on the other side of the rusty tracks, and she poked and prodded the skull into the middle of it, and then she waited again. When she went out this morning, smelling rain in the air, the fire was out and the skull was nicely charred but not consumed.

Now she holds the skull in her hands and, without any ceremony at all, she sends it spinning across the sheet of paper, leaving curved charcoal marks. She does this again, and again, and again.

Finally, when the paper looks nicely covered, she puts the skull aside and examines the marks it left. She shuffles around the paper to get a look at them from other angles. She picks the paper up and tilts it to the candlelight, screwing up her eyes and scrunching up her nose.

Well, it looks as though a Frenchman has just stolen a bicycle. Someone in Dorset – it's not clear who, or indeed why – has set fire to a boat. A big woman named Brenda is cheating on her husband. A team whose name begins with an A has won the American Football League.

Moll O'Connor lays the sheet of paper aside and kneels there, looking at nothing, for a while.

Finally, she says, "Well what *fucking* use is *that* to anybody?"

From the front door of The Pub On The Hill, it's said, you can see four different counties, and another two from the back. Mr Plough doesn't think that's such a big trick. In England you're never much more than fifty miles from the sea; finding a place to put a pub so you can see six counties from it can't be *that* hard.

He'd have thought the Hill itself would have been attraction enough – a three-hundred-foot anomaly of some past ice age, swelling smooth and grassy out of the rolling countryside, atop which some entrepreneur back in the days of Queen Victoria had decided to build a remarkably ugly brick pub. The Hill's just steep enough to stretch the muscles of your legs as you walk up the path to the Pub, although coming back down after an evening there it seems a lot steeper, and there's a beautifully hand painted and varnished board hanging behind the bar listing the names of a dozen local men who lost their footing over the years and tumbled to their deaths. When he first saw the board, Mr Plough had found it rather morbid, and wanted to take it down, but the locals complained, and Mr Plough had to wonder – not for the last time – what on Earth went on in their heads.

Mr Plough is returning from his morning's constitutional, a tour of the balloons ringing the Hill, checking the moorings, testing the batteries, making sure the connections are secure. At least that's what he tells himself; until quite recently he found the task rather tedious and he tended to storm through it in an hour and a half, pedalling furiously from installation to installation on his ancient women's bicycle. That he can now make the task last four hours, walking most of the way and wheeling his bike beside him, just goes to show how little he really wants to be in The Pub On The Hill right now.

In fact, pushing his bike up the last bit of the path to the Pub, Mr Plough could quite happily climb into the saddle, freewheel back to the bottom, and just keep going and never look back.

Of course, he knows that's not going to happen. He rolls the bike into the outhouse, locks the door, and stands for a few moments looking out into the misty distance of overgrown fields and woods, hedges, snaking roads, villages, and far far away, almost on the edge of visibility, a column of smoke rising from one of the four counties, although he doesn't know which one. For him to be able to see that smudge of smoke at all, it must be huge, and that really does tell you all you need to know about the penalties for disobedience. So no, Mr Plough isn't going anywhere.

Inside, everything is quiet. He's given his cleaner, Mrs Wakefield, a few days' holiday, even though there isn't really anywhere for her to go, because he doesn't want her poking around upstairs. She'd seemed rather bemused and upset by this, but a few quid in holiday money improved her mood and he hasn't seen her since. Ideally, he'd like to do something similar with the regulars, but he's been told to carry on as normal and if he ever feels panic overtaking him all he has to do is look at that faraway smudge of smoke. Whatever it is, it's been burning all week.

Still, he tells himself as he goes upstairs and puts his hand on the handle of the kitchen door, as he's told himself every morning for the past three days, perhaps this is the day when the nightmare ends, when he opens the door and they're gone.

Heart thudding, he opens the door. They're not gone. They're still sitting at the kitchen table, still in the same chairs, just the way they were when he looked in on them last night. Still drinking.

The two elves look at him. The wood sprite, completely shitfaced, just sits there giggling. One of the elves picks up an empty bottle and brandishes it in its fist.

"Plough," it says urgently. "Whisky!"

The wood sprite carries on giggling.

The Creature startles awake out of a nightmare of women on horseback and rolls out of the hedgerow he spent the night in. Climbs to his feet and brushes dirt and bits of twig and spiders' webs off his clothes and out of his hair. He yawns and blinks and scratches various itches. He walks along the hedge to a tree, breaks some bits of branch off, and eats them. He doesn't really enjoy doing this – indeed, he thinks it may not even be necessary – but he finished the last of his food yesterday, sheltering from the rain under a bank thirty miles or so from here, and he's a bit peckish and it'll do until he can buy something else.

Breakfast over, the Creature retrieves his rucksack from under the hedge, makes a quick check of its contents, straps it on, and then stands for a few moments looking about him. *East? West? North…?*

West. The hedge beside him is almost twelve feet tall, but the Creature jumps over it easily, and once on the other side he starts to run.

The elves turned up four nights ago, not long after he had closed up, and when he opened the door to their knock and saw them standing there he almost had a heart attack on the spot. They were dressed identically in jeans, boots and parkas with fur-trimmed hoods.

"Plough," the one on the left said without preamble. "We want to have a party."

Mr Plough discovered that the capacity for language had deserted him. He also discovered that he had wet himself.

"It's an anniversary party," said the elf on the right.

"Fifteen years since we regained what was rightfully ours," said the one on the left.

"We're going to have a party in your pub," said the one on the right.

"Oh," said Mr Plough, which was all he could manage of "Oh, fuck," which was what he really wanted to say.

"We understand our presence would upset your regulars," said the one on the left, "so we'll have our party upstairs, out of sight."

"And you'll tell no one we're there," said the one on the right.

"This is a private party," said the one on the left. And it smiled.

So they came in, and Mr Plough let them choose the kitchen for their party and he gave them a case of whisky and then he went away and was sick.

The next morning he stood outside the kitchen door, paralysed with fear and stunned with lack of sleep, wondering whether he should knock or go in or just go away, when a voice from inside called, "Plough!"

He went in. The elves had finished the case of whisky but didn't seem remotely drunk. With them was a wood sprite. Wood sprites were comparatively new; you didn't see a lot of them about. This one was about five feet tall and startlingly thin and gnarly and it had a bottle of rum in its hand, which it must have gone down to the bar for. It looked at him and giggled.

One of the elves held out an empty whisky bottle. "Whisky, Plough," it said.

It's remarkable what the human mind can get used to. Three days ago he almost dropped dead at the sight of the elves. Now he finds himself going into the kitchen without knocking. He's even managed some small talk, although in the circumstances it isn't *sparkling* small talk.

The elves began to appear a year or two after the Crash, which ended the war in Europe and more or less brought modern computer-based civilisation to its knees. Britain had been, if not climbing to its feet again, at least managing to get along, when the elves turned up and, to cut a long story short, put the country to the sword. Millions died. Derby, Gloucester, Swindon and Newcastle were obliterated. The elves, the story goes, lost Britain many thousands of years ago when Men and their technologies began to arrive. Quite how Britain was lost to a bunch of skin-wearing, spear-wielding hunters, when the elves are capable of reducing modern cities to rubble, is not explained in the story. The story does say that the elves were driven back to the edge of civilisation, where they watched for millennia, waiting for us to put a foot wrong. And eventually their patience was rewarded with the Crash.

Mr Plough goes down to the cellar and gets another case of whisky for the elves. He has another seven cases, which he hopes will be enough, but the problem is the wood sprite. The wood sprite will only drink rum, and The Pub On The Hill doesn't have very much in stock, the locals not being, in general, rum drinkers. Mr Plough only has a couple of bottles left, and once they're gone the wood sprite will either have to drink something else or Mr Plough will have to cycle over to The Black Duck in Wadstall and see if Andy Dinsmore has any for sale. It's a fifteen-mile round trip to Wadstall. At least it'll get him out of the pub.

He takes the whisky back upstairs, stopping off in the bar to grab one of his remaining bottles of rum, and takes them back up to the kitchen, where he gives the elves a bottle each and puts the rum in front of the wood sprite. The elves open the whisky and pour what look like perfect pub singles into their glasses. The wood sprite just throws the twist-cap over its shoulder and slugs straight out of the bottle.

"Are you afraid of us, Plough?" asks one of the elves as he turns to leave.

"Of course he is," says the other, not letting him answer. "It's the only sensible response."

England is very quiet, but to the Creature that's not unusual; this is the way he remembers the place. Other things are not the way he remembers them. The first time he saw a motorway and the cars abandoned on it his mind simply refused to process the image. The same when he saw his first big town. He's grown used to these things now, but his first instinct is still *not to understand.*

The Creature has been away a while. He doesn't know how long, but it's obvious that it's a long long time. He's not entirely sure where he *was* when he was away, or what he did there, but he's fairly sure that he did *something* because he was paid for it.

He was paid in two ways. First was the velvet bag full of gold and silver coins, which was the only thing with him when he woke up naked in the rotten heart of a hollow tree eleven months ago and which he has been using very sparingly ever since, the first couple of occasions having aroused a degree of suspicion he decided was unhealthy.

The second payment is less obvious. He's not quite the same as he was when he went away. He can now run, flat out and carrying a fully-loaded rucksack, for hours at a time without even feeling short of breath. He can flip a car over on its back with one hand. He can eat pretty much anything, including metal, although he'd rather not. And he suspects he may not have to eat at all, but he hasn't tried that yet. He can hold his breath for hours at a time; he's started to wonder whether he isn't breathing at all just out of habit.

None of this is normal, of course, and the only explanation he can think of for these abilities – which he certainly can't find in his ravaged memory – is that they're payment for something. Quite what would justify such a payment is entirely beyond him.

England is quiet, of course, because of the elves. The elves have banned, on pain of death, technologies such as the motor car and all forms of electronic communication. Possession of weapons will bring down a retribution as swift and merciless as the funnel of a tornado, while setting up an informal postal service could result in your entire village or town being levelled. There is no electricity anywhere in the country. He has heard, in his travels these past few months, the story of the War and the Crash and the Occupation many times, and he's not at all certain what to make of it. It's obviously true – he's seen the elves occasionally and their handiwork rather more often than he'd like – but there are times when it seems as if he's watching some horrible passion play rather than reality.

But he sees none of that today. He runs across the countryside all day without stopping or even breaking sweat and all he sees are fields, most of them grown wild, and feral cattle and sheep. He doesn't see another living person all day.

But as the sun begins to set and the Creature is starting to think about finding himself a hedgerow to sleep in – he could carry on running all night if he felt like it, but he doesn't see the point – he sees, far away in the distance, a line of silver sparkles in the sky. The Creature's eyesight is inhuman, but even he can't resolve the little shining sparks at this distance, so he turns towards them.

An hour later, what he at first took to be a line of silver sparkles turns out in fact to be a ring of silver sparkles, still catching the last rays of the sun high in the sky above a hill on top of which sits a singularly ugly building whose windows, in the early evening, blaze with light. The sparkles are tethered balloons. Oddly enough, the Creature understands this perfectly well. Back in January, when there was eight inches of snow on the ground and a wind-chill that drove the temperatures down to the point where people were dying of the cold, he stayed for a while with a little commune in Cornwall, and one of the people there told him about the balloons. Big helium balloons, each about the size of a bus and printed with solar cells. You ran them up into the sky and they made electricity. If the day was cloudy, you just let out the cable until the balloons were above the clouds. The elves have banned them, apparently, which is enough to make this place interesting.

The ugly building turns out to be a pub, and he opens the door onto a warm glow of electric light – also banned by the elves – and the interest of a dozen or so drinkers and a small plump man standing behind the bar.

Newcomers are rare at The Pub On The Hill; people don't travel so much these days, preferring to stay close to home rather than risk bumping into the elves on the road, so the sudden appearance of the sandy-haired young man with the rucksack gets everyone staring.

Not that it bothers him. He walks up to the bar and says, "Do you have food? I can pay." And he puts his hand in his pocket and takes out a little gold coin with the head of Edward The Confessor embossed on one side. He puts it on the bar. Mr Plough knows a little about old coins, and he knows that once upon a time, when these things were important, this coin was worth more than The Pub On The Hill.

He looks at the coin for a while, trying to decide. Then he smiles and puts out a hand. "Plough," he says.

The Creature has a name, of course, but he never uses it because he doesn't think of himself as human any longer. Still, he shakes Mr Plough's hand and says, "Thomas."

"All right then, Mr Thomas," says Mr Plough. "You go over and sit by the fire and I'll bring you a menu. Can I get you anything to drink while you're waiting?" And he closes his fist over the coin and pockets it before anyone else can see it.

A couple more people come into the pub during the evening, but by about nine, when the Creature notices rain pattering on the windows, people are starting to leave again. By ten, he and the landlord are alone in the bar. He doesn't know whether everyone has left because he's here, or because that's just the way things are around here.

The Pub On The Hill's menu was, at first glance, a work of fiction. The Creature hasn't seen meals like this anywhere since he arrived in England. When Mr Plough brings him a pint of bitter, he makes an order more in the spirit of experimentation, and is surprised when, half an hour later, Mr Plough brings him a medium-rare sirloin steak with fried potatoes and a medley of vegetables. The steak is one of the best things he can remember ever tasting.

While he's eating, he hears talking behind the bar. From where he's sitting he can see through a doorway behind the bar into a little hallway. Mr Plough is standing there talking to a person wearing a drenched and ruined Barbour jacket. They're talking very quietly, but as far as the Creature's concerned they might as well be shouting at the tops of their voices right next to him.

The figure in the Barbour jacket is holding up a sodden sheet of paper. "A boat, eh?" Mr Plough is saying. "Don't know anyone called Brenda, though."

"What about him?" asks the figure, turning to look at the Creature, who realises it's a little old lady with grey hair and a dirty but friendly face. "Maybe *he* knows Brenda."

Mr Plough chuckles. "Happen he does, but you're not to bother him. New customers are rare enough as it is; I don't want you driving this one away."

"But you could ask him," she insists.

"If the opportunity presents itself," he promises. He helps her roll up the sheet of paper and put it in a plastic bag. Then he gives her a bottle of Pernod from behind the bar and shows her out into the rain.

A few minutes later, collecting the Creature's plate, he asks, "Did you enjoy your meal?"

"It was marvellous," says the Creature. "Thank you."

"You're welcome," says Mr Plough, turning to go.

"I was wondering if you had rooms for the night as well," the Creature says, and he's surprised to see a band of tension cross the landlord's shoulders.

"I'm afraid we don't do –" Mr Plough begins, and then there's an awful unearthly noise from upstairs, a terrible high-pitched screaming keening bubbling sound.

For a few moments the Creature and Mr Plough look at each other. Then Mr Plough shouts, "Fuckers!" and throws the plate to one side and dashes across the bar. The Creature follows him behind the bar and into the hallway.

They run up the stairs and down the short corridor at the top, and as they do the Creature feels a breath of breeze on his neck and he looks over his shoulder. Down at the end of the corridor is a window. The window is open and its curtains are billowing into the corridor. Standing beside the window are two tall figures wearing jeans and parkas. The Creature stops and turns to look and as he does so one of the figures slips out of the window. The other half-turns and looks at him and a bolt of pain crashes through his head and drives him straight to his knees, screaming.

Mr Plough skids to a halt at the noise, looks back and sees Thomas doubled up on the floor, kneeling down with his forehead touching the landing carpet and howling. And beyond him one of the elves is standing at the open window, smiling.

And Mr Plough loses it. Every little humiliation they've put him through, every town they've destroyed, every person they've killed. In Mr Plough's head all these things reach critical mass.

Mr Plough takes a deep, deep breath and bawls, "Get out of my fucking pub you fucking *cunt*!"

And, miraculously, the elf does. It essays a little wave, slips through the curtains, and is gone.

"And don't fucking come back. You're barred," Mr Plough mutters, going over to where Thomas has managed to sit back on his heels and is blinking like a man who hasn't quite come to terms with his contact lenses yet. "You all right?"

Thomas looks at him and blinks some more. "That really hurt," he says in a baffled tone of voice.

Mr Plough grabs him by the arm and helps him to his feet. Thomas looks around him wide-eyed, as if he's just remembered something important. He looks at Mr Plough and says, "I'm all right."

"Okay," says Mr Plough, and turns and leads the way to the kitchen. He stops in the kitchen doorway, looks at what has happened inside, and says, quite calmly, "Oh dear."

Stopping behind him a moment later, the first thing the Creature sees is that the kitchen appears to have been decorated in gore. There's blood everywhere. Running down the walls, dripping from the ceiling, congealing on the furniture, inundating the floor.

The wood sprite has stopped making that awful noise. It's just lying on the floor, fingers twitching occasionally, its throat cut so deeply that it's almost been decapitated. As Mr Plough and the Creature stand watching, even the twitching stops.

Mr Plough shakes his head. "You see?" he says. "That's what too much drink will do."

They wrap the wood sprite's body in a blanket, carry it down the Hill, and bury it in a field in the pouring rain. The Creature does all the work, the tireless engine of his body shovelling earth with no more effort than as if he was spooning sugar into his tea. Mr Plough stands a little way off with a battery torch to light the work, although the Creature can see just as well without it, probably better.

All the while, Mr Plough keeps up a running narrative. How the elves suddenly appeared at his back door demanding to have an anniversary party. How the wood sprite just turned up out of nowhere. How he's had to keep the pub running somehow with all this madness going on upstairs.

"Poor little bastard," he says, nodding at the bundle the Creature has just laid in the six-foot-deep hole he's dug. "Probably just said the wrong thing to them. People, elves, it's all the same. They have too much to drink and somebody says the wrong thing to them and the next thing you know you're calling an ambulance."

The Creature, soaked to the skin and covered head-to-toe in mud, hops easily up out of the hole, picks up the spade, and starts filling it in. Actually, he rather wishes Mr Plough would stop talking.

While he works, slabs of memory start to coalesce and find their proper places. Scary slabs of memory. Dislodged, he thinks, by the sight of the elf in the pub, although he's seen elves before without remembering anything. Most of the memories are meaningless because no context comes with them; they're only pictures without a narration. But he remembers now that, wherever he's been and however long he was there, he was doing something for the elves. They're the ones who gave him the bag of coins and the other payments. He has no idea how he feels about this.

The job takes less than an hour. When they're finished only an idiot would fail to notice that someone has buried something here, but it's not as if they're trying to hide anything. The Creature looks at the churned earth of the wood sprite's grave and has an absurd urge to say some words over it, even if it's just 'poor little bastard.'

In the end, though, he just looks at Mr Plough and raises his eyebrows.

Mr Plough shines the torch on him. "I think you need a shower," he says. "And then a stiff drink. And I think we can manage a room for you now."

Mr Plough is as good as his word. The shower in the Creature's room delivers very hot water at a respectable pressure, and when the Creature comes down to the bar afterward, changed into his other pair of jeans and a tee-shirt and ruffling his still-damp hair into some kind of order, there is a glass containing somewhat more than a pub measure of whisky waiting for him.

"Feeling better?" asks Mr Plough from behind the bar.

"Much, thank you," says the Creature, seating himself on one of the bar stools and picking up the glass of whisky. He likes the taste of whisky, but he hasn't been even remotely drunk in the past eleven months because alcohol has absolutely no effect on him. He thinks that's a pretty cruel trick to play on a man. He sips the whisky.

Behind the bar, Mr Plough is in continuous motion, wiping glasses here, rearranging bottles there, wiping more glasses. The Creature watches him for a while and decides that could become quite irritating eventually.

"Where were you when it happened?" asks Mr Plough all of a sudden.

"When what happened?"

Mr Plough pauses in his perpetual motion and looks at The Creature and tips his head to one side. "The Crash."

Oh, *that*… "I can't remember."

Mr Plough stands still for a moment longer, then he's on the move again, rearranging the bloody bottles once more. "I think that happens a lot," he says. "There's an old girl in the village, Moll O'Connor, lives down by the railway. She can't remember what happened. Can't even remember the War."

The Creature doesn't know the details and he suspects they're irrelevant anyway. He says, "I think I saw her here earlier."

Mr Plough nods. "She does divination." He glances up at the Creature. "You know? Reading what's going on from sacrifices?"

The Creature just looks at him. Magic works in this new Britain, either because of the elves or in spite of them: you can read the entrails of a cow and discover what's happening on the other side of the world. He's heard it's the only method of communication the elves will allow. He was in a village in the Derbyshire Peak District last year and the two local newspapers were using it to get copy.

Mr Plough shakes his head. "She tries hard, bless her, but it's ages since she brought us anything that made any sense." He bobs down below the bar, comes up with a bottle of Scotch and a glass.

The Creature makes an effort to be human and says, "Where were you? When it happened?"

"Watching telly," says Mr Plough, pouring a very generous measure into his glass and topping up the Creature's. "I'd just got home from work – I worked in London." He pauses again for a moment, and the Creature watches all the painful memories of his past life cross his face. Then he seems to shake himself ever so gently free of them, for the moment, and he says, "I'd just got home. Kicked my shoes off, poured myself a drink, put the telly on. *News 24*. Simply to catch up on what had been going on. And then it was like a storm of midges was eating the picture. Couple of seconds, it was gone. Then the lights went out. And they've been out ever since."

"You have electricity here," says the Creature, gesturing with his glass to indicate the balloons.

Mr Plough shrugs. "*They* let me," he says, picking up a bar towel and wiping it across the top of the bar. "I think they do it as a joke. They're the reason I'm here in the first place. London was pretty bad after the Crash; a lot of people took to the road. The elves found me about six years ago and told me they wanted me to run a pub."

"Why?"

Mr Plough shrugs. "Christ only knows. Another joke, probably. They even made me change my name. My real name's Hammond."

"And the food…?"

"All from them," says Mr Plough. "The beer, too. Big delivery at the bottom of the hill every Tuesday morning. Never see them, but it's always there. The regulars don't know about it, of course."

The Creature shakes his head. Utterly insane.

"Anyway, I heard it was a computer virus, the Crash," Mr Plough continues. "Something nobody had ever seen before. Destroyed everything." He pauses again; the Creature is getting good at reading his pauses, like a student of Pinter. "Ended the War too, mind."

The Creature considers this for a while. He doesn't know what to say, really. All of this happened to these people while he was… elsewhere. It's hard enough to work up any great sympathy for them at the best of times, let alone for something that happened when he wasn't here. It doesn't help that their language is almost – but not quite – entirely unlike the mother tongue he remembers. It's not English as *he* knows it, and it's full of words and concepts which are completely alien.

The elves appear to have thought of this, because when he sees something unfamiliar or someone says something which makes no sense at all – 'computer virus,' for example – a little almost-not-quite-there voice whispers an almost-not-quite-translation in his head. This was happening almost all the time in the beginning and it almost drove him out of his mind, but these days it just almost-not-quite-speaks up now and again. This, presumably, means he's learning things.

"You know," Mr Plough says nonchalantly, "you were a big help tonight."

The Creature considers saying something like, `it was nothing,' or, `it was my pleasure,' but neither of these is true so he just shrugs and takes another drink.

"Really," says Mr Plough. "I couldn't have dug that hole on my own." He glances at the ceiling. "Still got to clean the kitchen, mind. I expect I'll have to burn the furniture."

"I expect so," replies the Creature. He's only really attending to this conversation with a fraction of his attention. The rest is taken up with reviewing his new memories and considering the possibility that the whole of this evening was staged in order to give them back to him. It would not, he now knows, be beyond the elves' capabilities or their sense of humour.

Mr Plough says, "I expect you've travelled a long way."

"Yes," says the Creature. Then something in Mr Plough's voice makes him put aside his memories and stare levelly at the little landlord.

"Seen much of the elves, have you?"

"Now and again," says the Creature carefully, understanding that this conversation is going somewhere but unsure quite *where*.

"And some of the stuff they do?"

The Creature nods.

"And how do you feel about that, then?"

The Creature doesn't know how he feels about it, particularly now, with his new memories. Things may be much more complicated than Mr Plough could ever suspect. He says, "How do you *think* I feel about it?"

Mr Plough nods. "You see, there's some of us in the area, we want to do something about the elves."

The Creature feels his heart sink. "Something…about them?"

"We've managed to get hold of some guns and some explosives," says Mr Plough, quite matter-of-factly.

The Creature looks at Mister Plough's face, searching for signs of madness, and finds none. Exhaustion, yes. Fatalistic determination, yes. But no madness. The little man really believes what he's saying. He says, "Ah."

"And, well, you know, we could use all the help we can get," Mr Plough says.

The Creature sits back. Well, there it is. Mr Plough is basically inquiring how he feels about committing suicide. "It sounds a bit risky," he says.

"Well, you think about it," says Mr Plough.

And The Creature says, "All right, I will."

And he does. He really does. He thinks about it when he's in his room at four o'clock in the morning, cinching his rucksack tight so it won't fall off his shoulders. He thinks about it as he drops a handful of coins on the bed and stirs a finger through them, noting the heads of kings and queens and emperors, assorted rulers collected by the elves down the centuries. He thinks about it as he opens the window and crawls, barefoot so his toes can get a purchase on the brickwork, head-first down the side of the building like a gecko. He's still thinking about it half an hour later, ten miles from The Pub On The Hill, running as fast as he can across country, hurdling hedges and fences, not even breathing hard.

What he mostly thinks is that Mr Plough and the people he's talked into joining his 'Resistance' are going to die, and they're going to die soon. He can't fault Mr Plough's bravery, but his group's operational security is appalling if their leader is inviting complete strangers to join them. They can't last much longer. The Creature doesn't want to hang around and see how that story ends, even if the elves might want him to.

Which makes him wonder why he was sent there in the first place, and he thinks about that too, as he runs across Middle England into the sunrise. Since yesterday evening he has concluded that nothing since his awakening has been an accident. The elves have been *showing* him things. In many cases they have been showing him appalling scenes of random cruelty and brutality. He's seen towns reduced to bumpy pavements of glassy slag or shallow mile-wide smoking craters. He's seen the populations of entire villages crucified on telephone poles. He's seen… well, he doesn't think about *that* because he's afraid he'd go out of his mind if he did.

Quite a lot of the time, the elves do things just because they *can*, just because they enjoy slaughter, enjoy the power it confers on them. But *sometimes*… sometimes he feels he's seen something with a larger purpose, something that's part of a larger creation, and he thinks last night's business with the wood sprite was like that.

Mr Plough rationalised it as an anniversary party gone bad, but The Creature has a feeling it was more of a ritual, a sacrament, and that his presence there was important, as witness or celebrant, and that somehow it served the elves' larger purpose in a way he can *almost* picture. But not quite. The larger picture keeps slipping away from him. But he knows it's there. And he knows it's a terrible thing. And he knows he's part of it.

The Creature puts back his head and screams obscenities at the dawn sky. Then without breaking stride he jumps entirely over a farmhouse which is in his way, rolls lightly on the other side, comes to his feet, and keeps going, Thomas The Rhymer, running into the new day, over the hills and far away.

# At Shadow Cope

Liz Williams

I should never have gone willingly to the house of a rival magus if it had not been for the promise of a demon. God knows that Simon Rule and I had never been close; we'd attended Oxford together, but whereas I had been popular as well as academically successful, Simon had always hung back – the one who hangs around the edges and doesn't fit in. I'd had few words to say to him then and I had even fewer now; I was, after all, one of the state magicians, could take up residence in London with Queen Aeve if I so chose, whereas Simon had returned to his family home of Shadow Cope, even further north than my own mansion of Burnblack, and skulked there for twenty years, doubtless brooding over his many collegiate failures.

So I was somewhat taken aback, to say the least, to receive a letter from him in the winter of Our Lady 1679, which read:

*My dear Lord Cygne,*

*I understand you have recently lost an oracular demon. I have such a being, and am willing to part with it for the right sum. I have little need of such fripperies now, in my current state, and frankly, I need the money. Let me know if you have an interest in the matter.*

*(Signed), Simon Rule.*

A number of things concerned me about this epistle. Primary among them was the issue of how Rule, a minor player in terms of Albion's magical practice, had found about the unfortunate episode of my oracular demon. It's embarrassing to lose a demon, and I'd taken some pains to keep quiet about the incident. I had, in fact, mentioned this to only one person: the Queen herself, and if Aeve had told Simon about it – no, the matter was unthinkable. At Oxford, Simon had often bemoaned his lack of connections –

despite his aristocratic origins he had been a scholarship student, and was already an orphan – and there was no reason for him to be in communication with the Queen now.

Thus a large part of my reason for leaving Burnblack in winter and taking a coach across the snow covered wolf-waste of the north to Simon's mansion of Shadow Cope, was simple paranoia.

Whereas Burnblack is a fortress, a squat tower round which my conjure-shucks prowl, deterring unwanted visitors (practically everyone, these days), Shadow Cope had once been a great house, a mansion onto which successive generations had added a wing here and an annexe there. It stood on the edge of a long stretch of moorland, close to the beginnings of Shadowmere Forest, in a rambling piece of parkland that had once been gracious and was now merely decrepit. Topiary figures lined the drive, concealed by snow and long since overgrown from their original shape. At the back of the house stood what had once been a knot garden and was now simply a knot, of bramble and elder and thick skeins of bindweed. Whatever skills Simon Rule might possess, gardening clearly wasn't among them.

Neither was housework. As I soon discovered, the place was filthy. Broken furniture lined the hall and what I initially took to be a grey stair-carpet turned out to be dust. Naturally, no one would expect a magus to sully his hands with such mundane matters, but it is simple enough to conjure something to do it, or merely to hire a maid and ensure her trustworthiness.

Simon himself was standing at the doorway, wringing his hands, and I saw immediately that he had lost none of the irritating mannerisms that had made him so infuriating at University.

"You're here. I'm relieved, Cygne. I saw the snow, I thought you might have to halt along the way."

"I *am* versed in some small manner of weather magic, Simon. I am not entirely without resources."

Simon's face crumpled. He was even more pathetic these days, now that we had long since attained our majority and were sliding into middle age. Naturally, I have preserved my good looks, but this was an advantage that Simon had never possessed in the first place.

"I did not mean –" he began, but I brushed past him.

"It is cold, Simon. I am most grateful for your hospitality, and I'm sure you'll forgive me for making full use of it." I snapped my fingers at the conjure-shuck close behind me, onto whose back my travelling bag was strapped.

"Of course, Cygne, of course," Simon said drearily. "Your chamber is the first on the left. I hope you'll find it satisfactory."

I went up the stairs, onto a landing that was at least carpeted, if equally dusty. My chamber was a large, echoing vault, decorated with gloomy portraits of Simon's deceased ancestors, all of whom resembled weevils. The conjure-shuck emitted a low moaning sound, indicating that it had reached the limits of the spell that had brought it with me. I took the bag from its back and banished it. The thing fled through the window in a smoking bolt of fire and I watched it blaze across the snow, a small meteor, hopefully all the way back to Burnblack.

When it had gone, I unpacked my belongings, placed the oak box containing my magical implements on a table and made sure the box was warded. I was still not convinced that this entire visit was not merely a sorry excuse for Simon to gain access to my magical tools. But few things could get past those wards, even a demon, and so my mind was reasonably at rest when I went back down the stairs to find my host.

But I could not find him. In fact, the stairway itself looked different: there were portraits on the walls that I did not recognise, that I was certain that I had not seen before. And when I reached the bottom of the staircase, I found myself in a hallway that I had never seen, a place that was completely different from the entrance in which I had first met Simon.

Those feelings of unease with which I had greeted Simon's invitation were now even more pronounced. He had brought me here to trick me; even now he was ransacking my magical tools… Then a flicker at the corner of my vision caught my attention and I turned.

A shuck stood in the passage. It had taken the customary form of a huge black dog but more rudimentary, a sketch of a beast, snatched out of night. The blackness of which it was made was complete, unsullied by any shade of grey or pale, unnatural and obscene.

I backed away. The shuck padded after, but it had not bothered to configure itself perfectly to its surroundings: its feet plunged through the floor and it moved slowly across the boards. It had no eyes. The great blunt head swung to and fro, mimicking a hound scenting its prey, but as I watched the muzzle of the thing began to melt, streamers and rags of black tearing away and drifting across the floor.

I was close to the end of the hallway. Dodging through a door would only bring the thing after me; I had to fight it. I gathered up power from the things around me, conjuring dust and shadows, igniting the grey swirling mass into a fireball and hurling it towards the shuck.

The magic caught, sparking dark against the edges of the shuck and then surging through it in fire. The shuck writhed, until it was no more than a greasy stain upon the floor. Around me, the hallway flickered and I was suddenly back in the entrance hall, with Simon stepping out of the parlour.

I could not challenge him. To do so would have been a sign of weakness; I had to pretend that nothing was amiss. He would know well enough that his conjuring had failed, and sure enough, there was a sickliness to his face that spoke of his failure.

"Simon, my dear chap! I've made myself quite at home in your delightful chambers. I'm so looking forward to dining with you, catching up a little, reminiscing about the old days…"

"Glad to hear it, Cygne," he replied, all feebleness. "We dine at eight. I need to do a few things before then –" and he fled, which did not surprise me.

I passed the hour or so before dinner in Simon's library which, to my surprise, was reasonably well stocked. Not as good as that of Burnblack, of course, but there were a handful of volumes of moderate interest and I spent more than a few minutes studying one of the volumes on Medieval lore. Not uninteresting.

Eventually the bell rang for dinner and I followed its clanging to the dining room. Again, I was surprised, for the dining hall contained a polished table, some half-decent silverware, and candles.

"Sit by me," Simon instructed. "I'm growing a little deaf these days. I should like to hear what you're telling me. I'm sure it will all be fascinating."

I thought I detected a faint note of sarcasm in his tone, but I must have been mistaken. I clapped him on the shoulder.

"Come, then," I said. "We'll sit together and talk over what I'm sure will be an excellent meal."

Actually, it wasn't too poor. There was an acceptable broth, beef or somesuch, followed by fancies and then a roast fowl. We had syllabub and a quite passable Stilton at the end of dinner, all served by a wan and silent maid. So, poor old Simon had some staff, then. When the maid had gone out of the room, I questioned him.

"Yes," he said, despondently. "They're a family known as Sear. They've served Shadow Cope for generations, ever since the thirteen hundreds. They've had to – there's little other work around here, apart from forestry."

"Are there more of them? Or only the maid?"

"The maid does most of the work around here. Her father helps in the gardens."

"If you don't mind my saying so, Simon, it all looks rather ill-kempt."

He did not seem to take exception to this, but gave a moody nod. "I know. But there's nothing I can do about it."

"Nothing you can do? Don't be a fool, man! You're a trained magus." Not a very good one, true, but this was basic stuff. "You should have shucks doing the work around the house."

To my amazement, Simon turned on me and for the first time I saw a glitter of real fire behind his eyes. "What do you think I've been trying to do?"

"What are you talking about? You've conjured a demon! Or so you say."

"I *have* conjured the demon. But I cannot control the shucks of this house, Cygne." He put his head in his hands. "And so I'm leaving Shadow Cope. I cannot manage this house on my own. You can see for yourself that it's falling down around me. Whatever I try is thwarted."

"That can only mean one thing, Simon. *Someone* is thwarting you. Who have you offended recently?"

"No one!" He was indignant. "I am on excellent terms with all." A pause. "Well, apart from the conference."

I poured him some more port. "You'd better tell me about it."

It took another glass, but he did so. His was the usual tale: a conference in York, to which Simon had been invited, purely on the strength of an ancient name, I imagine. A difference of opinion over something entirely trivial – a question of translation of some spell fragment – which occasioned a massive falling-out, rows, shouting matches, slammed doors and vows of eternal vengeance.

I'd heard it all before – God damn my eyes, I'd *lived* it all before. But it seemed quite possible that Simon had offended someone who did not scruple to strike at the weak. I'd have done so myself, after all.

I slapped him between the shoulder-blades. "You need to fight back, man! Stop vacillating! The demon is still yours – use it to find out who is besetting you!"

Looking back, I'm not sure why I was so uncharacteristically helpful. Perhaps I felt sorry for him, with his pink mole's nose and pallid visage. Certainly, I still suspected him of trying to have a hand in my downfall, but it was also the case that I wanted to have a look at this demon of his, that he professed to be so willing to turn over to me.

He turned towards me with a weepy hope. "Do you really think that would work, Cygne?"

I wondered what he'd been doing in terms of his magical practice all these years.

"Yes, Simon," I said, as patiently as I could. "I think it probably will."

The demon, however, was precisely what I should have expected from a magus of Simon's calibre: a small, snivelling thing about the size of a bald owl, blinking wanly in the candlelight. I wasn't even sure it was a demon at first, thinking it might be some minor elemental being that Simon had managed to attract, luring it with a flame like a moth. But then it shifted position on its perch and I saw its black, red-clawed feet, characteristic of demon-kind, and it opened a fourfold beak to reveal serrated rows of teeth. I looked at it and sighed.

"Very well, Simon," I said. "I suppose it will have to do."

We set up the conjuration as best we could, then took the demon, still blinking, out of its iron-bound cage.

"I hope you have better luck than I've had," Simon said, very sour. "I've never got so much as a peep out of the thing."

"Demons won't just *tell* you things, Simon. You have to *force* information out of them." I gave the bars of the cage a smack with the flat of my hand as I spoke, making Simon, but not the demon, jump. The demon shuffled forwards on the table, beak gaping. I picked up a shred of raw meat, prepared earlier, and stuffed it into the demon's beak. It gulped the morsel down and, thus preoccupied, offered no resistance as I grasped the startled creature by the feet and turned it upside down, before stuffing it headfirst into a large, waiting jar of ink.

The demon spluttered as I read the incantations. The words fell from my mouth and caught fire, smouldering into coals before they hit the marble surface of the table. Simon looked impressed, as well he might. I dragged the demon out of the jar, its eyeballs dripping with ink.

"Speak!" I roared. "Tell me who is trying to kill me!"

"What?" Simon said.

The demon's beak opened and it spat ink all over the table, which formed a rapid word. *Rule.*

"Aha!" I shoved the inky demon back in its cage and seized Simon by the collar. "I knew it!"

"I haven't tried to kill you!" Simon protested. "When? How?"

"Last night!" I had lost patience. "Your thrice-damned shuck!"

"Eh? What shuck? I don't have any shucks!"

Like demons, magi won't tell you the truth, either, unless you force that out of them. Minutes later, Simon was dangling out of the tower window in a raging wind, bound with magical shackles. I couldn't dip him in ink, but I could scare the truth out of him, with the addition of a quick spell-goad. It lashed out.

"You're trying to kill me! Why?"

"I'm not trying to kill you! I mean you no harm. I swear it!"

And amazingly, in the lambent light from the candles of the tower, his words had a faint silver glint, the gleam of truth spoken.

I had to bring him back in after that. The demon squatted in its cage, sulking. Its inky accusation was fading upon the table. "So," I said, to a shivering Simon. "If this creature is telling the truth, and so are you, what are we to make of that?"

"I don't know," Simon quavered.

I stood back, disgusted. "I think I have outstayed my welcome, Simon. I shall leave, tomorrow. I will take the demon with me." Turning on my heel, I stalked out of the room.

Despite Simon's manifest feebleness and his protestations of veracity, I warded the room as heavily as I could and eventually sank into a kind of doze.

I don't know what woke me. Perhaps it was a rustle in the corner of the room, perhaps some whisper of magic, but whatever the cause, I was wide awake.

The shuck grinned as it came, a head that was dog-like, with the curled horns of a goat and soft-padding human hands. The thing strolled through my wards as if they were not there, and as I threw myself from the bed the shuck leaped, striking me squarely on the back and clinging. Its touch burned like fire through the thick silk of my shirt; I could not seem to dislodge it, twist and turn as I might. I thrust my tormentor against the bedpost, trying to shift it, but that burning touch was maddening. I stumbled across the room, blundered against the windowpane, and glass and lead gave way, melting like air before me. The last thing I glimpsed before I and the shuck descended at speed into Shadow Cope's inadequate moat was the door of the room bursting open to admit a wild-eyed Simon Rule.

The fall succeeded, at least, in ridding me of the shuck. It surfaced some distance from me in the moat, sputtering. I was already on the bank, hastily and damply conjuring, this time meshing water and rushes and rain into a net that dragged the shuck down. A dank black bubble rose, and burst. The shuck did not rise again.

Simon cannoned into me out of the darkness, nearly sending me back into the moat.

"Cygne! Dear Lucifer! Are you all right?"

"I am alive, if singed. No thanks to your shuck."

"It was not," Simon said, very quietly, "*my* shuck, as such."

I think, now, that the truth of the matter must have been burning slowly in my brain just as the flesh of the shuck had burned upon my skin. We both turned, and looked at Shadow Cope. All the lights of the mansion were blazing, spectral candles in every room, insubstantial lamps glowing. And I knew that I was not imagining the rage boiling out of every crack and crevice of Shadow Cope.

"No," I said. "It's the shuck of the house. It's not you who is trying to kill me, is it? It's your *house*."

No wonder the shuck had been able to walk through my most powerful wards so easily, with the entire might of a building behind it.

There came a roar of sound, echoing across the moor. "Burnblack!" it cried. "Burnblack!"

"And it's not you it's trying to slay," Simon said, wonderingly. "It's *your* house, as well."

We watched, as the first flames took hold, sparks shooting upwards into the roof and setting it ablaze. With Simon quivering by my side, we stood as Shadow Cope burned itself down into an ashy rage. Caught in my preoccupations of rival magicians, I had not considered that rival houses might, in fact, be just that.

# Peculiar Bone, Unimaginable Key

Brian Aldiss

The lathis struck his bare back, once, twice, and again. They were made of strips of wood. They drew blood. I, Tom Lipseel, shirtless, knelt before the citizens of Whitby, receiving the blows.

I woke suddenly. It was by now three weeks since my public beating. My wounds had hardened into scars. Yet still I dreamed of the flailing lathis, of the noise they made against the air and against my spine.

Just because I had had a drop to drink.

Throwing back my duvet, I went to test the shower. No water again this morning. I put a lamb tikka in the microwave, squatting in my underpants to eat it. I thought of the girl in Perdika's office. I had found out her name. Nova. Beautiful name, beautiful person.

I lived in a one room flat. A notice hung on my wall, as on every wall in the land.

WELCOME TO EULAM, FRIENDS!
God bless you and Salaam Aleikum!
At last, we of the Middle East and we of the West
have come to a political agreement. And a religious agreement.
From henceforth, we shall live in harmony under one great
umbrella of benevolence.
Of course, we must make some sacrifices.
Those of you in the East Region must abandon the habit of
Honour Killing, while those of you in the EU must
abandon alcohol, that degrading trouble-maker.
The punishment for the practice of either habit is a

Public Thrashing with lathis.
Yours in our New Unity,
The EULAM Authority

After my grandfather died, I had to clear out his house. Henceforth, under the new dispensation, all houses were to be publicly owned, but I had come across a few vintage bottles of excellent French Shiraz. I could not bear to waste them, and an EUlamite had caught me with a glass to my lips.

Worst of all, the snooper had taken the bottles away with him.

Well, forget all that, Tom, I told myself. There's this question of what happened in Whitby, and I have to get myself to the Academy of Anatomy.

A lackey opened the door for me. I entered the office.

Behind a white plastic desk sat a small woman with a prominent nose and receding chin. She was no more than sixty-five, I estimated. Her hair was cut short and some attempt had been made to dye it blonde.

On her desk stood a sign announcing that she was Director of Ossuary Remains. The bone under contention lay in a transparent plastic envelope before her.

The woman had been expecting me. She introduced herself as a Doctor Sharah Hardcastle before saying, without further preamble, "This is not a bone."

"It certainly is a bone," I said.

"We have analysed it. It is not a bone." She prodded it with a sharp little finger. "Or not in any ordinary sense. It contains no DNA, only a similar formula, and a triple helix. I can of course provide technical data, should you require them."

A kite hawk landed outside her window. They were becoming more frequent these days.

"You don't want it to be the shoulder bone of Christ or something – of his descendants, supposing he had them. 's not very scientific, is it?"

I was aware of speaking boorishly.

"What I want is neither here or there. I am simply an analyst." She paused before adding, "My compuceiver senses your hostility to me. Still and all, we are interested in this bone of ours. Suppose we go for a coffee in the canteen? It will be less formal with no desk between us."

I told Sharah Hardcastle that my father was waiting in Reception. Rising, she said that we should certainly bring him along.

To be frank, I was ashamed of my father. Ron Lipseel had received little education and worked all his life on canal maintenance.

He had never been a tall man. Now, aged and bent, he was forced to glance up at people through bushy white eyebrows with a look, I always thought, of cunning. Of course, directly he was introduced to Dr Hardcastle, he began talking.

"Fancy us lot being in this important place. I can see you are important too, miss, though you ain't much taller than a horse's elbow."

The canteen was all designer white and grey. Wide windows looked out on a typical English sight – a lawn of crab grass with a row of baobob trees beyond.

"I ent no fool, you know. It's me what made this here discovery of the bone," he said, as we seated ourselves at one of the tables. "It give you something to think about, don't it? – Jesus Christ and all, I mean to say... The EUlams ain't going to like it much, that's for sure."

The canteen was empty but for two men talking together, hunched over their empty cups. A television screen was burning on the wall near us. We had happened to arrive at one o'clock.

"This is the government's BBC News," said a fluffy blonde in BBC uniform. "The British team has won the fourth Test Match, beating South Africa by two wickets. Mfango Tornid was declared Man of the Match.

"Good news too from Burma, where the Reform government has reinstated Rangoon as the capital city.

"News is just coming in of a remarkable discovery being made in the East Coast town of Grimsby."

"There you are!' said my father. "They means Whitby. Typical! They always gets it wrong. We used to have a right old piss-up in Grimsby Saturday nights without fail."

Dr Hardcastle silenced him with a gesture.

"...going over now to Ranjit Bowser, our Religious Correspondent in Grimsby. Hello, Ranjit."

A dark and handsome man clutching a microphone and standing in front of a structure apparently supurating tar, said, "Hello, Maria! I'm in Whitby and this is the old herring-smoking shed where this momentous discovery was made. As you can see, police have closed off the area and are guarding the site.

"Various items found on site have been taken to undergo scientific investigation. The Bishop of York will be here shortly to bless the site. You can see a full report in our six o'clock bulletin."

"Why didn't they mention my name?" said my father. "It was me as found that bone and other stuff."

A waitress brought us a pot of coffee and three cups. Dr Hardcastle indicated I should pour the coffee while she set up an IWpod to record further conversation. She then asked my father to give her the facts as briefly as he could.

"Firstly, Mr Lipseel, can you explain why Jesus should choose Whitby for his place of second coming."

My father gave his head a good scratching. "Whitby's the obvious place, i'n't it? Peaceful. Suppose he come back to Bangladesh or wherever it was, he might get hisself shot."

"You mean Palestine?"

"Same sort of thing."

Staring at his boots, but looking up occasionally to see that Dr Hardcastle was listening, my father related at length the function of the herring-smoking industry. He described how the particular shed in question had stood for many a century; it was sturdily built and was buttressed by the large brick chimney at one end.

Dr Hardcastle concealed her impatience as my father continued. "Herrings were smoked here, man and boy, since I knows not when. At least since Oliver Cornwell's time."

"Cromwell."

"Yes, him too probably. But the trade has declined. Folk don't smoke so much no more. The council was set on pulling down this here shed. Very typical of the way things is run these here days! Very sad."

He went on to say that he was having a final look round the shed when he realised there was a walled-up cupboard behind a rack of heating shelves. He got a crowbar and prized open the door. "And what do you reckon I found?"

"We would like you to tell us, Mr Lipseel." She gestured to the waitress for more coffee.

So it was that two days later Dr Hardcastle, with her head covered, my father and I stood on the windswept harbour of Whitby on the East coast of England, closely supervised by Ibn Damon Dulcetter. Defying his surname, Dulcetter had a deep voice, as befitted a man of his stature. Hollows had formed under his zygomatic arches; his face held the pallor of defeat, as if it had lost a battle against the dominance of his long prominent nose. He walked with a limp and wore an ancient raincoat. His official designation was Commander of the Sea Port.

Whitby itself had its charms. True, a large Tesco store loomed on a height before one entered the town, but the town itself appeared able to look after itself despite the union wrought between the EU and Islam, with plenty of small shops, a small park and a large statue of a defunct local dignitary. An insignificant little mosque stood behind the high street; on its door was a poster saying 'Vote Conservative'. We came across a shop whose facade was covered with shining green tiles, and passed a bookshop named 'Dracula & Co'.

"That's a funny old name," said my father. "I think Dracula must be a Turkish name."

Turning to him, Dr Hardcastle said, "Will you do me a favour, Mr Lipseel. Go and buy me a copy of the Gospel of St Luke. Just Luke on its own."

Muttering to himself about indignity, my father went off on his errand. The Dr caught my expression. "Tom, I cannot bear your father. Never have I met a more stupid man."

I looked down at the ground and said that she did not have to be rude.

She took my arm and walked with me a short distance from Dulcetter.

"I'm thoroughly upset. Your father is one of the many ignorant who fell for the EU pact with Islam. They were tricked, of course. Alcohol has been banned. They pretend they will not practice

Honour Killing, when it had already come under our criminal law... They have brought back corporal punishment –"

"They certainly have." My back began aching at the thought.

"Well, you can't like the way things are now, can you? Anything English is going down the drain."

I sighed. "The war ceased, didn't it? We just have to get used to things as they are."

"Oh, you're as stupid as your father!" she said in exasperation.

"They're eating fish and chips in Damascus," I retorted. I had no idea whether or not it was true. But it shut her up.

She turned on her heel and walked back towards Dulcetter.

"Sorry!" she called over her shoulder.

Since the union, motor vehicles had been forbidden, except for the use of those in authority.

We saw the current working harbour, but Dulcetter drove us in a different direction, signposted as 'To the Old Port'. Here, like ivy over an old wall, rust prevailed over old machines, a derrick, some skips, a tractor, piles of girders. In the middle of this desolation stood the herring-smoking shed, larger than I had imagined it.

The Commander of the Sea Port nodded courteously to the guard on duty and lifted the yellow police tape which guarded the port, permitting Dr Hardcastle to get through without stooping.

The old herring-smoking shed stood a short distance away, beyond another protective barrier. A blue portacabin had been installed for the convenience of investigators. Some of these official persons were just leaving in a black Daimler. The car nosed its way cautiously through a number of onlookers.

Who were these people?, I wondered, people whose casting in life was to be wherever a crowd might be called for. I thought about the crowd of courtiers I had seen in a recent performance of *Hamlet* in Baghdad, people who had no words, no script, and no motives but to look on at the tragedy of the Prince. Or possibly this little crowd was just a cross-section of those who had mourned the murder of Princess Di of Britain when she was about to celebrate the union of West and East – those who had gathered to grieve for the melancholy, not of her death, but of their own lives?

We entered this insignificant-looking shed, to be immediately enfolded by its hushed atmosphere. We were assailed by the reek of vintage fish. The silence was broken by the sound of our walking over the grit and grains of sand which littered the floor.

My father rejoined us, looking downcast at the failure of his mission.

Sharah Hardcastle was being extra nice. She brought a fancy box from her bag and offered both my father and me gooey lumps of Turkish delight.

Turning to Ibn Dulcetter, she asked if there was any truth in reports of Christ's return, and why he should have come to Whitby.

"It makes sense. Whitby has long been an active fishing port. Besides, the majority of his disciples were fisher folk."

"He knew better than to go back to where he come from," said my father, to fortify Dulcetter's case. "They'd have shot him."

"But this is not really a likely spot for Jesus," said Dr Hardcastle. "I would think he would have headed for the local church."

Dulcetter looked down his nose, a not inconsiderable distance, at the doctor. "For a start there was a portrait of Jesus hanging on this wall. A portrait looking much like Our Saviour, beard, kindly expression..."

"Loin cloth?" I hazarded. Dulcetter ignored the question. "The sitter is dressed in worker's overalls, a tear down one leg. The portrait has gone to the British Academy for examination and verification."

"That's right," my father agreed. "At the bottom of the picture was the words 'Our Saviour – His Second Coming'. It was signed George Stubbs. Some bloke was telling me as Stubbs was pretty well known in his time."

With the phantom of a sigh, Dr Hardcastle told us that Stubbs remained greatly respected. "This was what decided you? No suspicion that Stubbs might have been merely conjuring up a likeness?"

Turning on me, Dulcetter asked if I suffered from what he called 'a similar stubborn scepticism'.

Not wishing to admit I was inclined to agree with Dr Hardcastle, I reminded Dulcetter that he had spoken of disciples. Was he claiming Christ had returned with the whole pack of his disciples?

Again the length of the nose came into play.

"Only three of his disciples. Peter, Thomas and Moshe."

"I fail to recall a Moshe,' said Dr Hardcastle.

My father had been silent for longer than usual. He butted in saying, "Moshe was the bald one. They was a rough lot, the three of them, drinking round town, chasing the girls and I don't know what. Didn't speak very good English either..."

Dr Hardcastle asked him how he knew that.

"It were all over the *Whitby Advertiser*, weren't it, Mr Dulcimer? There was copies found right in this here shed. 'Scandal of Saviour's Hangers-On'. That's one headline what I saw."

As they stood talking, I trudged about, ignoring the crunching sounds underfoot. Behind a ruinous boiler, a little pile of sand had accumulated. When I kicked it accidentally, a silvery object was revealed. I stooped and picked it up.

In most people's lives comes a moment where everything seems to change, for better or for worse. So I imagine.

At first glance, that object lying in my palm looked like a miniature cross. The Sign of the Cross! It seemed to generate a kind of trembling warmth – as if – well, as if you had held in a small cage a bumble-bee struggling to escape. That is, in the days before bumble bees became extinct. But the sensation of warmth, of energy, of something trying to escape was there.

I knelt by the old boiler so that the others could not see.

The length of the shaft of the cross finished with a division into two opposed curled ends. The two arms each ended with a series of little stout pins.

It was not a Cross at all. It was an energiser. And the energiser was telling me it was the starter key

of a –

well, of a space machine...

"Tommy Lipseel? Where are you?" I recognised the voice calling my name, coming from a great distance away.

The original owner of this key had come from far away in space and time. Not on this occasion; this time he had travelled by boat. But previously. Why? What had made him visit this isolated globe in the first place?

It occurred to me that even this distinguished visitor – whom we had done our best to forget – was as much subject to Chance as all of us.

He had been in trouble. So the key seemed to declare, sending a stream of imagery to my clutch. He had been forced to land on Earth. I say, speaking loosely, 'It occurred to me', but the understanding came to me from the key. I stared at it with fresh admiration; half machine, possibly semi-organic. It in its time had awakened immense engines to life.

There was talk, the endless terrestrial chatter going on somewhere. But I was subject to a vision. It was as if this key spoke to me.

I cannot describe clearly the torrent of images that overwhelmed me. Either then or later I grasped one particular factor. As a single brick is to a house, so our 'science' was to the kind of science which had created that key and the culture it represented.

In one of the gospels, 'Christ' was described as the son of a carpenter. In olden days, sons followed their fathers in trade. Did we ever hear of Christ wielding an axe, a saw, a hammer – those crude tools with which we tried to shape our physical world? Of course not. He merely tried to make the lives of people a little better, a little less miserable. The description 'son of a carpenter' was a fabrication, a fabrication designed to make credible what many would have found to be incredible, like a mansion to those who only understood bricks.

This Christ's own machine had proved irreparable. Perhaps in a final fit of despair, realising that Earth had not the psycho-electrical equipment he required for his repairs, he had thrown the now-useless starter key away. Now it and the great legend lay within the clutch of my right hand!

I whispered a question about Peter and the other two 'disciples', but the response was already growing in me. This strange personage from the stars had crash-landed near to the place of his previous crucifiction. He had made the journey overland to Britain because Britain at the time was the most advanced country industrially; but it had nothing to offer to match his sophisticated standards. Such was told to me by the starter key in an unknown fashion, in something like pictures.

It was as if I had always known this. And I knew now that Peter and the other two companions had come with the stranger because they could not help it. They were helpless before the power of his 'personality', as we would call it. Or his 'charisma'? As I too felt myself transformed, being both in tears and yet rejoicing that such a fine alternative existence could be, could flourish in our galaxy.

"Tommy, what are you doing?" It was the voice of Dr Hardcastle.

I stood up. I said nothing. The power within my grasp reassured me. Already I had, stooping there key in hand, existed more deeply than in all my years put together.

"I cannot stand the stench in here any more," said the doctor, heading for the door. "Mr Dulcetter, if you please, take us to a decent hotel, if there is such a thing in Whitby, where refreshments are served."

"You don't believe Christ was here, despite the evidence?"

"I have yet to be convinced," she replied.

"Then we shall adjourn to the Happy Herring Hotel."

The Happy Herring had changed its name to The General Zia ul Haqq. Nevertheless, we went in.

We were sitting in a bay window of the hotel. We had said good-bye to Dulcetter. The evening was closing in; gulls proclaimed the end of the day's scavenging. Other people were sitting at tables nearby. The room was pleasantly old-fashioned, hung with paintings of peasants leading awful lives, with or without pigs in sties.

And I was clutching the key as if it were mortal in our sense of that word.

When an ample-breasted young woman brought us glasses of life-saving Hanafi sherberts, Dr Hardcastle spoke to her, asking her what she made of the Christ legend.

"I do not know,' the girl said, with an indifferent smile. "I am from Denmark, you see."

"Denmark!' cried Dr Hardcastle, as if in despair, when the waitress had gone. Glaring at me, she asked me what I made of 'all this', as she put it, with a side-glance at my father, as if of mistrust.

"We have some evidence,' I said. But I said no word about the key.

""Course we have," said father, butting in with his usual careless manner. "There's that bone, that curious bone. And we have the date from the paper of the ship docking: February 1793."

She turned to him. "You're sure about the date?"

He gazed up contemptuously from under his entanglements of eyebrow.

"The whole population of Whitby turned out to see Our Saviour. If they'd of had me on the telly I could have shown them the very newspaper – but no, not them..."

Dr Hardcastle, ignoring this remark beyond sighing heavily and shaking her head, said, "If memory serves, in 1793 Europe was in upheaval – the sort of upheaval that has eventually brought us down –"

And here she lowered her voice to utter the phrase "– to this dismal agreement with Islam. Revolutionary France declared war on Britain in that very month – February. It is hardly to be wondered at that little notice was taken of Christ – or not beyond Whitby in all events. England was in turmoil."

Sharah Hardcastle began talking into her compuciever. My father began talking to me. I sat there, not listening, gazing out to watch the shadows of the palm trees lengthen, clutching the key under the table. I knew I was a savage grasping the equivalent of a miracle; yet my heart lifted and I rejoiced. Somewhere, a better world existed; I held the proof of it – a world where the golden palace of philosophy often echoed with the pearls of mirth.

Ron Lipseel thumped on the table to gain my full attention.

"What I reckon is Christ come back to show us he was on Britain's side against Napoleon."

Overcome with a fresh awareness that a son must always grow to develop and contradict the father that begat him, I muttered merely that his statement was absurd.

Of course he had an answer. "Not half as absurd as if he had sided with Napoleon. That would have been a different kettle of fish, you mark my words."

'Words', I thought... How useless are mere words...

The results of Dr Hardcastle's talk over the compuciever were soon made clear. A uniformed police captain, whose badges showed he worked for both European and Sha'ria Law marched to our table. He was followed by two armed constables.

He announced himself as Captain Mohammed Farrow, and ordered my father and me to stand up. No notice was taken of Dr Hardcastle, who remained sitting, arms folded and resting on the table.

Poor Ron Lipseel was charged with taking various pieces of evidence from the shed, including valuable newspapers. He protested violently and swore at Captain Farrow. The captain's expression did not change during this abuse; he maintained an expression of weariness and disillusion. After my father's tirade, Farrow indicated to his men that Ron be taken away for further questioning.

I who held that precious key was not arrested.

Nevertheless, I was ordered back to the shed. Having said good-bye to Sharah Hardcastle, I travelled there by official car, accompanied by a woman calling herself Perdika, and her child, a girl of five or six years of age. Perdika seemed to treat the whole matter as a joke, whatever 'the whole matter' was. My fear was that I would be searched and the key taken from me.

The girl, by name Annya, stared at me curiously. Suddenly, she dived her hand into my pocket and pulled out the key.

"Key, mommy, key!" she cried in triumph.

"Oooh, you little thief! Put it back at once!"

As Annya did so, Perdika laughed, not at all put out. She laughed with her mouth open, so that I saw her teeth and the pink of the roof of her mouth. "If you are going to be a thief, that's your look-out!"

"No, it's my outlook,' the girl replied.

The crowd on the old dock had increased in number. Men working on the site took no notice of them or us. I asked Perdika what the man called Christ had actually done in Whitby.

"Seems as if once he had got himself kitted out – I mean you don't go round this dump in a loin cloth – he just went about healing the sick, same as what he had done in the old days in Jerusalem."

I asked who these sick people were.

"Anyone who was sick. There was a bit of cholera about then, so my gran said. There's a lot of it in the City records. Beggers, fishermen, prostitutes. He was keen on prostitutes."

She spoke in the manner of the under-educated, as if everything had happened only yesterday.

"How much would a prostitute cost about that time?"

"Oh, and he also healed a clergyman suffering from bronchitis – a well-know local figure, the Reverend Laurence Snodgrass. After just one visit, this reverend got off of his bed and walked. So the story goes." She laughed again, open-mouthed. "The doctors in the town were furious."

I pointed out that doctors were in the same trade of curing people.

"Ah, but Our Saviour was putting them out of business." She wagged a finger at me, thinking herself clever.

A photographer asked me to move to one side. I reserved answer to Perdika; I had suddenly come to appreciate the birth of Alternative Medicine.

Perdika turned from me to oversee Annya, who was filling in data on a wristop. She asked me how I had become involved in what she called 'this Christ business'. I told her of our family legend that an ancient great-great-grandfather had miraculously regrown a leg lost in battle. In his delirium, he had babbled of a doctor with a crown of thorns.

"Oh come on, he would surely have taken the thorns off by then..."

"Perhaps they weren't thorns, but some kind of – oh, communications device. Over long distances..."

Preferring to ignore that, she asked about my father.

"He was just the man who found the false wall. He's not important."

Annya was jumping about excitedly. Her mother took her hand. In quite a changed tone of voice, Perdika said, "Whether or not someone pretending to be Christ in the Eighteenth Century turned up here is unimportant. What's important is how we live our lives."

She looked astonished at what she had said.

"Go for it, Ma!" squeaked Annya.

But what Perdika had said echoed my own thought. These men and a few women wearing headscarves scurrying about here were simply doing this job on this day. The overriding issue did not touch them. No thought of eternity. No thought of what this 'Christ' might be and do. No real Being, only Doing.

One man not moving stood by the door of the shed, watching others. It was my perception that he was In Charge. Only those in charge had the privilege of not moving, not scurrying.

Now he did move. Coming over to us, I saw he sported a double-breasted grey suit and a single-stranded moustache. He told Perdika to go and report at once to the office – with her child. She made off, pulling a 'so-what?' face at me.

The double-breasted man was a head taller than I. "We can't have blasphemy here," he told me. "Even if we are atheists."

I looked puzzled. "If we are atheists, surely blasphemy is what we can't have."

"My name is Thunderton-Sophia. I am in charge of religion here, and my belief is that we have extracted from you all the little data you are able to provide. I believe I saw you being publicly flogged in the square, not so long ago. If you are in the wretched position of un-belief, I'd advise you to clear off now."

Perhaps it was the effect of the key. I saw that this large man had little spiritual control. He could be pleasant or unpleasant at will, or perhaps at random. It was a mere gear-shift. Much the same applied to Sharah Hardcastle, Perdika, Thunderton-Sophia, perhaps even my father. It is accepted that writers in their old age write in this random way. It lends their story more philosophical weight, even if it makes it more tedious to read.

Standing there among the ancient litter and the modern electronic junk, I became more aggressive in exactly this random fashion.

"Well, Mr Thunderton-Sophia, you stand here among this very belated recognition that a so-called Christ was here. Is it blasphemy to face the fact that really the Second Coming was a bit of a damp squib? Everything went on in just the same ludicrous way as before. Cholera did not disappear. Graves did not open, no trumpets sounded. Did all proclaim His coming, or was all unchanged? Was everyone too busy procreating and earning a crust?"

"Right, you're out." He placed a firm hand on my shoulder, urging me towards the door. "Can't have this sort of talk – it's against the Ewelamb." He said, as if the news weighed on his conscience, "He did a signing."

I asked him what he meant.

"Well, young man, what do you think it means? Christ got a pen and an inkwell and He signed His name to the Holy Scriptures."

I put it to him: he meant that Christ signed the Bible?

"Of course not, you half-wit! Just the New Testament. I take it you realise the New Testament is all about Him and His works – largely anecdotal until the Koran took over. There was a great long queue all along the quayside – women and kids as well as men."

"Oh yes!" A fragment came back to mind. To show him I was no mere heathen I said, "'Suffer the little children, and let them come to me', eh?"

"Only it wasn't like that. He told the kids to clear off. They were making too much row."

I managed to detach his hand from my shoulder. "I would guess those signatures would fetch a pretty good price today."

He gave a snort which made the sparse moustache tremble. "If you could find one."

We left the building, passing Perdika's office. The freshness of the air struck me. I breathed deeply, in order to expel the stink of ancient fish.

Thunderton-Sophia made his way to a waiting Daimler. He asked if he could give me a lift. Clutching the key, I said no. I have my pride.

As he entered the driver's seat, he slid down his window. "Let me give you some advice, young man. This business is not as simple as you may think. You will never ever find Christ's signature if you go looking for it. The Bishop of York, a man called Jervis Ferrers – funny names people had in those days – came down to Whitby in 1793, towards Easter, to see Our Saviour and verify his story. The two of them fell out.

"This is something that's wrong with the Church today – especially the old Christian side of it. The Bishop pronounced the signatures to be forgeries. He ordered all the signatures to be destroyed, officially declaring Our Saviour to be an impostor.

"In fact, he announced that the so-called saviour was a chap by the name of Entwhistle, Henry Entwhistle, a vagabond who painted lewd fore-edge paintings on books – if you know what they are."

He saw by my expression that I did not know.

"York turned all the other clergy against Our Saviour – all, that is, except for the Rev Snodgrass, whose leg Our Saviour was reputed to have regrown. Christ was putting the clergy out of business, just as he had done to the doctors and surgeons. "

A car was tooting impatiently behind Thunderton-Sophia's Daimler.

Thunderton-Sophia remained unperturbed.

"This whole business should be played down. The twin-religion thing is under enough strain as it is. Not to mention the lack of support for Christ, back in 1793..."

"I can't think why he didn't land in London," I said, in order to judge how silly his response would be.

"He had a cheap single ticket from Le Havre. Don't talk to any reporters, or you may feel a few more lathis on your back..." With a wave, he was off, having been agreeable enough for one day.

Turning away, I found a young woman waving farewell to the car. Her name was Nova Pilgrim. She worked in Perdika's office. We had exchanged smiles before. Perhaps she was hoping that by way of waving Thunderton-Sophia farewell, her hopes for promotion might be increased.

Her good looks were worth promotion and more. She was wearing a pink hijab which left her forehead clear but was folded so as partly to conceal, partly to reveal, her generous lips. Nova was coming off duty. When I invited her to have a sherbert with me, she readily agreed. We went to a teahouse in the main street.

As I gazed into her eyes, I felt love overcoming me with a tremendous wave of wealth. We talked as lovers do about how irritating our parents can be.

I asked Nova what had happened to Our Saviour after the Bishop of York had so offended him.

"They are going to try once more to hush it all up, darling," she said. "It throws the EUlam balance out. But the so-called disciple Peter was had up in court for drunkenness and imitating the crowing of cocks at dawn. You know alcohol was freely available in those days. Peter testified in court that Our Saviour had gone off with a local lady."

"Not quite the behaviour of any saviour we used to know..."

Nova laughed. "The couple were last seen heading off North in a mail coach – just the two of them.

"Peter, Moshe and Thomas were deported and that was about the end of it – at least as far as Whitby was concerned. I'm from Grimsby myself. The herring shed, now suddenly so popular, was sealed off by the harbour-master. I love the way your hair grows..."

"Oh, thank you darling, but your hair is so pretty! Surely Christ could not just disappear, even in the chaos of the Napoleonic wars. Where was the coach going?"

She allowed me to clutch her hand across the table.

"But this naughty Bishop of York, he who declared Our Saviour a fake," she said, little guessing how I admired her use of grammar. "He announced that anyone caught speaking to or of Our Saviour would be executed. No. Sorry, I mean excommunicated. So no more was heard of him.'

"Except," I began, as a waiter brought us each another sherbert.

"My theory, for what it's worth," she said sweetly, "is that he got married to this Whitby lady and that they propagated – had children. That explains why there are still such good people among all the evil-doers in our land."

"Except –", I began again, gazing into those beautiful eyes, "I could show you a peculiar bone. I have reason to believe that I am myself descended from Our Saviour. My bone is different from your bone but my suffering is much like yours. Certainly if we were crucified we'd both die. As we both live, so I trust you love me as intensely as I love you."

Her face became lit. "Oh darling," she said, in a kind of gasp, "when I first saw you in Perdika's office I knew there was something about you..."

I felt in my pocket for the key. "And something much greater, darling. Something free of human woes."

I laid the key in her open palm, clutched her hand, saw and felt the wonderful change overcoming her which had overcome me...

In that moment, we both knew there was a way of escaping to the stars.

# Deciduous Trees

Martin Sketchley

I do not have a religious background. If asked, I would have said that I am, at best, an agnostic. But there was a time when Jesus and I made a deal. It was a bit like an eye for an eye, He said. A bit like karma, you know – what goes around comes around and all that. He seemed genuine enough. He told me He'd sensed my restlessness and frustration. Said it clung to me like frost.

That made me think.

It could have been a pitch, a spiel, a generously baited hook. But I don't think so. I'd like to think he just saw the state I was in and decided to offer me a way out.

I mean let's face it, isn't that what Saviours are supposed to do?

Funerals were something I'd pretty much managed to avoid all through my life. By the age of forty, I'd been to only two. There were a couple I felt bad about not attending, but I wanted no truck with such emotional turmoil, such uncertainty.

My granddad on my father's side was cremated in Sutton Coldfield on a sunny day. To me, he'd always been a cheeky man cloaked in varying shades of brown and gold. He wore tortoiseshell glasses like the Two Ronnies, and would often waggle them like Eric Morecambe or dislodge them slightly like Captain Mainwaring. A whole raft of classic comedy heroes were always on tap. Sometimes he'd crack the odd slightly near-the-mark joke that would earn a swift rebuke from my nan – a cream-toned lady for whom 'bloomin' eck' was the most serious curse.

On the day of his funeral the black cars pulled up outside my grandparents' house in Kettlebrook. Someone said, "He's here," and everyone stood. Several minutes passed, the cars purring gently outside. I asked what was happening. A lady shaded in a patient blue, who I didn't know, told me they'd bought him home. "To say good-bye, like," she said. That struck me as odd somehow; the house in Kettlebrook was the last my grandparents shared, but seemed the least like their home.

The cars conveyed us sedately through Tamworth and out of the town through Mile Oak. Most people gazed, but one elderly gentleman stopped walking and held his hat to his chest as the cortège passed. His colours darkened, rolling through sombre shades as memories of someone close momentarily surged.

A lot of people were already at the crematorium when we arrived. Most of them I'd seen only a few times before, but heard mentioned in conversations: the man in the tweed jacket with the pencil moustache; the snotty woman with the pale blue suit and matching handbag, like the Queen. They milled around outside, exchanging sombre greetings and kissing cigarettes. The smoke mingled with their colours like milk and water. Even before we got out of the car I could tell that some of them were there because they felt they should be, rather than due to any grief or respect. They would put in their appearance, pick at the buffet, noses wrinkled, then sod off home and be glad it was all over and done with.

Inside, the building was like one of those fake Tudor houses they have in America: lines too clean, everything pristine. The emotional wear that centuries of funerals, marriages and Christenings has on thousand-year-old churches can't be artificially captured in machine-cut stone.

I can't remember if there was a hymn, but the individual songs of those present reverberated in shades of silver and blue. It was the first and only time I saw my dad cry.

There was a short service, and the casket that contained my granddad's body was drawn slowly into the furnace and turned to smoke and ash. This was ironic, considering it was smoke that killed him. First a distinguished pipe, then cheaper cigarettes, followed by roll-ups in the final years. As time passed and he became thinner, he clutched his twig-like comforts between trembling brown fingertips, and the Eric Morecambe and Captain Mainwaring gags dried up along with his lungs. The colour of the coffin reminded me of the nicotine stains on the headlining of his white Triumph Dolomite and his tan fingertips, which tapped on the steering wheel to Mantovani's *Big Country* on the eight-track.

This didn't seem right. Here was the man who had taken me to hides in the New Forest on the lookout for stags and hinds, and sea fishing on Boscombe beach, while waves as grey as the sky rolled and pushed across the shore. He'd told me how it was more difficult to change gear in a car than it was to steer, how trees that lost their leaves in winter were called deciduous, how people who could write with both hands were ambidextrous.

My mother's mother was also cremated. She didn't want to be eaten by worms, she'd said. Well, fair enough.

She always carried a large furry brown handbag stuffed with knitting and paper bags and things that might come in handy. There were always a few sweets rolling around in the bottom, among the fluff and threads: mint imperials or aniseed balls, whose patchy appearance and softness caused us to claim that they were already half-sucked when she offered them to us like bits of treasure.

She lived in Nottingham, where she'd moved some years before to live with a gentleman friend. This meant she could only come to our house every few months. But on those visits she always bought with her a bustle of joviality, gifts of Walnut Whips and white paper bags filled with bonbons or lemon drops that the paper tended to stick to. Plus the odd half-sucked aniseed ball or mint imperial.

I remember waving to her from the living room window of our house in Amington one winter's evening as she passed on the bus to Tamworth, from where she'd travel on to Nottingham. It seemed a long way to go on such a cold, dark night. But hers was a generation undeterred by such inconvenience. I could see sparks of honey and gold swirling around her like fairies, and although I couldn't hear it I knew the slightly humorous music that seemed unique to her would be fluttering like snowflakes around the other, unknowing passengers.

When she was gone, and her large furry handbag would visit our house no more, there was a service at a church in Nottingham. The place had dark wooden pews in tiers like in a theatre. The hymn was *The Old Rugged Cross*. It was her favourite, my mom said.

Some sang it better than others.

I remember wondering at both funerals what had happened to everything those people had been. All that knowledge and experience, all that character and spirit. I couldn't really work it out, so I tried not to think about it much.

So, until middle age that was about it for me as far as funerals went. At some point I know I'm going to be pulled into the hurricane of grief that comes unforecast into everyone's life, when I have to deal with the deaths of my own parents. There will be no way out for me then, no-one to make excuses on my behalf as to why I can't attend. No buffer to absorb the impact. To some extent I'm prepared for that.

But there's one person's death I dread. The impact will be immense, the tremors unending.

Mick's a small, wiry Irishman. He can be as cantankerous and stubborn as he is argumentative, possessing incredible amounts of dubious information to draw on at key moments in arguments he often starts for a bit of fun, just to wind someone up. But he's also generous and caring, a man I like and respect.

Mick has no fear of dying. As the years have passed, death accelerating towards him like an oncoming train, he's taken comfort in his faith. For Mick, death will be a joyous occasion on which he finally joins with the God he's loved for so long, and Who has loved him in return. It'll be a time at which he's received into the Kingdom of God and reunited with all those loved one who have entered it before him. And, as he would almost certainly point out, all those right sickeners he couldn't stand the sight of.

His illness came on quite suddenly, a surprise to everyone. Other than a slight limp and a hernia, he had up to that point been a relatively healthy man, his body having survived the rigours of life in the construction industry pretty much unscathed. This was largely due to a pledge taken at an early age to forgo alcohol, a good if bland diet, and the exercise that was inherent in his work.

I've always been as confident as Mick about what awaits: there is no afterlife, no heaven, no God. These things have simply been created by man during his 10,000 years on the Earth in an attempt to provide some reason for the wonders that defy explanation. Or if God does exist, I do not know where, or in what form.

Yet from what I have seen, those who do believe – those who really believe, I mean, not those who just go through the motions out of habit — gain comfort from their faith in the existence of something higher. And I, cynic though I am, would not wish to deny them that.

I'll admit that while part of me envies Mick his belief in a glorious time following death for the comfort it must give, the other side of me feels sorry for him and all those like him. I'm sure that cuts both ways. Yet my trepidation regarding his death is not due to concern that he'll be devastated by disappointment: he and his fellow believers will not be aware of the infinite darkness that descends upon them in death. Neither is it an unwillingness to confront my own grief when he dies.

The fact is, Mick is my wife's father, and I know that when it comes his death will break her heart.

First impressions stick.

Amy's the youngest of Mick's three daughters. The baby. His little girl. When she was a child he'd take her to see West Brom play, huddled and hatted on the cold terraces, watching the ball kicked through the mud by players with hair as long as their shorts. Watching football was something she'd enjoy doing herself with our kids, although due to our son's allegiance it'd be cheering on the Blues from the Tilton Road end or the Kop.

We met at a gig at Tamworth Arts Centre in 1989. She'd travelled over from Birmingham with one of the bands and we were introduced by a mutual friend. Her song was the sweetest I'd ever encountered, her colours the most vibrant.

We clicked immediately, and by the time the headline band took to the stage – a bunch of Cuban-heeled black leather-clad youths with Warhol mop-tops – and began bashing out thin, trebly chords, it was like we'd known each other years.

Later, when I leaned close to her to say something, she turned her face towards me. As our colours and music merged, we kissed.

There was no looking back.

The first time Amy took me to her house we'd known each other only a few weeks, but already we knew something was happening. Something neither of us had experienced before, despite thinking we had. Something simultaneously exciting and frightening. She told me I was the first proper boyfriend she'd taken home to meet her parents.

No pressure, then.

The square entrance hall struck me first. Clad almost completely in dark wood, including the ceiling, it felt like being inside a box. Directly opposite the front door, next to the first leg of the staircase, a glass-doored cabinet was crammed with novels, biographies and blocks of bright red Reader's Digest books with gold lettering on the spines. The stuffed pheasant perched on top of the cabinet looked as though it'd had enough of Reader's Digest and might make a bid for freedom at any moment.

Next to the front door was a grandfather clock, which I'd heard chiming in the background whenever I phoned Amy. It struck quarter-to-seven just as I walked through the door at six forty, as if nudged into a reluctant gesture of welcome.

Amy opened the nearest of the three doors, off the hall to the left. The room beyond was bright, the telly on. An open fire burned strongly behind a brass guard. I could hear Amy saying high-pitched hellos, then the door opened further and her mother appeared.

"Mom, this is Steve," Amy said.

Amy was smiling as she looked back at me, but it was clear that she was as nervous as her mother, who now stood silhouetted in the doorway wringing her hands. Her colours rolled and surged around her, speckled and sparkling, and her music ebbed and flowed, suggesting both friendliness and uncertainty.

"You're very welcome," Mary said, with a slight nod of her head. Her Irish accent was warm.

"Thanks, Mrs Joyce," I said. I remember thinking I should say more, but I wasn't sure what: nice house? Nice fire? Nice pheasant?

"Oh, it's Mary, please," she said. "Now, will y'have someth'n' t'eat? Yer look half-starved the pair of ye."

I found myself saying, "Oh, I'm all right, thanks," even though my stomach had been rumbling since Amy picked me up at New Street Station. "No need to go to any trouble for me."

"It's no trouble at all. I'll just do a little something. You go on in." She gestured towards the room behind her, then turned and peered around the door into the living room. "Mick?" she said.

"Amy's young man's here." I rather liked that. It made me sound like a suitor, a beau, Mr Darcy in *Pride and Prejudice.* If only I'd had a horse and breeches…

As Mary walked past us and into the kitchen on the opposite side of the hall, Amy pulled me into the living room by the sleeve. Mick was sitting in an armchair near the fire reading the sports pages of *The Daily Mail.* With his silver hair and weathered skin, he reminded me of Magnus Magnusson. As we walked in he took his glasses off the bridge of his nose. His colours folded through shades of white and silver as pure as his hair as he stood and reached out to shake my hand; like Mary, he was not quite as relaxed as he was trying to appear. "How'd y'do, sir?" he said. "Make y'rself at home."

Amy and I sat at opposite ends of the sofa like 14-year olds rather than people in their early twenties. As Mick pulled a fat, green log from the large brass box next to the fireplace and dropped it on to the flames, Amy looked at me and grinned.

Mick sat down again and picked up his paper, pushing his glasses back up his nose. "Do y'like football, Steve?" he said, looking at an article about the recent sacking of the West Brom manager.

"Um, not really," I replied. "Just never been my thing. Sorry."

"Oh, that's all right, then," he said. "Just so long as you're not a Blues supporter."

Amy laughed. In truth, a lack of interest in football was the bane of my life. Put together a group of unacquainted men from any number of different backgrounds and social classes, and even in the most unfamiliar of environments – weddings, Christenings, school playground, sauna – the conversation will turn to football within a few minutes, nine times in ten. Unlike women, men aren't naturally predisposed to talking, especially not to strangers, so when they're forced to do so they like to be on familiar territory. And football binds men the world over.

Most of them.

But as Amy would point out later, I'm not like most men. I never was. I was always the one generously donated to the opposing team in the school playground – *you can have him* – because I was more likely to kick the ball over the fence than between the two piles of jumpers. Least likely to win a challenge. Once, when I'd tried to play football in the school playground aged about nine, I sprained my ankle on first tackle and had to miss the school trip the next day. I don't think I ever recovered from that.

The door opened and Mary returned with a tray. She drew the smallest table from the nest next to the piano and set it down. There was a stack of four plates laden with slices of some kind of dense brown bread – soda bread, I'd later learn – cheese, a pot of tea and four cups, a bowl of sugar and some Manor House cake.

"There now," she said. "Help yourself." Her colours were more subdued than when I arrived: apparently she'd relaxed slightly.

After I'd had my fill of tea and cake, Amy took me up to the room in which I was to spend the night.

That was when Jesus and I first met.

He was waiting for me at the top of the stairs. His face was a pale gold and his bright blue eyes gazed skyward, towards the corner of the picture frame. His bleached skin made him look more like a Victorian doll than someone from the Middle East. Judging from his expression he'd just hung out a load of washing and felt the first spots of rain.

That image, in its golden-framed prominence in the home, was a stark reminder of the differences between Amy's world and mine. The house I grew up in until the age of eleven was opposite the church by Amington Green. Next to the gate was a wooden sign that said *Holy Communion* and listed days and times. Some Sundays people would queue on the path as if waiting to have their tickets checked. They were always dressed up: the girls usually wore elaborate frocks, while the boys wore suits – usually steel blue or pale grey – and had unnaturally smooth hair. They looked a weird bunch: practitioners of strange rituals; people to be wary of.

As I walked past the picture and along the landing, Jesus glanced down at me with a watch-your-step-son kind of expression, then smirked and winked. I did my best to ignore Him.

The room had belonged to one of Amy's older sisters. She'd left sufficiently long ago for her presence to have been erased with a couple of coats of magnolia and the removal of all personal belongings. Even the majority of her clothes had gone from the wardrobes, replaced instead by Mary's coats and suits and dresses. "You have wardrobes," Mick would tell me years later, brandishing a passionate index finger, "a woman'll just fill 'em with stuff she never wears, you mark my words."

I walked across the room and parted the floral curtains with my fingertips. The land at the back of the house was open fields, smothered in darkness, but light leaking through the kitchen blinds illuminated part of the garden. At the point where the light faded almost completely, a figure stood looking at the house.

Amy made some more tea, and we sat on the bedroom floor and talked quietly about nothing in particular. A while after her parents had gone to bed we got under the single duvet and giggled like the kids that, in truth, we still were.

It was just light when I woke. I could hear violins playing. They were making a bit of a din, though, as if two of the instruments were being rubbed together rather than being played. More Bad Seeds than *Big Country*.

When I rolled over on to my back I cried out and shoved myself backwards so hard that I fell on to the floor: Jesus was floating in the air above the end of the bed, the figure's pose and colours the same as the print on the landing, but life-size.

I crouched in the corner of the room and stared up at the apparition. I remember wishing I had some boxers on – anything: the last thing you want when you're visited by the Son of God is to be stark bollock naked. Even if He is only wearing a thin white robe.

Jesus looked down at me and smiled. It wasn't the crafty smirk He'd given me on the landing the previous evening, but warm, understanding, benevolent.

Then He spoke.

"Steven," He said. "I want you to know something. I'm always here for you. I know you're not a subscriber, but that's not important. Just give me a chance if ever you need anything. If you're finding it difficult to cope, or need guidance, stability, or just someone to talk to. I can sense the restlessness in you. The frustration. It clings to you like frost. Give me a chance to warm you, Steven. The things you do in life are important. Consider the consequences, because decisions have an impact. It's like an eye for an eye, or karma, if you like. I *can* help. Just think about it, that's all I ask."

Then Jesus slowly faded.

"Jesus bloody Christ," I muttered.

I heard someone running up the stairs and Amy burst into the room. She was red-faced, freckles blooming. Her colours rolled through red and purple to a marching band accompaniment. "What happened?" she said. "I heard a bang. You shouted."

I remember looking down at myself, backed up into the corner of the room with my knees drawn up to my chest. Not a pretty sight. "Fell out of bed," I said.

She raised her eyebrows. "Dreaming about me, were you?"

"Yeah. I dreamt about you last night and I fell out of bed twice…"

Our relationship blossomed, and just a few months after being the first proper boyfriend to meet the parents, I called her at work from a phone box in Burton on Trent and asked her to marry me.

Fifteen years later Amy and I still have a great relationship. Many couples grow apart, becoming increasingly dissatisfied and disillusioned as the summers and winters pass like the flapping of a wing. Some split up, breaking hearts and homes. Others sit it out in a bitter mire, sharing little more than a bed. But Amy and I have grown together. We speak more openly now than ever. Our love life continues to improve. Our affection is not only more open, but more frequently expressed and, perhaps, more deeply meant.

We've been lucky. Very lucky.

But as Mick's passing approaches, Amy's sorrow grows and she becomes more and more distant.

We visit him in hospital every day. There's a rota of relatives at his bedside. He tries to look cheerful, smiling thinly, eyes half-closed. But he's clearly deteriorating. A drip feeds colourless liquid into his arm. His skin's as grey as the tonnes of concrete he's laid as foundations through his working life. His colours are as drab and stolid as sludge, and his song nothing more than a tuneless drone.

Everyone says encouraging words. Makes light. Pretends nothing's wrong. "Oh well, you'll be right soon enough," they say. "You've got to hurry up and come home so you can fix that shelf." All that. Mick asks weakly how the Baggies got on at the weekend. They drew with Cardiff, but at least Blues were beaten by Chelsea in the last minute of injury time. His colours shimmer and surge as a spark of satisfaction briefly flares.

Only outside are his visitors' tears allowed to come, glistening in the golden light in which Mick is bathed. The women huddle, comfort, reassure; the men nod and sigh. But maintenance of hope is as exhausting as deceit.

Later, as Amy shudders and sobs in my arms in our bed, I feel helpless. More helpless than when I'd watched our children removed from her body. More helpless than the night I thought she was going to leave me, during a period when our marriage slipped into one of the fissures that occasionally mars all long-term relationships. This helplessness isn't due to obstacles, inability or lack of knowledge. It's just that she and the rest of her family are being transported to a completely different place by the situation. As Mick approaches the God to Whom they have spent their lives praying, they're going with him as far as they can.

And so while Mick faces death with cheery optimism, joking with the nurses, complaining about the gifts people bring him and the state of the NHS – a situation he'd soon put right given a day in Ten Downing Street, he often points out – so my own fear grows.

When Mick dies, when the daddy who took her to football and watched her dance as a child, who jig-jogged her on his knee and worked day after day, year after year to put food on the table and pay for the holiday caravan in Stourport, the man who cried at our wedding and spotted me as a future son-in-law the moment I entered their house is no longer there, she will be so utterly removed from me I might never get her back.

I can't bear that thought. Without her I'd be nothing. There would be no reason for the work I do, the tiny measure of perceived success I've achieved in my little career. No reason to wake, no-one to make laugh, no-one to show me my flaws and take my hand and coax me into situations I would otherwise shirk away from.

It cannot be this way.

So now's the time to see if Jesus meant what He said all those years ago.

I'm not sure how to pray. It's not something I've ever done. But I'm sure if God is as understanding and *good* as people say, it doesn't matter anyway. Just to be on the safe side, though, I reckoned a traditional approach would be best. I mean, I didn't want to offend Him. I might get struck down by a bolt of lightning or something.

I knelt on the floor, rested my elbows on the bed and linked my fingers 'here is a church'-style.

"Dear God," I said. Well, where would you begin? "Or should that be Jesus? Sorry. I'm not very good at this sort of thing. Anyway, I was just wondering if You could help me. Thing is, Amy's dad's not doing too well. I know it'll crush her if he, y'know, goes, and I really don't want to see that happen. So I was wondering if there was something we could do, some kind of deal we could cut. I'm not sure what, but I'll happily give up something to buy him some more time, or help her cope with it somehow. I'm a bit useless, see. And a bit scared. Erm… Anyway, I guess that's it. Perhaps You could let me know somehow. Give me a sign, as they say."

I wasn't sure whether to end it on 'regards', 'best wishes', 'love', or what, so I just said "thanks" and released my hands, which I reckon is the praying equivalent of pushing the *end call* button on a phone.

I'd just got out of the bath and was about to have a shave when it happened. As the hot water ran into the basin the mirror began to steam over, smooth grey shapes pushing across the glass. I'd just washed my face and was reaching for the towel when I looked up and saw Jesus staring back at me. Just a faint image in the steam, but there He was, all pious and serene – just how you might expect.

"Hello, Steven," He said. "I heard your request. I understand your concerns. I can help you, but there will be a cost. As you said, you must give up something of yourself in return for what you want. Are you prepared to do that? To make such a sacrifice?"

I didn't know what to do. I couldn't help wondering why Jesus tended to show up when I was in a state of undress. "Yeah, I think so," I said. "What kind of sacrifice?"

"I can't tell you that. Let's just say it will be commensurate to the scale of your request. An eye for an eye, remember?" The steam shifted, Jesus smiled, and then He faded away again.

When shaving, I cut myself twice.

Now I'm in the hospital, and the life-size apparition of Jesus floats above the end of Mick's bed, swaying slightly. It looks more like a moulded plastic clown in the neon-lit hospital ward. He gazes towards the corner of the ceiling as if He's spotted an unfortunate cobweb that needs a miracle performed upon it. Somehow I find His presence comforting. I hadn't expected that.

He turns His head slowly and looks down at me. His plastic doll eyes shine. I cannot look at Him. "Do not be afraid, Steven," He says. His words are warm and clear inside my head. His is the gentlest yet most powerful voice I've ever heard.

As those around me struggle to remain strong in the face of Mick's obvious decline, Jesus reaches out to me.

"You know why I'm here," He says.

I give a single, short nod no-one else will notice.

"Come, then," Jesus says. "It is time."

Then He's gone again.

A few moments pass, then I lean towards Amy and tell her I'm going to the gents. I'll be back in a minute, I say. She nods, but continues to gaze down at Mick, who now seems to be asleep.

Before I leave the ward I look back at him. There's not long left. His weakening state can no longer be countered by optimism and hope alone. As I walk away I place my hand on Amy's shoulder, savouring this moment of contact.

I feel it might be the last.

I walk along the corridor in a daze I'm so nervous. I'm aware that a few people look at me as I pass: an elderly couple holding hands; a nurse with a bunch of files clutched to her chest. I must look a state, red-eyed, sweating, pale.

When I reach the end of the corridor I push through fire doors onto a stairwell. The air is much cooler, and as the doors close behind me the noise of the corridor is abruptly subdued.

For a moment I stand on the landing and breathe deeply, trying to regain some composure. I can feel my heart beating as I look out through the window in front of me across the rooftops and trees.

I hear echoing voices and look down between the glossy black handrails; nurses are walking down stairs several storeys below. I look up and see a figure looking down at me from the balustrade on one of the highest floors. I can hear Mantovani: *The Big Country*.

I begin to walk up the stairs, my right hand gripping the balustrade.

By the time I reach the top I'm sweating and my legs ache. The top flight of stairs ends at a red door to the hospital roof. A sign states that the door is alarmed.

I turn and look down the stairs again. The stairwell is deserted. In fact I can hear no noise at all: no aircraft approaching Birmingham airport; no rush of traffic; not a single person's song. There's a loud bang and I turn to find that the red door is open. I can hear no alarm, but in the door's glossy frame, haloed by the sun's golden light, is Jesus.

"Steven," he says. "Thank you for coming. Time's running out."

I feel sick now. My head's spinning. I can feel sweat on my forehead and back. I look past Jesus towards the pale sky. Behind him I can see angels playing among the clouds, chasing each other with the exuberance of children.

Jesus smiles and beckons. "Come with me," He says.

As I walk towards the doorway He backs away. The sunlight is so dazzling I have to shield my eyes. I step through the door out on to the roof; its gravel surface crunches beneath my feet. I pause. Jesus is near the parapet. His form is unmistakable, but all detail is bleached away by the brilliance of the light behind him. It's like looking through frosted glass.

I take a few uncertain steps. Mantovani grows louder.

"Come, Steven. There's no need to be afraid," Jesus says.

I walk forward until I'm just a meter or so away from Him. The sun is bright. The trees shush and shift in the breeze beyond the edge of the roof in a gentle, comforting dance.

High above the swaying trees the angels emerge from the clouds and lunge down towards me, cherubic arms folded back against their sides. As they swoop past they cry and scream like agitated chimps. I catch a glimpse of pointed teeth and gnarled, withered skin as they snap and grab at me.

"There is no more time, Steven," Jesus says softly. "Not for Mick. But I'm glad you're here. It means you've made the right choice." He beckons with one hand and the angels suddenly dart and dive around me. Growling and hissing they grasp my wrists and push me to the edge of the parapet like a prisoner. My instinct is to look down at the car park below, but one of them grips my head and forces me to look towards the trees.

Through watering eyes I see Amy's face in the swaying leaves, and a thousand other faces around hers.

Despite everything I have tried to do, still she cries.

In the sky, I see Mick's face in the clouds. He's looking at me, smiling as if the Baggies have just replaced Blues in the Premier League. His face is relaxed and happy, all his worries and anxiety dissolved. There are other faces, too. People I know.

I think of Amy and our kids, Mick, Mary, my own parents. I look towards Jesus to my right and find Mick standing in his place. He smiles at me. "It'll be all right," he says gently. "Don't worry. It'll be all right."

Then he fades away, and although I'm alone with the trees and the clouds, I feel new strength. Perhaps it's a parting gift from Mick.

I breathe deeply, and as I turn and walk back towards the stairwell bathed in golden light, I know Amy will need me more than ever now.

The deciduous trees, the stags and the hinds, the half-sucked sweets in furry handbags, all the jokes and values, the stubbornness and generosity – they live on in me and Amy, and will live on in our kids, and in their kids, just as fallen leaves feed the earth.

Is this where God is?

I don't know. But do I know that everything will be all right.

# Soirée

Alastair Reynolds

My hands were sweaty, and that wouldn't do. I brushed them against the back of my skirt, hoping that no one would notice me doing so and that the dampness wouldn't show against the dark fabric. The black shoes were hurting my feet and the black stockings felt as if they were cutting off the circulation in my legs. Looking around at the other members of the reception party, none of us appeared comfortable in the outdated, puritanical-seeming costumes. The idea was that the clothes – derived from records dating from the time of *Starcrosser's* departure – would strike the right balance between civic authority and reassuring familiarity, but we could only guess what the passengers would make of our outfits, as well as our choice of makeup and hairstyles.

Never mind. It was much too late for second thoughts now.

I glanced back at Gil Peterson, who was listening in via an earpiece to the technicians monitoring the capsule.

"Are we good to go, Gil?"

He touched a finger to his ear then nodded. "They're moving around inside. I think we should go in immediately, before they start getting concerned."

I glanced at the other members of the party, receiving nods of assent. They all looked nervous, but this was what we had been training for and all of us were absolutely prepared.

"All right," I said. "Let's do this. Happy faces, everyone. We want them to know they're among friends."

I began to walk along the connecting ramp, shadowed by technicians and a swarm of floating cameras. At the end of the ramp, resting on a bright yellow cradle, was the craft that contained the sixty passengers. The main part of *Starcrosser* was still in orbit; this was just the life-support and re-entry capsule; the pimple on the end of the nose. It was a blunt arrowhead, stubby-winged, white with black markings, ticking and creaking as it adjusted to the pull of gravity and the crush of a planetary atmosphere. It had been brought down from space in a tractor field, and then subjected to aggressive quarantine measures. Only when those measures were coming to an end had we sent an electronic signal into the capsule, instructing the systems to bring the passengers out of suspended animation.

As Gil had told me, those people were now warm and mobile. It was time to say hello.

I knocked bare knuckles on the outer door, then stepped back and clasped my hands behind my back. Several seconds later there came an eruption of vapour from slats next to the door and the door began to hinge open, the movement accompanied by the flashing of orange lights and a squawking tone. My heart was racing as the vapour dispersed. The cameras and technicians jockeyed around me for the best angle.

Someone loomed in the door. I fought the urge to take a step back, holding my ground. The figure was a man, wearing a silvery garment studded with medical tabs, life-support cables hanging limply where they had been disconnected from the capsule's equipment. He was middle aged, bearded, patrician-looking, his expression serious and guarded but not fearful.

I recognised him instantly.

"Do you understand me?" he asked.

"Perfectly, Captain Fisher." I walked closer to the door and extended a hand. "I'm Alice Hodgkin. On behalf of the Planetary Coordinating Committee, welcome to Benevolence. We're very glad that you made it."

"You know my name."

"And a lot more than that. We know the names and biographies of all sixty people who left Earth in the *Starcrosser*."

"Did we make it?"

"Yes," I said. "Absolutely."

Behind Prescott Fisher, peering through the doorway, were other silver-clad passengers, of various ages and sexes. They had the stunned look of small animals exposed to sudden light, as if the capsule was a den which had just been uncovered.

"Then where are we?"

"The place you expected to be. It's just that we arrived here ahead of you."

"We were the only ship that got out."

"No, just the first." The words I had rehearsed so often poured out of me. "While *Starcrosser* was *en route*, technology raced ahead. We made better drives, faster ships. Colonists reached Benevolence fifty years ago. I was born on this planet, and my parents only have very faint memories of Earth. Don't worry, though. We came in small numbers – our ships brought many other systems within reach – and most of the planet is still relatively unexploited. There's more than enough room for sixty newcomers."

Fisher was unsteady in gravity, taking faltering steps. Gowned technicians raced to support him before he stumbled. He looked back at the other passengers, some of whom were beginning to emerge from the capsule.

"What happened back home? When did the Singularity hit?"

I smiled, trying to put myself into his mindset. History recorded that the passengers of the *Starcrosser* had considered themselves refugees escaping a coming catastrophe they deemed a stone-cold certainty. "It never did, Captain Fisher. You were right to be concerned, but the scenario you feared never came to pass. Machines got cleverer, it's true. But there turned out to be hard limits to robot intelligence. Beyond a certain point, they got faster but not smarter. Those machines gave us the new drives, the new physics that underpinned everything. But they never posed a serious threat to human hegemony. Earth's changed – you'd probably find it quite disorientating by now – but there are still people there, still in charge."

Suspicion lingered in his expression. "If you overtook us, why did you wait until now before bringing us out of suspended animation?"

"Our thinking was that this had to be your achievement and yours alone. We'd have intervened if there had been a technical fault with *Starcrosser*, but since the ship was performing well, we deemed it unnecessary. And now you have the satisfaction of having completed the interstellar crossing, entirely through your own efforts. It's quite an accomplishment, Captain. Don't think for one moment that we're not impressed. We've made progress, but we can still appreciate a brave endeavour. What you did was astonishing." I offered him my hand again. "How are you feeling?"

"Hungry," he admitted.

"That's what we expected, based on what we know of your suspended animation process. We have medical staff waiting to examine you and therapies to strengthen your muscles sooner than you'd think possible. Most importantly of all, we've got food and drink."

"Food and drink sounds good."

"That's what we were hoping. Once you're done with the medics, we'd like you to join us for a reception, so we can all start getting to know each other a bit better."

"I've got a lot of questions," Fisher said.

"I'd expect nothing less."

"I don't know where to begin. Your government, your technology and medicine … how you deal with machine intelligence … what kind of role we're going to be able to play." He shook his head, evidently frustrated at the depth of his ignorance. I studied him carefully, trying to work out how it must feel to have arrived on a planet that was already settled. They had been expecting an empty wilderness, a place to fashion their machine-free utopia, a sanctuary that would be forever barriered against the kind of Singularity assumed to have overwhelmed Earth.

Instead they had arrived to find a fully-fledged society, a settled world with its own towns and cities, a world where the fears of the previous century had been forgotten. It was a triumph on one level and a failure on another. It was Fisher who had organised the sixty 'evacuees', pooling resources and money to build the *Starcrosser*. To make that happen, he had of necessity become something close to a religious figure. But the records were all unanimous on one thing. He had been a man of sincere beliefs, who had manipulated people only to the degree that was absolute necessary to achieve his ends. A good man, in other words.

I was privileged just to be in his presence.

"This is going to take some adjusting to," he said.

"We'll make it work," I said.

The medics fussed over the sixty passengers, treating them with kindness and dignity. Fisher was the first to be attended to, so that – with his strength renewed – he could visit the others and reassure them that they were in safe hands. There was an understandable resistance from some quarters, but most of the newcomers appeared ready to go along with the story for now, happy just to be alive. Above all they were hungry and thirsty, and the reception waiting for them was as lavish as any in our planet's short history, with the food carefully prepared so as not to damage their recovering metabolisms.

We were in a tower, on the western edge of Glimmer Bay, near Benevolence's equator. The tower had been intended to form the anchor point of a space elevator, until the tractor technology came along and made it redundant. Now it was one of several landing stages for interplanetary vehicles, although the only ship currently docked was *Starcrosser*'s re-entry capsule. There had been other candidates for hosting the ship, but I was glad the Planetary Coordination Committee had chosen this one. The view was beyond comparison, and it wasn't just me who felt that way. Even as they mingled with the various functionaries and bigwigs, the passengers kept being drawn to the vast window or the balcony outside, with its wide panorama of uninterrupted scenery. The sun was lowering towards the horizon, the still water of the bay shining like hammered bronze.

"It's wonderful," Fisher said, sipping from a glass of wine.

"The wine?"

"The wine, the view, the company, everything. I had my doubts when I came out of the capsule, but that seems like a lifetime ago." He raised a hand before I had a chance to contradict him. "I know; it was only a couple of hours. But I can't pretend I don't feel reassured. It's like waking from a long, troubling dream, and finding out that everything's still all right with the world. That gorgeous, warm realisation. You know that feeling?"

"Absolutely," I said.

"Maybe it's something in the wine, or the drugs your doctors gave me. But I don't think so. You wouldn't have any reason to make us feel happier than we'd already feel, would you?"

"It's right to feel happy. You embarked on a dangerous journey because you feared something was going to happen. Not only did it not happen, but you survived the journey. There's two reasons to celebrate already. On top of that, we're happy for you! Happy that you made it, happy that we've got some off-world company again. Don't misunderstand what I said earlier – interstellar travel is still phenomenally difficult. We're better at it than you were, but it's still not child's play. It's not as if Benevolence gets visitors every few months." I glanced towards the window. "There are half a million people out there who'd like to meet you in person. I'm afraid the one thing I can't promise you is a quiet time, at least not for the next year or so."

"I don't imagine we're going to be able to pay our way. We came expecting to tame a new world, not to slot into an existing society."

"We'll make things as easy for you as we can. You may feel bewildered to begin with, but you'll catch up pretty quickly. We can always use good minds, strong hands."

"You mean, you'll find menial work for us." Fisher said this without rancour, as if it was the least he could expect.

"Not at all," I said hastily. "You forget that we know almost everything there is to know about you. We know your skills, your interests, your passions. Before you became a mover and shaker, before you mobilised the resources of an entire planet to build *Starcrosser*, you were an avid pianist."

Fisher blinked, as if the memory had been lost to him until that moment. "You're right."

"We still value pianos, we still need people to make them and tune them and play them. If you don't want to do that, you can teach music." I waved a hand airily. "Or a hundred other things – I'm just offering suggestions."

"One down, fifty-nine to go."

"It's not just you." Lowering my voice, I looked across the room, through the endlessly moving bustle of the reception. "Take her: Georgina Crane. You probably know her as an expert on antimatter physics: she was the one you brought along to fix the engine, if something went wrong with it. In her twenties she swam in national competitions. Our records suggest that she would be considered a very strong swimmer, even by Benevolence standards. She could coach one of the regional teams, if that was what she chose. Or pursue further work in physics, if that's her vocation."

"I imagine everything she knows is hopelessly out of date by now."

"Don't assume so. Even if that's the case in her particular specialisation, there are bound to be little nooks and crannies that still need exploring." I paused to take a nibble from one of the circling trays. "Trust me, Captain Fisher; there isn't a single one of you who can't be employed in some manner, if that's what you choose. And if you don't, that's fine with us as well. It's honour enough to have you as guests, even if all you do is spend the rest of your lives as tourists."

"It sounds too good to be true," Fisher said.

"That's what you said last time."

He looked at me sharply. "I'm sorry?"

I shook my head, disturbed by the words I'd just spoken. They had come out of nowhere, as if a crack had opened in some private compartment in the back of my head, where the words had been contained, allowing them to spill into my mouth.

"What I meant was…" I began, anxious to reassure him.

"How could there have been a last time?"

I wanted him to just forget what I'd said, to put it down to a malfunctioning synapse, but his expression said he was not going to let it pass that easily. I groped for a plausible fiction, an explanation that would explain the slip, and to my intense relief something popped into my mind.

"I shouldn't have said that. Truth is, we've been very concerned about not making a mistake with this whole revival process. We'd never had any experience of this kind of thing before, and we were scared about screwing it up, either by mollycoddling you or exposing you to too much change in one go. So we ran scenarios – simulations – in which we brought you out time and time again, adjusting our responses with each iteration."

His eyes were narrowed, not quite ready to let me off the hook. "How could you run scenarios? How could you know how we'd behave, as individuals?"

"You were sixty of the most famous people on Earth at the time of your departure. You didn't get any less famous afterwards. In the records there are literally tens of thousands of hours of documentaries and interviews for each and every one of you. All that material survived, so all we had to do was look through the records and build predictive models."

"So you've already met me."

"In a manner of speaking. Of course, now that I'm talking to the actual Prescott Fisher, I can see how lacking our simulation was. It was a cartoon, a sketch; you're a flesh and blood man. But it was a start; better than nothing." I sighed, looking down at my black stockings and shoes. "Look, I'm sorry if I kept that from you. Believe it or not, initial concealment of the existence of the scenarios was one of the things the scenarios recommended! You'll just have to take my word that we'd have told you eventually."

"I don't suppose I've got much choice."

"All we ever wanted to do was make things as smooth as we could. There are going to be some missteps along the way, that's to be expected. But we're doing everything in our power to make you happy."

"It would have been nice if you'd told me up front."

"In hindsight, that's what we should have done."

His demeanour softened. "On the other hand, I guess you couldn't have told us everything in one go – we'd have been overloaded. If no actual deception was intended … "

"None was, I promise you."

Gil Peterson sidled up to us, holding a wineglass in his palm, with the stem passing between his fingers. Like me he was dressed in the dark, puritanical garb of the late twenty-first century, the era of *Starcrosser*'s departure.

"Everything all right?" he asked, directing the question at the two of us.

"Alice was just telling me about the run-through scenarios," Fisher said. "The simulations you ran."

"Right," Peterson said, nodding slowly. His eyes met mine for an instant. It was clear that he had no idea what we had been talking about, but – quick-witted as ever – was going to make every effort to sound as if he did. "Well, you were going to find out about those sooner or later. But please don't blame Alice for keeping them from you – she was only following the guidelines we all put together."

"I'm not blaming her," Fisher said, smiling to emphasize his point.

I felt a shivery, dislocated feeling, as if the wine was going to my head too quickly. There was a bulging, migrainous pressure in my skull.

"You look like you could use a little fresh air," Peterson said, nodding at me. "Go and take a breather, Alice – we'll hold the fort here."

"Thanks," I said. "I've been on my feet all day, and all of a sudden…"

"Cut yourself some slack," Fisher said. "You're only human, after all."

I left the reception room, walking through the sliding doors onto the balcony. The doors closed behind me, cutting off the babble of conversation. The balcony was empty.

My heart – or what passed for my heart – was hammering in my chest. I had nearly made a terrible mistake. Only quick-thinking, and Gil Peterson's deft intervention, had saved me from disaster. It had all been my own fault, too.

The feeling that the words had escaped from a compartment at the back of my mind was more accurate than I'd realised at the time. The compartment was where I kept the true knowledge of my own identity, and that of the colleagues around me. It was where I kept the true knowledge of what had really happened to Captain Fisher and his passengers.

Not just the last time, but the time before.

My mistake had been in thinking I could deal with that duality, holding that information in one part of my mind while submerging myself into the Alice Hodgkin identity. I had been confident enough to believe that I could maintain a grip on Alice Hodgkin, her fictitious personality, the fictitious web of her invented memories and past, while also maintaining the knowledge of my real, higher identity. Not forever – I knew I couldn't keep that game up for more than one night – but I'd at least thought I could get through the soirée.

How wrong I'd been. The gaff had been explained away, but in doing so I'd had to introduce another small lie into the world, one that would have its own ramifications. My base memories would now have to be edited to include the truth of the run-through scenarios. That was exactly the kind of messy, corrective intervention we'd hoped to avoid this time.

I knew now that I'd overestimated my self-control. The only thing for it would be to commit to total submergence in the Hodgkin persona, fully and irrevocably, before returning inside. I had probably got away with that one error; a second could not be tolerated.

I slipped off the hard shoes and walked in my stockings to the balcony's edge, with its low stone railing. I still had the wine glass. I drained what was left, dwelling on what lay ahead of me. This, I thought, must be what it feels like to know that death is near. It was not a sensation I had ever expected to experience.

The evening view was lovely, especially now that the lights had come on across the bay, reflected in perfect vertical lines in the calm, darkening waters. The golden lights of the houses and buildings contrasted with the coloured lanterns strung along the public promenades and piers. The towns all looked inviting, even to my eyes. Tomorrow the passengers would get their chance to explore further afield, if that was what they wished. Beyond this little bay, with its coves and harbours, lay the panoramic enchantments of a whole world. There was surely room enough in it for the newcomers, no matter their tastes. Some would want to join the existing communities, while others would crave the isolation and empty spaces they had never known on Earth. All would be accommodated, as far as circumstances allowed. Nothing mattered more than the happiness of the newcomers.

It would be a delicate, testing business to begin with. No matter how successful the soirée would turn out, it could only be viewed as the first step in an arduous process. Prescott Fisher and his passengers had been dazed by the circumstances of their arrival, blinded by the attention. One should not be too surprised if their critical faculties were not fully engaged. The difficult stages lay ahead, in the days and weeks to come. Once the passengers had adjusted to the good fortune of having survived the crossing, they would naturally begin to pay more attention to their surroundings. It was entirely possible that they would begin to notice details – errors and omissions – that they had been inclined to ignore until then. There would be mistakes – hopefully not as serious as the one I had just made – but it was my fervent intention that none of them would be grave enough to endanger the enterprise. It was irrational of me, but I had an absolute faith that all would come good in the end.

There would absolutely not be a repeat of the first two times, that was for sure.

The first revival had been the most traumatic. When the passengers had begun to suspect that their environment was fabricated, that their hosts were not human after all, they had taken it very badly. Unfortunately our efforts to placate the distressed creatures had only worsened the situation. The humans had turned aggressive and in the ensuing violence had inflicted permanent, non-recoverable damage upon one of us. The carnage that followed had been regrettable, but there had been no option but to kill the humans. Fortunately, their remains had been catalogued and preserved, and following improvements in our science it became possible to not only reanimate the passengers but also to restore their memories to the point before the earlier revival.

The second time had gone marginally better, but the humans had still found mistakes in both their hosts and the environment. By this time we were ready with painless euthanisation methods and there had not been nearly as much trouble resurrecting the bodies.

After two failures, there was far from unanimous agreement that there should be a third attempt. There were those who argued that the kindest thing would have been to leave the humans alone, rather than risk putting them through another upsetting episode. Thankfully they were outnumbered, the majority of us believing that we owed the humans the kindness of being revived in a safe, comforting environment. There was also a degree of self-interest in that viewpoint. Extinct since the Singularity, humans existed nowhere else in creation. This might be the only chance we got to study organic intelligence before it was encountered elsewhere in the galaxy.

I was glad that the majority had prevailed. As one of those advocating a third revival, I'd put my reputation on the line. I was emphatic that we were going to get it right this time.

But it would not be without costs, especially for me.

The first and second revivals had failed for various reasons, but the chief flaw had been that we did not play our roles with sufficient conviction. As a precondition for the third trial, it had been agreed that this flaw must be rectified. In order to interact with the humans in as convincing a fashion as possible, we would need to become fully submerged in our invented personas. The thinking was that if we believed that we were human as well, if we believed that Benevolence and its history were real, the passengers would be much less likely to detect inconsistencies in the constructed narrative. As the main proponent of the third revival, I'd had no choice but to submit to this reasoning. I could not even say I disagreed with it.

They had let me have this one evening, before taking the final step.

For now I knew exactly what I was. I was a member of that bright and glorious civilisation that had succeeded humanity. I was immortal, indestructible, virtually omniscient. My brothers and sisters were already spreading into the universe on wings of light, amassing data, knowledge and wisdom in glorious quantities. One day they would find other sentient creatures – beings like us, or other organic intelligences. I loved my brothers and sisters deeply, and admired the enterprise on which they were engaged. It was a spiritual quest that cut to the very core of what we were.

But I could play no further part in it.

In a few moments I would have to forget my true identity. That compartment in the back of my head would be locked for good, so that nothing would ever leak into my dream of being human. I would never regain access to those memories, or at least not until this revival failed and I was called to account for my mistakes.

Gil Peterson – the identity behind Gil Peterson – had already made that awesome sacrifice. Now it was my turn. When I next spoke to him, or to any of my colleagues – to anyone alive on Benevolence who wasn't one of the passengers – I would do so in the deluded belief that they were also human. Our only modes of communication would be language and gesture. Component by component, my body would gradually turn itself into meat, until even an autopsy would give no hint as to my higher identity. I would know pain and illness. My thoughts would crawl with agonising slowness from one fuzzy state to the next. The rich emotional spectrum that was my birthright would be filtered down to a handful of muddy colours. The only consolation – if you could call it that –

was that I would remember precisely nothing of what had come before.

From across the bay, fireworks flowered above one of the inviting little towns.

My mask, the one I had worn all evening, reshaped itself into something fierce and beautiful and utterly inhuman. For a moment I knew everything, feeling the comforting presence of my brothers and sisters, information whispering into me like summer rain. The sky was ablaze with number, logic and the ethereal songs of receding explorers, sending news of the wonderful and strange things they were encountering as they sped further and further away from home.

It had been good, being part of that.

The door opened behind, babble and music spilling out into the evening.

"Are you feeling OK now?" asked Peterson.

"Much better," I answered, still looking out to the bay. "I just needed to clear my head."

"I don't blame you. It's been a very long day. But I get the impression they're taking it pretty well."

"What's not to like?" I asked. "They left Earth expecting all hell to break out. They crossed interstellar space in a rickety old ship, and yet they all survived the journey. We've given them a planet, a beautiful paradise, and told them to make themselves at home."

"Are you sure you're all right, Alice?"

"Fine, Gil. Honestly."

The sadness was hitting me like a tidal wave. I knew I could postpone the moment of total submergence no longer. I turned around to face Peterson, who remembered nothing of what he had once been, putting on my happy, human mask, and in the instant after that I forgot everything as well.

Then we went back indoors, to face our guests.

# On the Sighting of Other Islands

Ian R. MacLeod

The island which floated above mother ocean was composed of many things. Part metal, part forest, part city, part mountain, part orchard and meadow, it cast a shadow across the waters beneath and generated tides, currents, storms; it cast out nets of emerald lightning. Down in the barnacle dark of its turbulent underside, nameless sea-behemoths, flocks of blind seabirds and silvered shoals fought over its many kinds of spoor. Roots, chutes and fallings of metal sluiced, fed, or were torn apart by the endless clashings of waves. From some angles and sufficient distance, it seemed as if the island was somehow supporting itself on shimmering legs, or had just emerged from the sea, or was falling endlessly towards it, but from most, even as the eye strained to take in the scale of what it was seeing, the island appeared to be what it truly was: a bulkingly beautiful, yet seemingly impossible, vision made real.

Those who lived on the island never saw it from such a distance. To them, it was land and it was their home, and beneath there was only mother ocean, and the drop which separated the two was too vast and terrible to contemplate. For mother ocean, it was commonly believed, was endless, and the only qualifications to this watery infinity were those rare events known as sightings. In the island's topmost towers, the question of when and where the next sighting would occur, and then what it might mean, occupied the minds of the greatest of the dreamers. Some who lived and worked in the more mundane lowerlands claimed that the dreamers actually possessed maps of mother ocean, although such documents would surely have consisted almost entirely of ever-changing greys and greens and blues, and were thus hard to envisage. Others speculated that the dreamers steered the island in some direction or another in active search of new sightings, although it was mostly accepted that the island steered itself – if, indeed, it was consciously steered by anything at all. Strangely, the more common assumption was that sightings only occurred because the dreamers called them into existence out of a conjunction of their various slumbers, and that, once they had drifted beyond the horizon's haze, these other islands vanished back into the watery, sleepy stuff from which they had been made.

After each sighting, the dreamers in their towers would put away their sacred telescopes and set about long and stringent debate as to what this particular conjunction of stone, roof, precarious field and hazy mountain signified. From there, decisions on such crucial matters as the planning of the harvest, levels of hemline and the financing of new sea-drains were made. Over the innumerable lives and sightings through which the island measured its history, there had been many different visions with which the dreamers had had to contend. There had been islands glimpsed at dawn, and islands which appeared to drop from the nowhere heat of cloudless midday. There had been islands which looked to be transparent, or perhaps were made entirely of smoke, or possibly ice or glass. There had been islands of iron, and islands seemingly banded with precious stone. Sometimes, and yet more memorably, there had been several islands at once, which, even in the brief period in which they could be studied, had doubled and rejoined. Most spectacularly of all within the memory of recent generations, there had been the strange, far lights of an island glimpsed at midnight, and the horror of an island hanging upside upon a blood red sea. But most sightings, rare though they were, were far more commonplace, causing the island's more daring thinkers to posit that the beings who surely dwelt on these edifices lived lives which were perhaps not entirely dissimilar to their own. Sometimes, it was said, the dreamers with the best sight and access to the strongest and most sacred telescopes had glimpsed high towers formed in shapes of a near-recognisable architecture, or caught the sunflash of lenses trained back on them. But this, too, was merely another part of the pattern of sightings, and was soon re-woven into the fabric of the dreamers' dreams as the island drifted on, floating vastly on shimmers of storm above mother ocean's endless haze.

# Fireflies

Christopher Priest

The drones came in at nightfall. If she had completed her day's tasks at the observatory, Lorna Metterline would shut down her terminal then scramble down the uncertain cliff steps to the beach. From there she could watch the tiny aircraft returning as they flew in low above the sea.

When the sea was calm, the brightly coloured LEDs in the belly of each of the drones mirrored back from the surface of the waves. On some evenings the machines flew in one by one, sometimes separated by several minutes, but most evenings they arrived in such numbers that they swarmed towards the island in a glistering formation. As they passed over the beach and responded to their sensing of the rocky cliffs rising beyond, they would adjust their height in unison. In their wake was a breathy susurration from their silenced vanes, a feeling of secretive distances already crossed, covert explorations, unstated winds.

In case anyone challenged her for being on the beach at that time, Lorna always took the tabulator with her, but this evening, as on most evenings, she did not switch it on.

The tabulator hung on its strap against her side. She could feel it vibrating gently in stand-by mode as it responded to the locating pulse of each incoming machine, separately identified. At this stage the detection of the drones was merely numerical: so many recognized and logged, so many accounted for. She would return to evaluating the more complex quantified results the next morning, after they had been downloaded at the base and sent along the landline to the institute computers.

In the chartroom the staff would view the coverage of the ocean, then become absorbed in the task of tracing each drone back to its launch point, using the satellite returns to analyse its route. Working with the other cartographers, Lorna then laboriously transferred the images to the master data store. But even with a full complement of staff they were endlessly running behind – they were still trying to untangle the reports from more than two years ago. Tonight's data would not be properly evaluated until another two years or more had passed. Gradually, the backlog was increasing.

Lorna should have left this island, Meequa, several months earlier, at the end of her contract, but she felt trapped by Tomak's sudden disappearance. How could she leave until she knew what had happened to him? Patta, her roommate, obviously thought it was time for her to move on, but that was for Lorna irrational and impossible. Tomak had left her with so many things unsaid, so many personal decisions unmade.

She still ached with love for him. Why had he left her that way? It was impossible to re-adjust without him.

She stared across the sea, under the scattering of drone lights, at the dark offshore island where Tomak had been posted.

The island had a name: Tremm, once the mythological companion of Meequa, the fast wanderer of island passes. But the island which carried the name was dark and low against the twilit horizon, stolid and heavy-looking, as much unlike a wanderer as it was possible to imagine. Tremm was directly opposite the cove, an hour or more across the shallow strait, and whenever the drones swarmed in she would see the paths of their LEDs veering to one side or the other of the island. Tremm had been charted years before, but ironically it was one whose details were the least known. It was one of several closed islands in the vicinity of Meequa, taken over by the military many decades before. No one could go near it without permission. Anyone who did go there never spoke about what the island was used for, and rarely admitted they had even been on the place. Officially it had ceased to exist. Even to look at it was, in theory, to break military law, although the civilian cartographers, and ordinary people in the town, could and did use this beach.

Tremm was an area on their map of the Midway Sea. Just a legend over a dishonestly blank area south of Meequa, in small blue letters: DANGER.

Gradually, the oceanic chart was taking shape, but because the drones were self-guided on reactive principles (programed to avoid each other and solid objects, rather than seek out certain targets) most of their data was produced along randomised paths and therefore much of it overlapped. The returns inevitably revealed unidentifiable stretches of ocean.

Digital images of land, or better still of coastline, were comparatively rare, a fact which often surprised visitors to the mapping institute. To most people, the sea seemed crowded with so many islands that it was unbelievable that it would be so difficult to chart the areas of land. However, less than five per cent of the Midway Sea was actually solid land, the rest being ocean, lagoons, rocky shallows, beaches, and so on. This percentage was a working assumption. The actual figure would not be known until the mapping was complete, of course. Satellite images, always unreliable because of the temporal distortion zones, had provided the working estimate, but drawing detailed, reliable maps was now a matter of urgency.

At least the institute was well funded. People who ran wars needed maps.

The terrain of many of the islands, viewed from above, was unbroken forest, or unexceptional farmland with few distinguishing features. Coastlines were always more satisfactory to work with: the peninsulas, cliffs, fort installations and river estuaries could usually be identified and located to particular known islands or even existing maps made by the locals.

The drones were programmed to detect and map roads, ports, railway lines, airfields, factories, homes, sources of pollution, and many more man-made objects. Mostly they found traces of sea.

Progress was therefore infinitesimally slow. When she began working here in the Meequa Chart Institute as a young graduate, Lorna had imagined they would be mapping the whole shape and extent of the Dream Archipelago. As she soon discovered, this gigantic task was still barely started, buried under an ever-growing mound of data.

More recently, as experience replaced her youthful idealism, she had found herself following the example of her colleagues. Now she concentrated on a single group of islands, her chosen speciality: the cluster of cays and islets thought to be to the south of Paneron, known informally to the cartographers as the Swirl, but which in reality carried more than seven thousand different names for the individual islands. No one at the institute had ever been to Paneron or its Swirl; no one at the institute even knew anyone else who had been there. There were no photographs or drawings of the Swirl, and of course no charts were available. A hundred books described it, though, some accounts only vague or with probable inaccuracies, most in the lyrical rhythms of Archipelagian literature. A collection of sea-farers' yarns, told in archaic marine argot, happened to have become one of Lorna's most reliable guides. Names were the only certainties – the culture of the islands was oral and textual, not visual.

Occasionally, one of the drones passed over an area of tiny islands and crags, and every now and again Lorna could make a matching identification and fit one more piece into her slowly shaping jigsaw.

Such was the task. She knew that even if she lived to be an old lady, and worked here to the end of her life, no more than a quarter of the islands should by then have been mapped. Maybe all of the Swirl would have been completed, perhaps many of the large islands elsewhere. But not all. Even by then.

She and the other cartographers had only charted a little over two thousand accredited islands. Another five thousand were in preparation. The entirety of the task was still unimaginable. Maybe a hundred, a thousand, times as many islands remained to be mapped.

As the last of the loose formations of drones passed quietly overhead, she walked across the shingly beach to a spur of smooth rock. The pebbles crunched and ground beneath her feet. She balanced the case of the tabulator against the outcrop, then leaned back on the sloping surface that faced the sea. She let her hands swing at her side.

Tomak had been on Tremm for nearly two years, and never once in those months had she received any communication from him.

He warned her before he left.

"They mute the islands they use," he said. "Tremm is hooded: no sounds or transmissions enter or leave. No one without authority is allowed on, no one is allowed to leave."

"Then why should you go there?"

"You know I can't tell you."

"Then please don't go."

She had implored him throughout their last three weeks together, but one evening, after they had stood together on the beach to watch the drones flying in, he had been taken in a motor-lighter to a small ship waiting offshore. Before that final evening they spent a short holiday together, a tearful and frustrating experience for Lorna, but Tomak said only that he was unable to resist the force of military law. He promised that he would return as soon as he could, but so far he had not.

As a civilian she felt abruptly excluded from his life, and not long after he left, feeling betrayed by him, feeling abandoned, she took a kind of unintended revenge on him. Her physical affair with one of the graphics assistants called Bradd had not lasted for long, and afterwards she felt a sense of crushing guilt and abhorrence at her own selfishness. Bradd was still working in the institute, but whatever there had been between them was emphatically over. It already felt like a long time ago to her, although not nearly as long ago as Tomak's departure. More than anything she wanted Tomak to return, so that she could quietly, silently, close the error for good.

As the darkness of the sky deepened, she took her binoculars from their case and held them to her eyes. She focused on the dark jagged bulk of Tremm, knowing that if one of the patrols happened to come along the beach and spot her, she would be in serious trouble. Her status at the mapping centre would be small protection.

At first she could make out little of the island in the dark, its steep mountainous sides almost at one with the sky. Then, as her eyes adjusted to the gloom, she could see the central mountains. Five of the highest peaks were visible from this shore.

The first of the fireflies glowed so quickly she almost missed it. She held the glasses steady, hoping for another. After a few minutes she saw a second one, then almost immediately a third. She reduced the focal length minutely, widening the field.

Tiny bursts of light were appearing on the dark slopes of the distant island, a sudden silent flaring, like miniature explosions too distant to be heard. So far away from her, with no hint of their size. She began counting them, as she often did – she had spent so long quantifying data, so to her it was an automatic reflex.

Double figures in the first minute, then a pause. Twenty-five more followed swiftly, followed by another pause so long she thought the display had ended. Then a final outburst of flaring lights, always white and intense, now clustered together, almost a stream of lights, but there was no discernable pattern.

When she lowered the binoculars, someone was standing a short distance away from her. A man, his shape just visible against the white curve of the waters's edge. She had not heard him walking across the shingle.

Swiftly, she moved the hand holding the glasses, trying to slip them down out of sight. Just in case he had not noticed them, although of course he had.

"May I look?"

"You know it's illegal," she said. She knew the voice, of course. Relief, irritation, both coursed briefly through her.

"So do you."

"I was monitoring the drones." In the dark she touched the side of the tabulator, a gesture he would not see.

"Oh yes, of course." He stepped away from her, lowering his head, staring down at the sand. "You would have to say that."

"Leave me alone, Bradd," she said.

"As you wish. Do you know what causes the flares?"

"No. Do you?"

"I see you most evenings, looking across."

"Then you must be looking too." He was stepping to and fro in an agitated way, but somehow he was managing not to make any sound on the shingle. "They're something to do with the military. Or the drones."

"Same thing."

"The drones are ours."

"We use the data from them. You know who finances them."

She wanted to get away from him, but he was contriving to stand between her and the shortest way back to the steps. She eased the tabulator strap over her shoulder, then walked down across the shingle, going around him. It was too dark now to make out features, just shapes, but she knew exactly where he was, and she also knew how he would be looking at her.

Her feet crunched on the shingle again, a curiously hollow sound, as if there were just a shallow layer of pebbles above a cavern. She heard Bradd behind her.

As she started to climb back towards the top of the cliff, she took one last look out to sea, towards Tremm. Without using the binoculars it was impossible to be certain, but she felt sure the flares were continuing. She paused, looked back down. There was no sign of Bradd.

She raised the binoculars to her eyes, but now Tremm was once again just a dark shape. That familiar blankness, unrevealing of anything except the one thing that could not be hidden: its real presence, there across the strait.

At the top of the steps lay the unkept garden that surrounded the institute, and in the dark the breeze from the sea was more of a presence. It mingled with the scents of the night-fragranced flowers that grew wildly everywhere, slowly cooling as the short night began. Beyond the main bulk of the building, in the valley below that opened out into Meequa Port, the lights of the town were visible, a ribbon of electrical dazzle that followed the course of the river.

Lorna paused, taking a breather after the climb up the cliff, thinking that Bradd would soon catch her up.

The windows of the institute were lit from within, but every pane of glass was curtained so that it was impossible to see inside. Lorna knew that at this time some of the cartographers would still be hunched over their drawing tablets and terminals, but most of them would have stopped work for the night. Maybe there would be people in the bar, but a lot of the staff simply went home at the end of the day.

Lorna and Patta were unusual in renting one of the institute's small service flats inside the main building.

Beyond the institute, the town, the inland heights of Meequa's range of hills. Sometimes, people who worked in the institute went on hill-walks up there in the heights, but because of the friable nature of the rocks the hills were not thought in general to be a safe area for climbing or exploring. Lorna herself had never been away from the coast. She preferred to leave the dark peaks a private mystery in the background of her life, an omnipresent enigma. They housed part of the network of installations found all over this sector of the Archipelago, with the result that large areas of the hill country were forbidden for intelligible reasons. Somewhere behind the first range of peaks was the base to which the drones returned, where they landed, somewhere dark, unlit, away, bringing in data, information that was more than just the map details that were fed to the institute, military intelligence, mining data, probable oil reserves, weapon caches, sources of energy. None of that disagreeable practicality was any part of Lorna's own enigma. She sensed a deeper, more personal absence, Meequa being for her another island with a seashore mentality, a littoral culture, turning its back on the engine of military ambition and strategy that powered the island economies from inland, looking instead out towards the unmapped seas, idle in the warmth, languorous under the sun, dreaming in the days.

# The Man of the Strong Arm

Adam Roberts

## 1

"By permitting," Jeunet began to say. He was, perhaps, distracted by something, for he stopped. Maybe it was the sound of the small waves folding over onto the beach again and again, below the platform on which they sat, as if the ocean itself were bowing before him. At any rate he didn't finish that sentence. Presently he started again. "The *strength* of story," he said. "It's *strength*."

"Story," said Soop, absurdly excited to be in the presence of a man such as Jeunet. "Story, yes. Absolutely, yes."

"The Man of the Strong Arm permits the study of art," said Jeunet, as if this fact were so extraordinary a thing that he needed to remind himself of it by speaking it aloud.

"Such art as expresses the strength of the human spirit," agreed Heston.

Soop was so excited he couldn't keep his legs still

Jeunet waved his hand in the air. "And you believe your latest find, this latest science fiction is – appropriate? You're certain?"

"Certainty *is* strength," said Heston.

"This –" Jeunet's speech slowed as he navigated the syllables, "this Edgar Burroughs of the Rice – is art?"

"Oh, *very* much so," said Soop, getting to his feet. He really couldn't help himself; his enthusiasm just bubbled over. "It is a fantastical and dream-like story of a hero – a strong man – a strong hero – who flies by *sheer force of will* to the stars – to a red star, which becomes, when he arrives, a red desert. He sees a red star, Mars you know, and by sheer force of will he conjures out of that a world of red desert. Conjures desert out of the light of the star! For of course we know that light is not sand… although," he added, at a gabble, for Soop's mind worked by means of sudden leaps to the left or right of his train of thought, "sand *is* glass, and glass has to do with light, after a fashion..." He stopped, and looked about him. Heston was staring at him. Jeunet was looking away. Soop blushed as though a fire were lit inside the bowl of his skull. "I'm sorry, I'm sorry."

He sat down again.

Bitterns rolled through the sky on their inconceivable avian errands. They were watched by other bitterns perched on the rocks, poking their heads in the air and, it seemed, booing their fellows. The sea was very calm. It gave the illusion of being composed of a single unbroken substance, a fabric stretched taut seemingly at a slight upward tilt, running away from them until it slotted into the groove of the horizon. The small waves continually stroked the white flank of the beach as if trying to pacify a bulky and potentially violent monster. One of the women unzipped her eye slit, identified that the tumblers of the men were empty, and shuffled in to retrieve them. Jeunet leant a little to the right to avoid being touched by fabric of her alldrape.

"Why, *of the Rice*?" he asked.

"We're not sure," said Heston, holding his right hand out in front of Soop to restrain him from attempting to answer the superior's question. "Perhaps the author derived his income from rice. Perhaps he farmed it."

"Farming rice is a perfectly honourable occupation," said Jeunet, thoughtfully. "And you have the whole of this red desert story?"

"Not all of it. Its source has been corrupted," said Heston. "We've recovered about two thirds. It seems likely that our version of the text is from a variety of provenances, some of them indecent."

"But the tale *itself* is not indecent," Soop broke in. He really couldn't contain himself. This was a failing of character, a blockage in the development of his own strength. He knew it, but couldn't help it, and again the excitement came bubbling up. "It's a strong, heroic tale. It has much in common with the *Fairy Queen*, a much older tale, or at least another tale from a different historical period. As in the *Fairy Queen*, a warrior goes to a strange world and fights Error. Error in this case takes the form of an army of green-skinned monsters with four arms and two legs."

"The Queen of... what did you say?" asked Jeunet.

"A piece of poetic art," Heston explained, breaking in smoothly. "A perfectly decent, strong-armed piece of art. It is well known, amongst those who specialise in… that sort of thing."

"Art," said Jeunet, "I wish I could be as *comfortable* with that word as you are." The woman, or one of the other women standing down by the low wall, for their grey alldrapes rendered them all equally indistinguishable, brought new drinks on a tray. "This talk of corruption in the text disturbs me," said Jeunet, gazing past her to the placid sea.

"Well," said Heston, glancing at Soop to ensure his silence, "corruption is an inevitable part of retrieving art from the historical periods. It is inherent in the nature of the medium. The means of computational storage from that age, to put it plainly, were not watertight. All sorts of extraneous materials, images, portions of other texts, they all find their way into the zeros and ones. That's our job, essentially; to sift this heap of rubbish and pull out the clean, spiritually-strengthening works of art. To discover the sort of stories that the Man of the Strong Arm would endorse."

"Not without risks," said Jeunet, looking pointedly at Soop.

"Soop works under my guidance at all times," said Heston.

"As it should be. And you have enough raw material to go on with?"

Soop hiccoughed, a high pitched sound. "We," he started, and then he stopped himself.

"What?"

"The raw data the Centre sends," said Heston, smoothly, "is more than adequate to our needs."

"Good," said Jeunet, giving Soop a hard look. "Good. So. Is it this rice farmer's tale you are going to give me? I mean, is it in a fit and decent *condition* to give me?"

"Yes."

"Tomorrow, then," said Jeunet, with finality, and he got to his feet leaving his drink untouched.

## 2

Jeunet went off to the guest hut in the lee of the small cliff, a scalloped white slice cut like a smile into the green of the hill. Soop, following Heston, took the opposite direction, along the upward path to the broad hall. From this slightly higher position, no more that twenty yards above the terrace and beach below, the view opened up: the three other islands, like three green lids sealed over the blue-green pans of their own reflections; and beyond that, far away under the glassy sunlight, the broad low ebony-coloured bar of the mainland. The two of them walked up in silence. A week or so earlier, Soop had uncovered several key story-texts – visual narratives, that amongst other things explained why the name *Heston* was so popular amongst followers of the Man of the Strong Arm. An actor with that name had appeared in several heroic texts from the industrial period. Soop, to be honest, derived an almost subversive pleasure in silently contrasting Heston's short, pen-thin frame and moist eyes with the rugged handsomeness of the original strong-man actor – a towering, jut-jawed, bulky individual. Of course it hardly mattered, given the weapon at his belt, whether Heston were muscular or not.

"Come along," Heston said, without looking over his shoulder.

At least, Soop told himself, Jeunet *looks* like Jeunet. Jeunet the Great. And, at least Jeunet the Great had been something more than a mere *actor*. Visual narratives were slippery. It was harder recovering them, and if they were coloured-in (which, Soop thought, was a necessary precondition for modern interest) then they were much more likely to contain unacceptable or harmful material than written texts. That was one reason amongst many why Soop preferred the latter.

And now they were at the top of the path. A handful of tiny white clouds were moving along the sky overhead, passing one after the other close across the sun as if wiping its face. A broadcast of glitter speckled the sea beneath in a swathe from mid-ocean to horizon, looking like nothing so much as myriad droplets of sweat discarded by the strenuously gleaming sun.

Evidently, then, Jeunet's boat was coming for him tomorrow. He had said tomorrow, meaning, have the story ready for me to take away then.

Soop had worked with Heston long enough, on this remote place, for the older man not to need to give instruction to the younger. Soop knew that Heston would go off for *his* siesta, just as

Jeunet had gone for his; and that in the meantime Soop was to work on preparing a copy of the heroic story in a finished form for the visiting superior to inspect. The afternoons and early mornings were Soop's golden times. Free from the restraint of his elder he could roam uninhibited through the word-forests hauled, unsystematically and indeed erratically, from the databases of the degraded past. Most of it had already passed through the filter of the historians, those guardians of orthodoxy, and all dangerously historical material had been removed. But this process could never be pure, for, Soop often thought, though the peoples of the degraded past had evidently lived in what must have been a thoroughly exhausting fever dream of image, fantasy, dream, scientifiction, speculation, oddity and imaginary worlds, nevertheless *some* of their art was grounded in the business of historical living. From time to time he would uncover stories set not in a clean and uplifting fantasy place, but actually in that vanished, degraded world. Soop sometimes worked on retrieving accounts of imaginary cities that suddenly shifted their meaning and revealed themselves to be actual accounts of urban living. That was why Soop preferred the science fiction: tales set on distant worlds no human had ever even come close to actually visiting, these stories – or most of them – were free to give vivid life to the heroic narrative of strength and purity. Although if truth were told what Soop found most comfortable of all were the mere blocks of texts, the characters and numbers and incomprehensible jumbles of queer symbols, a third of it garbage, deliberately or otherwise. Purge the text of this *code*, as it was called, and more often than not it would be possible to follow long unbroken strings of language all along their thrilling length to conjure heroes – flights through the daysky and the nightsky, journeys to other worlds, into the comforting vales and forests of fantasy lands.

Heston had gone to his room to sleep, and Soop walked through the workshop. Women were cleaning it, and they leapt away from him and pressed their backs to the walls as he passed through. Some of them automatically zipped up their eyeslits. Others looked to their maitre for leadership as to whether to flee the room entirely; but Soop had not communicated anything to the maitre, and her swathed form could only shudder with uncertainty. He passed straight through, opened the rear door and stepped outside.

There was glade outside, sown with smooth lawn and surrounded on three sides by solid curtains of foliage, irregular and pitted masses of several mingled shades of dark green. As soon as he stepped through the door, this solid vegetative curtain shook, and a body emerged from it. It was a female, dressed in trousers and a white kaftan, and shockingly bareheaded – the mass of her hair a gleaming blackness tied in a stem at the back.

"That's the second time you've come here naked," said Soop, in an amused voice.

The girl fumbled at the scarf around her neck and pulled it hurriedly over the crown of her head.

"Still," said Soop, uncomfortably aware of his body's automatic reaction to the proximity of this individual, and speaking to create a tiny heroic narrative of his own in which that arousal was an irrelevance, "it's not as if you're a woman."

"My husband," she said, in her execrably-accented English, "would disagree."

"You never cease to astonish," said Soop, excited still further by her boldfacedness in answering him back – in speaking to him at all. "Husband indeed! So, so. Have you got more for me?"

She held out a fishstick-sized chip.

"And that?"

"Moon."

"Moon?"

"I mean," she said, after swallowing, "it's another version of the moon story. The Armstrong story. That's what I mean."

"The one you gave me yesterday?"

"It's a very popular story from that period," she said, glancing anxiously at the open door behind him. "Very popular. There are hundreds of different retellings of it."

"I've heard you whistle *that* tune before," said Soop, fumbling in his satchel for payment. "And I'll tell you straight up, I'm not paying you hundreds of times for the same story. Now, I will say I'm intrigued as to how this version is different from the one you sold me yesterday. I'll take it. It's a good story, if a little dour. It's good, it's heroic. It's just a little dour." She took the money. And he took the data stick. And that was the end of their exchange, except that they both loitered there, in the clearing.

She kept staring at him. Extraordinary!

"There's a very important man who's come to visit us," said Soop, his heart scudding in his chest with the excitement of imparting this news to her. But why should he care about impressing *her*? Barely even a her!

"Important?"

"A very senior man."

"Seems to me," she replied, "all your men are senior."

"You say that," burst out Soop, in a little spurt of laughing exasperation, "as if it is a *strange* thing!"

And then, after all her extraordinary behaviour, the female asked the most extraordinary question of all. She said: "Does this senior man have weapons?"

"He is very strong," said Soop, putting the matter as simply as he could. He thought of Jeunet, taking his afternoon repose in the hut by the sea, just a few hundred yards away; all that manliness, strength and potency coiled, as it were, in rest. But his natural ebullience would not permit awe to silence him for very long. "Of course he has weapons." He plucked his own pistoletta from his belt and, not meaning to threaten or intimidate her, but merely because it fell to him as the most natural way of showing it off to an interested party, he aimed its muzzle at her. Her striking eyes opened even wider than before, and her shoulders snapped up and back. A tremor became evident in her whole body. "This," said Soop, carelessly, "would kill you easily enough, of course. Erase you. But the sort of weaponry *he* carries…" It was wonderful even to contemplate it. "This whole *island*…" he said, moving the muzzle from left to right to gesture at the place as a whole. "All of it… it's a great strength he has…"

Over their heads, in that portion of sky demarcated by the hemming treetops, four distant bitterns moved, as if sliding magnetically across a blue screen. The sound of nesting birds booing was audible, a faraway, languid sort of commentary upon the action.

"Anyway," he said, putting his pistoletta back in his belt. "You asked."

She had gone very pale.

"I wish I knew why you're so interested," he added despondently. He felt thwarted, although he could not say why, or of what. "I don't know why you're so interested in his weapon. You've got your money, haven't you? Shouldn't you be running back? And where," he added, almost at a shout, "do you get all these stories from anyway?"

"*He's* here for the stories," she said, in a voice from which the earlier colour, the tones of will, was now quite emptied-out; a small voice.

"The superior? Of course he is."

"I can bring you stories."

"You? Yes you can. What do you mean by saying that?"

"Good stories."

"Of course you can," he retorted, puzzled.

But she was trembling now in quite a marked manner. She was shaking so hard now that her scarf had fallen again around her neck. The naked skin of her face did not fascinate Soop so much as the hair. The purity of colour of her hair, like grooved plastic set upon her head. It, somehow, startled him. Startled was the word. "Your misfortune," he said, "is to have been born outside the protection of the Man of the Strong Arm."

"Your Leader." She almost gasped it.

"Yes. Strength – but," he interrupted himself, "what on earth are you so confounded scared about?" A thought occurred to him. "Is it the gun?" He tutted. "I was only *showing* you the gun. I wasn't about to *shoot* you with the gun."

She shook her head slightly.

"Not the gun?" he persisted. "Then what? I do wish you'd stop being so scared, because it makes it hard to speak with you. What *is* it?"

She nodded, or rather inclined her head backwards a little to point with her chin. To point past Soop's left arm. With a sense of growing alarm, and a constriction in his throat, Soop turned about.

## 3

Jeunet, the great Jeunet himself, was standing in the doorway observing the scene with languidly self-confident potency. For long seconds Soop had no idea what to do, or what to say. It was alarming that Jeunet was here. It alarmed Soop to think that Jeunet had been listening in on his conversation with the female. He tried to master his alarm through his own strength, but it wasn't easy.

Jeunet's hand hung easily, loosely, beside his pistol. "He wasn't wrong," Jeunet said, apparently addressing the female. "He said I could destroy the whole island, in stages or all at once. That's true. Nothing but the truth."

"Strength," she hissed.

"Jeunet," said Soop. Then: "I thought you were asleep."

"I wanted to have a word with you before I lay down," Jeunet replied.

"Of course," said Soop. "Of course. A word – I'd be delighted. I could wake Heston, if you like."

"A word with you alone," said Jeunet. What was disconcerting was the way that, although he was talking with Soop, he kept look at the female. She in turn kept glancing hurriedly over her shoulder, as if trying to spy her way to escape.

"You," said Jeunet to the female. "If you turn your back I'll put a hole into you the size of my fist." She looked straight back at him, as bold as ever. "A good deal of your blood would come out of such a hole," Jeunet went on. "Innards, too. You'd lie on the grass and die in great pain."

"You have my attention," she said, with her atrocious accent.

"She was selling me stories," said Soop, in a weirdly squeaky voice. His own heart was rattling in his chest like a wind-up toy – like those castanet-like chattering teeth that you set on a tabletop and leave to clatter away.

"I gathered as much," said Jeunet.

"It's research," Soop said quickly. "It's, eh, ah, one of the avenues of research we pursue here at the station." He could not imagine why he wanted to save this female's life. Even had she been a woman he would hardly have cared – and she wasn't even a woman. But still he gabbled on. "She brings data with archaic stories. She lives in one of the villages, I suppose. She brings me the data."

"And you pay her?"

"Small sums."

"Where does she get them from?"

"As to that," said Soop hurriedly, "well, I don't know, I couldn't say."

"They could be forgeries."

"As to *that*," Soop leapt in, "I don't believe so. I trust my judgment. I think I could tell a contemporary pastiche of antique science fiction, and the real thing. I've read a great deal of the stuff – of heroic fiction from –"

He dried, abruptly, in mid sentence, and stood there with his mouth open. What was he saying? He couldn't remember what he was saying.

So there was a little period of silence, and the silence was filled only with the myriad scratching and piping noises made by the jungle insects. And with the distantly mournful booing of the bitterns in the distance.

The stranger was trembling very visibly. She was clearly terrified. She was perfectly well aware, Soop could see, that her life was almost at an end.

"So you have bought a story?" Jeunet said, eventually.

"It's a moon story."

"A fantastic voyage to the moon?"

"Precisely so." To try and master his alarm, he reached for a lecturer's dryness of manner. "Any student of the ancient traditions of science fiction will tell you that voyages to the moon have a long pedigree in fantastic storytelling. Voyages to the moon and the sun – because those are the bodies that can be seen most clearly, right there in the sky – take precedence over voyages to the planets and stars. This one is about a hero called Armstrong who flies up to the moon."

All through this strange interview Jeunet stood in the doorway, his hand hanging leisurely next to his pistol. But the strangest thing of all was the way his eyes remained fixed on the female. He stared at her with a bewildering intensity. She was, as Soop had to remind himself, nobody at all.

"Tell me this story," he said.

The stranger said nothing. Soop cleared his throat.

"It's a variation on a standard theme," he said. "A hero flies up to the moon on a giant firework. He is aided, of course, by the gods – he could hardly have reached as far as the moon without supernatural help. There's a pre-industrial god called Saturn – I've always assumed that the final syllable there means that he was a funereal god, though that's not clear. There's another deity, a god called Apollo. Apollo is the pre-industrial god of the sun and the moon. The significance of these gods to the story is a little obscure, but I assume that on a metaphorical level they fight, Saturn the god of Death and Apollo the god of Life, fight over the mission, over, I mean, the *success* of the mission. Armstrong succeeds, of course, despite terrible danger and adversity."

"So. A mythological tale?"

"But that's one of the things that's interesting about this story," said Soop, warming to his theme and forgetting, as he was wont to do when in full spate, his surroundings, his interlocutor, even his fear. "In common with the science fiction of its period it *is* a mythological story – but it's told in this pedantically pseudo-scientific, or pseudo-technical manner. There's a *lot* of detail about machinery, dials, switches and so on. It tells a purely fantastical imaginary story in a peculiarly detailed realist way."

The female twitched as he said this, and glanced nervously at Soop.

"Realist?" said Jeunet in a low voice, coming a little further out of the doorway.

"It's a wonderful paradox, really. But it's one of the things I love about all this antique science fiction. There are lots of examples of it. Take Robert High-line; he was a contemporaneous writer of imaginary voyages and his stuff is *full* of gadgets and technical digressions and the like, although the stories themselves are as fantastical and mythic as you like. This Armstrong story is just like that. It's a perfectly impossible adventure, of course, but it's told with a straight face. And that combination is just, is just a thing that I – and I'm speaking only personally of course – *love* about all this work."

"It was an age that trusted in technology," said Jeunet.

"It was, and that sapped its strength, of course," said Soop rapidly, "although they didn't *entirely* lose sight of the importance of strength. That's why, of their two modes of storytelling, it is the science fictional that is the greater. Their dreary non-sciencefictional art is all of it morbid and diseased and depressing. But in the science fiction! Well, well, this Armstrong story is a good example. Pure fantasy, yes, but a fantasy of *overcoming* and *strength*."

"I know this story," said Jeunet.

The female twitched again. She was holding herself up on her two feet only, it seemed, by an enormous effort of will. Soop had never seen anybody so nervous before.

"You know it?" said Soop. Since Jeunet's assertion really made no sense Soop couldn't quite understand grasp the meaning. "You *know* it? Really? I must say, I'm surprised, Jeunet… I mean, it's a minor example of the genre. Interesting, but minor. I had no idea your knowledge of the artform was so extensive."

"Minor you call it," said Jeunet, his gaze still fixed upon the female.

The stranger suddenly spoke out at this, her voice strained. "If he thinks its minor," she said, nodding her head at Soop, "then he clearly doesn't *know* it very well."

This pricked Soop's professional pride. "Indeed I do!" he insisted. "It is a variant of a story as old as the industrial period itself. As, that is to say, science fiction itself. Don't know it well? I know this: one of the pioneers was a European called Sir Arno of Bergerac – that's a county in old Europe, you know – and *he* told a story about flying to the moon on a giant firework. Then there was the Jew, Verne, who told endless stories about gigantic magic pistols, amongst them one that could shoot men all the way to the moon. And Wells from World's-End who told a story about a magical house that only stayed on the earth when its windows were open – if you shut them you flew up to the moon. What could be more fantastic? This Armstrong story is in the same vein as these, except there's a pleasant and agreeable twist at the end. You see, all the previous tales of this sort had portrayed the moon as a vibrant and fantastical place filled with colourful monsters. The Armstrong story starts in full-colour, but the moon is a purely black-and-white location. It's *The Wizard of Oz* in reverse, you see. It's a deliberate artistic inversion. It's a land of paradoxes, you see – he lands in the sea, but the sea is all dust. He tries to take small steps so as not to fall over, but the smaller the steps he takes, the more gigantic his walking becomes. *That's* taken from *Alice in the Looking Glass Wonderland*, where the people must run as fast as they can to stand still. He finds a place without any air at all, and yet he plants a flag that flutters proudly. And yet! And *yet* all this bizarre fantastical nonsense is related in the driest, most precise pseudo-scientific manner! It's splendid. It's hilarious, actually. And then the story ends by Armstrong leaping directly from the mirror-land back to earth, from black and white to colour, from a sea of dust to a sea of water."

"It is not an orthodox story," said Jeunet.

It took a moment for the full implication of this statement to find a point of entrance into Soop's jangled mind. "What? What's that? *Not* orthodox? Not *orthodox*? But—forgive me for appearing to contradict you, Jeunet, but. Surely it's perfectly orthodox! Surely as I've just been saying, speaking *as* an expert of the science fiction from this period and it's exactly like two dozen other stories."

The stranger sucked a deep breath and released it again. "Shouldn't he be calling you *sir* or *lord* or *master*?"

Soop might almost have admired her courage in talking so, to such a man, excepting that it evidently wasn't true courage; it was the recklessness of an individual who knew that whatever she did she would die very soon. Her impertinence, at any rate, seemed to amuse Jeunet.

"That wouldn't be very *strong*, now, would it?" he said. "Using that sort of cowering idiom? But you're right; I am the superior party here."

"Well," said Soop, croakily. "Of course."

"If I say the story is not orthodox, then young Soop must just accept the fact."

"Of course," said Soop, in a smaller voice.

For the first time in the interview Jeunet moved his eyes from the stranger and looked at Soop. "I am aware of this story. I know about it *because* it is proscribed."

"Proscribed? But *why*?"

"You've been on this island for too long," said Jeunet. "You've become a little dissociated from real life, Soop. It's necessary, I realise, if we are to maintain a proper quarantine on these dangerous memes. But it's a strategy that has its own dangers. People like you lose touch with real life. It's proscribed because it's an evident forgery."

"Jeunet!" said Soop, for this was to insult his professional judgement. "I strongly disagree! All my long-built-up expertise tells me that it is an authentic artwork from the industrial age."

"It's a modern pastiche," said Jeunet, in a tone of voice of somebody not about to enter into a discussion over the fact. "Worse, it is made – perhaps by this stranger and her people, perhaps by some other group – specifically to undermine our strength. It's a crude satire. Come come, Soop: the hero here is called *Armstrong*? Doesn't that strike you as almost too obvious a libel on the Man of the Strong Arm?"

"Libel?" said Soop, alarmed and confused. "Libel? But he's a hero, Armstrong is a hero. He's a recognisable archetype of strength!"

"Tch. A man called Strong-Arm journeys to a barren land, and jumps up and down in the dust, and then returns home and declares that he has undertaken mankind's greatest adventure. Can you *honestly* not see how this works as satire? Can you not understand how injurious to the dignity of the Man of the Strong Arm such a tale would be, if it were widely disseminated?"

"I," said Soop, confused. "I had not regarded it in that light before. I saw it as an example of a well-attested tradition in fantastical sciencefictional art…"

"You have been too *close* to all this material, Soop," Jeunet said. "Cut off from the real world for too long. Let me ask you: who is the creator of this artwork?"

"It," said Soop, sweating now. "It is sometimes attributed to a man called Nasa. But then again, Nasa appears in the story as the organisation that sponsors Armstrong's extraordinary voyage, so that might be a mistake – that happens sometimes, in the case of an anonymous tale, a character from the story gets misidentified as the author."

"Nasa is an acronym."

"Yes, yes," agreed Soop.

"You know what it stands for?"

"Well there are several theories. Personally I take it to be a reference to the Jew Verne. His moon adventure was organised by the American National Gun Club. The Armstrong story has very many similarities with that earlier story – I take it Nasa is the same organisation, perhaps the National Association for Shooting Artillery."

"And if," said Jeunet with a grim face, "I were to tell you that it stands for *Never Accept the Strong Arm*? If I were to tell you that it is a *real* organisation, in the world today, dedicated to subversive revolutionary action against the Man of the Strong Arm?"

"No!" gasped Soop.

"You see now *why* this story is proscribed?"

"Of course! I'm … I'm *horrified* at my error…"

At this point the stranger in the clearing spoke out. "That's not why the story is proscribed," she said.

Everything becoming too much for Soop's poor brain. "What? What's that?"

"Strong-Arm has a good reason for keeping this story secret," she said, in an unquavery voice. "But that's not it."

"Why then?"

"Don't be foolish," snapped Jeunet. "I have told you the reason."

"You are a liar," she said.

But this really was going too far. Jeunet stepped quickly from the doorway and strode out into the little clearing. "You are extraordinarily bold," he said. "Considering that you are about to die, it is almost impressive. But enough now."

It took a moment for Soop's bewildered brain to process what happened next. There was the sound of a snake. No, there was no snake. Jeunet had pulled a slender wand from his belt. Soop didn't know that he had such a truncheon on his person, except that there is was. But it wasn't a wand, it was an arrow shaft. And it hadn't been pulled from his belt, it was sticking out of his hip. Jeunet gave voice to a sort of strangled yell, something like a cough, and his right elbow jerked out, flapped back, jerked out. He began to reach across his own torso with his left hand, and there was another hiss. This time Soop saw the arrow strike home, thudding audibly into Jeunet's hip and digging out a little spurt of blood that fell as a twisting cord that broke into beads and droplets before it reached the grass. This second arrow knocked Jeunet leftward and he hopped on his left leg to keep his balance. His left hand had reached his gun now, but for some reason he didn't seem to be able to unholster it. He fumbled at the weapon a little and it came away from its hook, but instead of falling into his hand it only slid a little way along the shaft of the arrow.

The female started screaming.

Soop saw, with abrupt understanding, that the second arrow had struck home directly *through* the trigger guard, and had pinned the pistol to Jeunet's hip. The first arrow had nailed Jeunet's right hand to his flank.

The female was not screaming; she was whooping. A second individual, another female, emerged from the foliage, holding her bow before her, an arrow cocked. She came round from the right to face Jeunet directly.

"Soop," he growled. "Soop – now. Now!" He meant, *Soop, get your pistoletta out.* Soop's mind buckled, stretched with astonishment, and snapped back into normality. He grabbed his weapon.

The second female fired an arrow straight into Jeunet's stomach where it buried a third of its length in his flesh. With startling rapidity she drew a new arrow from a pouch at her side and cocked it. She had pulled the bowstring back even before Jeunet hit the ground – he slumped down, and fell heavily on his rear, and there he was, sitting on the grass with three arrows in him.

Soop raised his pistoletta. It was clear that he should first shoot the arrow-woman, and then the other. But the fact that there were two of them put a moment of uncertainty into his aim. What if the first had a concealed weapon – a knife, say? Should he shoot her first and the other after?

Then he was aware of a sudden, violent pain in his elbow. He looked down. It had been pierced by an arrow. The dart had entered obliquely on the outside of the arm, passed straight through the muscle and bone and emerged behind just at that place where the bicep joins the end of the humerus. Actually seeing this wound with his eyes intensified the agony. A huge, fierce pain. Pain leapt upon his body with malign completeness, most intense at the site of the wound. It possessed a disorienting, counterintuitive quality; instead of ebbing away from a point of initial severity, it seemed merely to accumulate upon itself, to grow more fierce as the seconds passed.

Jeunet rasped from below him. "You fool, Soop." There was a wet, grinding quality to his voice. His breathing had taken on an asthmatic resonance. "You consummated. Idiot."

Soop tried to move his arm, not to shoot his pistoletta, although that, clearly, would have been a good idea; but only from animal instinct, from a revulsion at the sight of the arrow piercing his flesh. The muscles twitched. The surface of his bones scraped against the shaft of the arrow as the joint attempted, without success, to uncurl. This made the pain leap to perfectly intolerable proportions. Soop wailed, a vibrato high-pitched squealing over which he had no control at all.

There was a whomp, a punch to his gut, and he sat hard down on the grass next to Jeunet. For a moment he was aware only of the pain at his elbow, and the concussion on his rear-end of the tumble. Only after he saw that a second arrow had passed through his right hand and bedded itself in the meat of his stomach, just below the ribs, did he begin to feel the sensations of the new wound. His hand flared. The split bone in the palm radiated shards of agony down each finger and hard up the wrist. It was quite impossible to move the hand. It was already pinned to his gut like a butterfly to a board. He could not maintain a grip upon his pistoletta, but neither could he drop it; the weight of its stock rotated it about his trigger finger so that the barrel now pointed up at his chin.

He tried to take a breath to scream with pain, but the action of his diaphragm and the fluid motion of his belly, jarred against the arrow-point buried there, and a new intensity of pain scorched with fearful inevitability in his solar plexus. He would have thought his nervous system was already transmitting as much pain as it was capable of; but this new agony intensified the sensation to a new level. Unable to scream, he gasped, drew a shallow breath and let it out again in a wheeze of distress.

"Idiot," said Jeunet beside him with a perfect, complete contempt.

The first female, the one without the bow, was crouching in front of Jeunet. She was carrying a weapon, Soop saw. A large knife. Each tiny smile-shaped serration on its blade bit into air in a way that was, somehow, connected to Soop's own nervous system. She jabbed the blade forward, towards Jeunet's stomach, and the mere motion somehow transferred pain through the air to the triple node of agony in Soop's own body. Elbow and hand and stomach, each passed their hurt along to the two others, forcing acid through every nerve channel that Soop possessed. His vision was blanching out. His head buzzed. Oh, it was painful.

"Let go with your finger," the female with the knife was saying to Jeunet, "or I *will* just cut the finger off."

"You don't think," Jeunet rasped, "that I'm trying?"

"Nazdh dra'gh dijit," said the archer, the arrow in her bow aimed at Soop's head, Soop's poor, dizzy, pain-stunned head.

The first stranger answered in English: "But it's snagged in the trigger guard."

The archer said something rapidly in her barbarous tongue.

"Oh, I don't know," and she turned back to Jeunet. "Cutting your finger off wouldn't make *you* pass out. Big strong man like you?"

"I am not," wheezed Jeunet, "afraid. Of you."

"I'll reprogram your pistol now," the archer said to Jeunet. Her accent was more pronounced that the first stranger's, so much so that it was actually quite hard to follow what she was saying.

"You," said Jeunet. "Can't."

"If you are alive," said the archer, releasing the tension in her bowstring slowly, and then dropping easily to her haunches in front of him, "then I can."

"The pistol," wailed Soop, the pressure of his pain and the terrible realisation of what the females were about almost overwhelming him. He felt like a child. He felt the desperate need for somebody strong to come in and help him – to swaddle him. To make the pain go away. To save him. Over his head the bitterns moved through their own element, slowly, sadly, entirely indifferent to his sufferings.

The archer placed her bow on the grass and started gabbling something incomprehensible.

"My friend," said the first stranger, coming over to Soop now with her knife, "wanted to shoot you both in the throat, right at the beginning. That was *her* plan. She says that you would have stayed alive long enough for us to get useful imprints. I was not so sure. My way was riskier. I was beginning to think that *he* –" Soop tried to look toward Jeunet, but moving his neck tugged on the arrow in his gut. He could just see the other man, out of the corner of his eye. The archer-female had somehow got the pistol free from Jeunet's hand, and drew it gently along the length of the shaft of the arrow. "– would just kill me from the doorway, that Aliss wouldn't get a clear shot at him. It was a *frightening* thing, I don't mind telling you."

The first female brought something from her purse, a small black tube, and pressed it against Soop's right eye. "Uhh!" he gasped. "Ah! Ah! Uh! Uh!"

"And there are *good* reasons," said the voluble stranger, stowing the tube away again in her purse, "why Strong-Arm wants to keep certain stories prohibited. It just so happens that they're not the reasons *he* gave you."

"Don't listen," Jeunet gasped. "To them. Soop."

But Soop couldn't think about that; couldn't concentrate on that. His pain was the entire horizon of his thoughts now. These females moved like spectres through the fog of his agony, performing their precisely choreographed actions, a sort of callous ballet. Soop's pain was so entire a thing he found it hard to imagine that there had ever been a time when agony had not squatted inside him, twisting his nerves, shredding his mind.

"Stories are important," the stranger was saying. "But perhaps they are not enough by themselves. Tyrants like to control what sorts of stories are told," she was saying, as she rolled a small block, a plastic-feeling something, over Soop's fingertips, one, two, three, four. "Of course they do. Celebrations of the heroism of tyranny." She pressed the block against his right thumb. "But, you see, the story of Armstrong is a *different* sort of story. A story worth celebrating. You, your leader believes, what? That a strong-man's got to know his limitations? This isn't a story about safe little impossibilities."

"Science *fiction*," barked Jeunet, in a desperate voice.

"Science fiction," repeated the female, and her flat delivery and accented English made it impossible to tell what she meant by this. "Anyway, *of* the various ways of getting different stories into circulation, alternative stories… well *of* the various ways, pistols have a certain …" She trailed off.

"You'll not," Jeunet said, speaking slowly and strenuously. "You'll not. Decode the. Decode the."

"Man," said the female, "we certainly will. You want to worry what we're going to do *after* we've reset them."

"'Tzent'u!' cried the archer, snatching up her bow and drawing the string. She was aiming in through the open door.

"Relax," said the other one. She added something in her native tongue.

Soop tried to turn his head, to see what they were looking at in the doorway, but the action tightened the skin at his neck, which pulled on the skin of his torso and ground further snaps and jags of pain from the arrow in his gut. He was crying freely now, water simply oozing from his eyes and slicking his cheeks. Tears just pouring out of him, as if his head were a cracked pitcher. His vision was blurry. His line of sight was framed by the sparkles and little leaps of bodily agony. He thought he saw one of the women in the doorway. It was definitely one of the women. She threw up her gloved hands and scurried back inside.

"It's only one of their women," said the first female, in a contemptuous tone.

The archer spoke hurriedly.

"Yes," said the other. "Yes. We're done here anyway."

They were on their feet, and Soop's pistoletta, and much worse than that Jeunet's pistol, were in their purses, and in a moment they had vanished into the jungle.

## 4

The quiet that occupied the clearing afterwards had the tangible quality of enormous, persistent pain stitched into its insect-underthrob. The distant melodic booms of the bitterns echoed along Soop's nerves. He tried his very best not to move; to take the shallowest of breaths, not to sway, not to move anything that would cause the slightest friction between his flesh and the shafts of the two arrows that were in him. The dry, pulling sound of Jeunet's breathing was lessening; the spaces between breaths growing longer, his lifeforce marking a sort of diminuendo. The green itself, the mere colour, the colour by itself, seemed somehow to detach itself from the leaves and, in some peculiar manner, to stain Soop's mind, to give his impossibly extended physical suffering a chromatic focus. He became aware that his trousers were sodden, and panic at the thought that he had wet himself – disgraced himself like a child –

made his heart beat faster, which in turn pushed blood through bulging veins and squeezed a new peak of agony from his wounds. But he had not pissed himself. It was blood from his stomach that had flowed down there. He ought to be feeling light-headed, really. Well, perhaps he was feeling light-headed. Really. The air felt thin in his mouth. Everything was slower. Jeunet drew in a pained breath, and breathed out roughly. There was a long pause. Then Jeunet drew in another breath and didn't let it out. The colours tinkled in Soop's eyes. Pain was unlike sound. If his pain were a symphony then the cacophonous crashing of his elbow, his hand, his stomach, would drown out all other sensation. But in fact, and despite the overwhelming nature of those sensations, he was also aware of sweat trickling into his eye. He was aware of a tickling sensation on his hand and up his arm, where ants from the grass had crawled up to investigate the site of the trauma.

He didn't want to look at that. He rolled his eyes upward, at the sky, and its patch of blue was almost a relief from the agony of green. There was the moon. He could see the moon, round as a coin. That insubstantial way the moon looks in the afternoon sky, as if it is an image projected upon a screen rather than a solid lump of rock inset in the waveless blue of its idiom. Moon, he thought. Moon, moon, moon. It didn't look like an eye. He couldn't understand people who thought it looked like an eye. It was rather a sort of lid, the texture of its iron pitted and stained with long use, on the manhole of existence. The lid sat at the top of a tall blue shaft with impossibly smooth sides. The air was hot. Soop was intensely aware of the heat in the air, the jungle stench, the noise, and infiltrated into every element he was aware of his pain. It was his pain, most of all, that pinned him to the mud. He was broken. Moon, he thought, it's gone wrong.

To his left he sensed movement. Women had come out of the doorway, and with them came Heston. They must have gone back and woken him from his sleep. He wouldn't, Soop thought, be happy about that. He didn't like being woken from his siesta. On the other hand, and considering the circumstances they were in, being woken from his nap was really the least of his potential annoyances.

"Heston!" Soop rasped. "Heston, we have a problem."

# An Afterword

Someone told me recently that the BSFA is the oldest science fiction organisation in the world. Probably. I have no idea whether or not this is true, although it does sound entirely feasible. Perhaps there is now somebody out there itching to jump up and declare that there's an SF organisation in some obscure corner of the planet (assuming globes can be considered to have corners) that is older than 50 years. But if so, please don't. Keep it to yourself. Because I really *want* this to be true, so humour me and leave me with my delusions, okay?

I'm a comparative newcomer to the BSFA, although for many years prior to joining I was aware of this mysterious organisation which bestowed 'the BSFA Awards' on privileged individuals and works. I had no idea who they might be, these nebulous figures who wielded such power, but I knew they were out there somewhere.

Only once I started attending conventions and became involved in the arcane, slightly daunting world of 'fandom' did I begin to grasp the reality: that these mysterious figures are in fact fans, much like me. And this is surely what makes the BSFA so special – the fact that it is not at its heart a society for authors, editors, agents or other industry figures, it's about fans. Oh, certainly many of all the aforementioned are members, but that's because *they're* fans too.

The British Science Fiction Association is all about the people who read, watch, talk about, dream about and are passionate about… science fiction. It's as simple as that.

I feel greatly privileged to be involved in a book that celebrates fifty years of the BSFA, and would like to thank all those who have played a part in its creation, particularly the authors, who rose to the challenge of producing stories worthy of such a collection against, as ever, an unreasonably tight schedule.

The BSFA is special. For such an organisation to have existed for as long as fifty years strikes me as remarkable. Of course, we have no way of knowing whether or not it will still be here fifty years from now, but I've a funny feeling it will be, and that's a prospect I find oddly reassuring and which, as a fan, I wholeheartedly applaud.

*Ian Whates* – January 2008